This book is respectfully dedicated to the memories of Brian Ainsworth, John Bailey, Jim Briggs, Don Haigh-Ellery and most especially Trevor Russell.

DOCTOR WHO

SPIRAL SCRATCH

GARY RUSSELL

BBC
BOOKS

DOCTOR WHO:
SPIRAL SCRATCH

Published by BBC Books, BBC Worldwide Ltd,
Woodlands, 80 Wood Lane, London W12 0TT

First published 2005
Copyright © Gary Russell 2005
The moral right of the author has been asserted.

Original series broadcast on BBC television
Format © BBC 1963
'Doctor Who' and 'TARDIS' are trademarks
of the British Broadcasting Corporation

ISBN 0 563 48626 0

Commissioning editors: Shirley Patton and Stuart Cooper
Editor and creative consultant: Justin Richards
Project editor: Vicki Vrint

Cover imaging by Black Sheep © BBC 2005
Printed and bound in Great Britain by Clays Ltd, St Ives plc

For more information about this and other BBC books,
please visit our website at www.bbcshop.com

Chapter One
I Need

'I need you to go to the planet Earth in 1958 and save the universe.'
'I need you to go to the planet Huttan in 2267 and save the universe.'
'I need you to go to the planet Janus 8 in 66.98 and save the universe.'
'I need you to go to the planet Schyllus in 4387 and save the universe.'
'I need you to go to the planet Narrah in 2721 and save the universe.'
'I need you to go to the planet C'h'zzz in 3263 and save the universe.'
'I need you to go to the planet Luminos in 2005 and save the universe.'
'I need you to go to the planet Yestobahl in 1494 and save the universe.'
'I need you to go to the planet Helios 3 in 5738 and save the universe.'

Chapter Two
Real World

It was the hottest harvest-time that the Goodewife Barber could remember. It was also one of the most productive, and the squire overseeing the village, Richard de Calne, would be pleased. Beans, wheat and root vegetables were plentiful. Wulpit would be safe from famine during the winter months.

'Have you seen Shepherd Mullen today?' asked a voice beside her.

Startled, the Goodewife nearly dropped her hoe, but steadied herself in time.

'Oh good morning, Brother Ralph,' she said. 'I did not hear your approach.' Then she scanned the horizon, but saw no sign of the shepherd. 'That is quite strange,' she continued. 'He was here earlier, I am sure of it. I saw him talking to one of the village girls, Daisy, not half the morning ago.'

Brother Ralph shrugged. 'It is of no matter, Goodewife. I thank you for your time.' He turned away and then back again. 'Oh, and many apologies for disturbing you so.'

Goodewife Barber laughed the hearty laugh of a woman who eats well. 'Do not worry so, Brother. It is an honour to be visited by one from the monastery. We look forward to celebrating the festival of the harvest with your abbot and your fellow monks shortly. Only a few more days, I should imagine.' She stopped and put her hoe down, laying it next to the bean-filled sieve already on the ground. 'May I ask a question, Brother?'

Ralph nodded his assent.

'Why are you looking for the shepherd? Have more of his flock breached your grounds? My husband has, I believe, already mended the fence once this month.'

Ralph laughed and shielded his eyes from the sunlight as he gazed around. 'Nothing like that. No, we are thinking of adding to our own flock of sheep and goats, and the Abbot requested I seek the good shepherd's advice.'

Goodewife Barber reached down for her hoe again and then froze.

'Do you hear that?' Ralph asked, answering the question she was about to pose him.

'What can it be?' she said, looking around, trying to see if it was Daisy or one of the other children in the fields. But they all seemed similarly bewildered. 'Where is it coming from?'

'All around us,' breathed Ralph. 'Like the sound a man's heart makes in his ears after he has run a great distance.'

The noise was loud enough that they clasped their hands to their ears and the Goodewife was aware that Brother Ralph was crying out in some pain, when suddenly it stopped.

The immediacy of the silence was almost as painful, but that passed.

As the confused villagers made sure their fellows were perfectly well, a cry could be heard.

Not a cry of pain or anguish but one of surprise, followed by 'Come! Quickly, come!'

'That's the shepherd,' Goodewife Barber said to Ralph as they began a hesitant walk towards the voice. A second call, however, had them hurry their pace, joined as they were by Daisy, a couple of her friends and one or two other Goodewives – and one of the men, Twisted Jude, who was unable to work for the Squire due to his tortured spine.

After a few moments, the group found themselves over-looking one of the specially dug wolf-pits, designed to trap wild beasts that might attack their sheep, chickens or other livestock. On the far side, it seemed as if the ground had given way slightly, disappearing into a hole, all but forming a green cave.

The shepherd, Mullen, was trying to make the entrance larger and realising he had an audience, implored them for some help.

'Why, good shepherd,' called Jude. 'Have you lost a sheep?'

'No,' cried the shepherd. 'But I can hear sounds in here. Children, possibly!'

At that, the women, girls and Twisted Jude began clambering down the pit's side, ignoring the dirt and thorns that smeared and scratched at them.

Brother Ralph was about to join them when Goodewife Barber looked up at him. 'Fetch the Squire,' she shouted. 'And the Abbot! His services may be needed,' she added, crossing herself as she spoke.

Watching Ralph run off, the Goodewife turned her attention to the shepherd and, easing some of the enthusiastic but weak girls aside, she began pulling clumps of earth away, astonished at how much grass and other greenery there was by this earth fall. After all, the wolf-pits tended to keep their exposed earth, and naught but a few weeds usually crawled their way through the disturbed ground to seek the sunlight.

She put this out of her mind as, sure enough, a child's sob could be heard from within.

'Did you hear that noise, like a hundred hearts?' Shepherd Mullen asked as they tore away sods and clods.

The Goodewife nodded. 'Brother Ralph also likened it to a heart's beat,' she panted.

The shepherd looked around, as if expecting the young monk to aid them in their digging, but Goodewife Barber explained she'd sent him back to fetch authority.

Twisted Jude tried to get close enough to help, but the shepherd eased him back. 'You may do yourself more damage, friend Jude,' he said.

Jude looked pained but accepted the truth.

Poor Jude, the Goodewife thought. Once he had been as strong and capable as any man of Wulpit, but an accident on horseback had ended his usefulness as the Squire's horseman, and these days he was more commonly seen talking to the village's youngest children, telling them the stories and rhymes that they needed to hear. Seeing him stood there, unable to do anything, she noticed what might almost have been a flash of anger cross his face, but she knew it to be at his own physical hindrance rather than at the shepherd's advice.

The sob came again.

'It is all right, my lovely,' she called into the darkness. 'Help is at hand.'

As they continued scrabbling, the shepherd began talking again. 'I was stood atop the pit when that noise started, and that's when this hole, this cavern just appeared,' he was saying between pants and deep breaths. 'I watched as it just... well, it just fell in on itself, revealing the cave. And this grass and stuff, I swear it wasn't there before.'

'Did you see the children fall in?'

'No,' said the shepherd. 'No, and they're not any children I know. They started crying as soon as that noise ended.'

The Goodewife was confused. She had just assumed these were a couple of village children. Even Wikes, where the Squire resided in the Great Hall, was some way away and certainly too far for children to walk without someone raising an alarm.

Shepherd Mullen seemed to be reading her mind. 'Could they have come from the village by King Edmund's resting place?'

'Even further away,' she said, and then called into the gloom once more. 'Can you see us yet? Can you see the light?'

But just a sob, a boy this time she thought, was the only response.

'I can see something,' Twisted Jude muttered. 'There, to the left of the hole. In there!'

Shepherd Mullen reached into where Twisted Jude had indicated and called back. 'I have something... someone.'

And with a tug, he all but dragged a boy of maybe fourteen or fifteen summers through the undergrowth and mud, and almost fell backwards with the strain.

A second later, a girl, a year or two younger, crawled through the same hole, and immediately grabbed for the youth the shepherd was holding.

The cry of victory and cheer of success that was started up by the onlookers died in their throats as they saw the newcomers.

Both were dressed only in thick furred gloves and boots, but otherwise they were completely naked. Their hair was long and matted with dirt and weeds, and their eyes were wide with a mixture of fear and astonishment.

But that was nothing to the astonishment that Goodewife Barber and her villagers felt.

The skin of the two naked children was bright green!

* * *

Within the hour, the Goodewife Barber had been joined by her husband, Erwick, at the Hall, where Richard de Calne had put the strange children to rest in one of the many rooms.

Now the two of them, along with Shepherd Mullen and Twisted Jude were awaiting the arrival of the Abbot and some of the monks to discuss what should be done.

'Elfenkind,' Twisted Jude had called them, but the Squire had said there were no such things as elves and faeries.

The Goodewife Barber was not entirely convinced by the dismissal. This part of Suffolk had played host to many such sightings of strange and inexplicable people and events, according to legend.

Right back in the days of the Norman invaders, stories had circulated of changelings and suchlike. Whether they were England's own imps or indeed had been brought over by William of Normandy, no one was sure, but either way, the omens were rarely positive.

'At the moment the children are sleeping,' de Calne said softly, as if he might wake them accidentally. 'When they awaken and have been fed and bathed, then we shall ask how they came to be in the Forest of Wulpit.'

'And how they come to have the hue of that forest,' said a stentorian voice from the doorway.

It was the Abbot, and Goodewife Barber could see Brother Ralph and another behind him. After a second, she realised it was Brother Lucien, a man who was as disliked by the villagers as much as Ralph was admired.

De Calne bowed sociably to the Abbot and welcomed him into the room, offering him an ornate seat by the fire. Brother Ralph was carrying some wood, which he placed in the flames, further heating the room immediately. It was sweet-smelling wood, probably cedar, which made the Goodewife relax somewhat. She believed it had the same effect on the others as even Twisted Jude ceased looking quite so agitated by the thought of green children.

'They cannot be the Lord's children,' said Brother Lucien. 'The Lord would not let his people be unclothed before the young daughters of the local villages.'

The Abbot shrugged. 'That is one opinion,' he stated. 'However, without the facts at hand, we should not judge too quickly. Our Lord may have sent these children to test us. To test our fidelity.'

Shepherd Mullen was horrified. 'Why would the Lord doubt the people of Anglia like this? We are God-fearing and abased before him each Lord's Day.'

'Perhaps we are being challenged on our harvest,' said Twisted Jude. 'Mayhaps the Lord looks unfavourably on our tilling of the land.'

Erwick Barber spoke, and his wife found herself proud of his calmness.

'I believe I agree with the Squire. We should wait until the children are awake and find answers then. Supposition,' and he glanced over at the Abbot, 'however well-intentioned, will not give us answers. And without answers, we cannot find the truth.'

'Without questions,' said the Abbot, 'we cannot recognise answers.'

With his left foot, de Calne nudged a log back into the flames, which was in danger of dropping to the woollen-rug-covered hearth. 'I shall awaken the children,' he announced. 'They have slept for two hours now.' He turned to go, and then looked back at the assembled group. 'I make one demand.'

'Indeed?' asked the Abbot.

De Calne took a deep breath. 'As Squire, the wellbeing, both spiritually and practically, of the villages in Edmund's part of Anglia is my responsibility. Therefore, no matter what we may learn this day, we keep it between ourselves. Anyone not agreeing to this should leave the Hall forthwith.' He stared at the Abbot for a moment, almost as if he were challenging the Lord's representative, before departing the room.

Brother Lucien approached the Abbot. 'I am sure the Squire meant no disrespect, Master Abbot.'

The Abbot smiled and looked at the others. Goodewife Barber took her husband's hand in hers. She felt as if the Abbot was gazing directly into her soul, searching her for answers. However, he just said: 'Oh I am quite sure Richard de Calne offers me the respect he feels I deserve. He has no time for the Church. We are tolerated here, but not welcome.'

Erwick opened his mouth, as if to contradict the Abbot, but the Goodewife squeezed his hand tighter, hoping to stop him. They both knew the Abbot was correct – the Squire's convictions and fealty towards the Lord were well known in Wulpit and the other villages. She was just surprised the Abbot did not seem offended. Or demand retribution.

'Nevertheless,' he continued, 'nevertheless, I respect him enough to accept his views, as he acknowledges mine. Ours.' The Abbot looked kindly up at Lucien from his seat. 'Neither I nor the Lord can demand his obedience. Indeed, one who questions, who disagrees, can contribute just as much as those who follow blindly. The Squire is, by nature, a man who asks questions. The sign of an intelligent man who deserves his position in society and the respect of others.'

Brother Ralph started forward. 'But Master Abbot, surely...'

'Brother Ralph. Accept that the Squire has a role to play in our lives, and that he must play it as he sees fit. The Lord shall judge him at his appointed time, not you or I.'

The door reopened, to admit de Calne and the two green children, now dressed in woollen smocks to cover their dignity, but not the green hue of their faces or hands.

Erwick, who had not actually seen them before, recoiled slightly, but his wife still held his hand tightly, willing him to be strong.

'Who are you, child?' the Abbot said in a suddenly serene and welcoming voice. 'Where do you come from?'

The boy, whom the Abbot had addressed, just stared. Not rudely, the Goodewife Barber believed, but in complete incomprehension. He looked from the Abbot, to de Calne then to the girl.

The Abbot then addressed her with the same questions, same tone. He received the same response. Or rather, the lack of one. He took her arm, tugging slightly as if that might provoke a reaction. Which it did. She yelled some incomprehensible words and tried to pull away.

Immediately the boy reached out, tenderly, to the girl, gripping her shoulder and catching her eye. No words, not even a sigh passed between them, yet the girl was calm in an instant, lowering her eyes to the floor as if in shame for her outburst.

The boy let her shoulder go and took a sharp breath, as if in a momentary spasm of pain. But it passed in an instant and he, like the girl, resumed staring at the crowd in wide-eyed innocence.

'Perhaps they do not speak our language,' offered Twisted Jude. 'Perhaps they speak a green language.'

De Calne nodded at this. 'If they are from another country, across the seas perhaps, that might explain much.' He looked across at the Goodewife. 'Goodewife Barber, in my kitchens are some hams and mutton, warming on the fire. Would you fetch them?'

The Goodewife immediately did as she was bid, although she was slightly alarmed that she might miss something important.

She made her way to the kitchen and swiftly found the meats, nestling in a pot of bubbling water. She took the pot from the fire and found a plate to place the meats upon.

In a store cupboard she also found some carrots, green beans and a turnip. She cut the latter into manageable chunks and put them on a separate plate, then carried the food back to the main room.

It was evident that she had missed nothing of import – even the Abbot was beginning to look frustrated.

Brother Lucien was just suggesting that discipline might be appropriate. 'A whip to the boy's back might make him speak,' he said cruelly.

'No!' the Goodewife said. 'He's only a boy, and is scared.'

'What is there for him to be scared of?' Lucien asked. 'It is we who should be afeared of him and his discoloured appearance.'

'And just suppose,' she reasoned, 'that where he is from, everyone is green. What must he make of a group of grown-ups with pale pink skins? I do not believe I would be ready to reveal all about myself if our places were reversed.'

'As always, the Goodewife Barber speaks sense,' said de Calne. He reached over and took the plates from her and held them before the children.

Both looked at the meats in abject horror and the younger one, the girl, started fretting and trying to pull away.

The Squire instantly passed the plate back to the Goodewife, who quickly hid it. The children relaxed almost immediately and began digging into the vegetables, specifically the green beans and turnip.

The boy picked up a bean pod, staring at it suspiciously. Goodewife Barber reached forward and eased it from him with a smile, snapping it open to reveal the mottled pink beans inside. The boy smiled at her and she realised it was the first time she had seen either of them smile. Seeing her brother's reaction (Goodewife Barber had mentally decided the children were siblings), the girl grinned as well, whilst eating greedily.

The Abbot watched the proceedings with, the Goodewife thought, almost detached amusement. As if he was seeing something else in these poor, confused, green children.

Twisted Jude picked up a dropped carrot and passed it to the boy, who seemed to notice the former horseman for the first time. He frowned, looking Twisted Jude up and down, and the older man flinched slightly. However much he was used to getting a reaction to his injuries, this new green boy's confusion was startling. It was almost as if the boy were staring not just at Jude, but through him, spotting his shattered bones, curious as to why the man stooped at an angle whereas everyone else stood upright.

And the Goodewife realised he was giving Jude the same, slightly scolding look he'd given his sister a few moments earlier when the Abbot had tried questioning them.

He reached out to the horseman and took Jude's big left hand in both his small ones, and stared deep into Jude's eyes. After a few seconds, surely no more than that, Goodewife Barber felt lightheaded. She couldn't explain it, but a wave of what she could only tell herself later was pure calmness, goodness even, washed over her. It was as if something was entering her body, making her smile and feel content, as well as revitalised. She actually felt the tiredness of the day ease from her bones.

For Twisted Jude, the effect was greater. With a slight gasp, he dropped to one knee, without breaking the boy's gaze.

The Goodewife was aware of Brothers Ralph and Lucien stepping forward, but without thinking she put up an arm to slow them, and saw that the girl was similarly holding her beloved Erwick back as well.

De Calne and the shepherd were stood closer to the Abbot and merely watched the tableau unfolding before them.

Unfolding was a good description, the Goodewife decided, as that's exactly what Twisted Jude did. As he stood up, a deep, contented sigh escaped from his lips and he closed his eyes, took a deep breath and stood upright.

Straight up.

For the first time in three years.

And Goodewife Barber could see the tears trickling down Jude's face as he realised what had happened. Like the others in the room, till the day he died, he would never understand *how* it happened, or why even. But he certainly understood that this strange green boy had somehow repaired his damaged bones and muscles, reinvigorating his heart, lungs and everything else in the process. Jude would say later that he felt that ten years had been shorn off his life, not just the three since the accident.

The effect on the boy was, however, similarly quick. He fell to the floor silently, his sister at his side in an instant, although she snarled as Erwick finally approached them both.

For a moment Goodewife Barber feared for her husband, so savage was the guttural cry from the girl, but as before the boy weakly raised an arm, and placed his flattened palm on the girl's shoulder and nodded at her. She calmed in an instant, and the boy succumbed to sleep.

* * *

For many weeks, none who had witnessed the miracle could bear to talk of it in the village. Twisted Jude returned to the Squire's stables, and the Abbot and the brothers stayed in the monastery, presumably going through their books and scrolls to see if such miracles had ever been seen since the death of the Lord Jesus Christ.

The Barbers often went to the Squire's Hall to see the children, and formed quite a bond with them.

Only the shepherd, Mullen, kept his distance. Unlike the Abbot, he was sceptical about the inherent goodness of such miracles and wondered what price they would all pay for Jude's recovery.

The price, as it transpired, was not paid by the villagers at all, but by the boy. Richard de Calne had given the children the names of his grandparents, Dominique and Julien, and gradually introduced them into the village. Neither spoke English, but they seemed to understand it all the same.

Dominique was given to temper, not entirely becoming in a young lady, but de Calne and everyone in Wulpit forgave her. Julien, however, remained uniquely capable of halting his sister's tirades with a soft touch, and de Calne offered the suggestion to the Barbers and Jude one evening that, just as the boy's touched had healed his horseman, so it healed the girl's temper.

'Some kind of saint?' offered de Calne, and heard the gasps of his guests. 'Oh don't pretend you haven't thought it yourselves.'

'But the Abbot...' started Jude.

'The Abbot is...' de Calne took a deep breath. He was clearly going to say something else, but changed his mind and instead said: 'The Abbot is a good man, but put yourself in his place. He, like all good men, has his scriptures and books, and believes in the one true God. These children challenge that faith, and as a result he is choosing to ignore them.'

'We should be grateful,' Goodewife Barber offered, 'that he has not proclaimed them the Devil or worse.'

'Worse? There is nothing worse,' said Jude.

De Calne shrugged. 'Either way, in case you had not noticed, neither he nor Lucien, nor any bar Ralph, have returned to Wulpit since their arrival. And whilst that holds no fears for me - as the Abbot has often said, I am not a God-fearing man - I am aware that the villagers are alarmed by this.'

Erwick nodded. 'I have heard many mutterings over the past few weeks.'

De Calne took a breath. 'It is my intention to go away for a while. Jude, you shall oversee the estate in my absence; Erwick, you shall be Headman of the village. And you, Goodewife Barber... Edith if I may?' With a slight flush, Goodewife Barber nodded her acceptance of the use of her given name. 'You, Edith, must keep the children of the village in learning. With Jude now back in my service and with the new duties I have given him, the schooling of the young ones has fallen away. I should like you to take charge of that. Is that clear everyone?'

'Where will you go?' asked the Goodewife.

De Calne put a finger to his lips. 'I tell you this. I fear for the green children, for Julien and Dominique. I fear the Abbot, I fear the kings and I fear one or two in Wulpit.'

'Shepherd Mullen?' asked Jude.

De Calne nodded. 'It is better for the children, for you and indeed for myself if I keep my ultimate destination a secret. But I shall be back before the spring, with or without the green children.'

He stopped as the door opposite them opened, letting a draught rush into the room.

And Goodewife Barber realised her shiver wasn't just because of the air; the look on Dominique's face as she stood framed in the doorway had sent a chill through her.

'Is it Julien?' asked the Squire. The girl nodded and as one the adults rose and headed up the stairs, telling Dominique to stay in her room.

And in his room, they discovered Julien, lying on his bed. As one, the onlookers gasped. His pallor was not so much green now, more a normal flesh colour, but he was sweating.

'Julien, what has happened?' de Calne asked, knowing he would receive no answer.

So he, along with everyone else in the room, was shocked to receive one. Not from Julien's mouth but from... from somewhere else. It was in their heads, in their minds, and they could see from his eyes that it was indeed Julien speaking, but his lips never moved.

'My sister and I came here by accident. We found the five-sided cave and climbed in. To explore. We were brought out by you. The light here, it is so bright. Where we are from, it is darker, more as it is before nightfall here.'

'Twilight,' de Calne breathed. 'A land of perpetual twilight...'

Julien continued his mind-speak. 'I thank you for looking after us, but I am dying. I need to go home, back to the cave so we can find the five-sided exit to our own world.'

'Own world?' Jude was confused. 'What other world?'

'Do they look normal? Do they look human to you?' snapped the Squire. 'I mean, do they?'

Jude shrugged.

'We do not understand where we are,' Julien continued. 'My sister and I are grateful, but I will die if I do not get home. My sister likewise, although she is stronger than I, she has much of my life-energy within her.'

'From when you touch her? When you calm her?' asked Erwick.

The boy nodded. 'My gift to her. She can be... aggressive. Not right in one so young.' He pointed at Jude. 'I hope you continue to live a good life, my friend.'

Jude widened his eyes. 'Did curing my ills... did that add to yours?'

'I do what I do because I can. Because I must,' Julien replied. 'But please, I need to go home. Back to the world of Lamprey. My sister too.' His eyes implored. 'Please?'

And then he was asleep.

A deep, deep sleep that, despite their attempts, none could awaken him from.

Without a word, the Squire wrapped the boy in his blankets and hoisted him up, draping him over his shoulder. 'Edith, get Dominique, we must go to the cave.'

As quickly as they could, they got to the cave, but word had got out. They had been seen leaving the Hall and, unlike others, they were not travelling on horseback. By the time they reached the cave, a good crowd had gathered. The Squire neither knew nor cared if they were there to cheer or scold him, he just knew he had to get the children to the cave...

Which proved a problem. An insurmountable one.

Standing before the cave mouth were Shepherd Mullen and Brother Lucien. Brother Ralph was there too, but he was imploring the other two to go away. Mullen was gesticulating at him with his shepherd's crook.

The three in the pit; others grouped above, blocking the way to the woods. Goodewife Barber didn't like what she was seeing. It was like a cockfight.

'What's going on?' bellowed the Squire.

'That child is the spawn of evil,' Lucien replied.

'Should've killed them when they first arrived,' agreed Mullen. 'My fault for helping them crawl out.'

'Are you people mad?' Jude asked. 'Look at the good they have done me!'

And Brother Lucien smiled his cold, dark smile. 'Maybe, Jude, you too should go. Maybe you too are part of the Devil now.'

'Aye,' added the shepherd.

Goodewife Barber looked at the assembled villagers above the ridge of the pit, their numbers growing by the minute.

'What has taken your minds?' she asked. 'They are children, they cannot hurt you. Why are you scared?'

'Why are you wanting to put them back in a cave? Normal children don't live in a cave,' was Lucien's retort.

De Calne just ignored them, walking down the slope towards the cave mouth.

And then he stopped.

It had been sealed up with rocks and stones. Cemented together by straw and mud, which had dried.

'I did it a week ago,' Mullen said, adding a none-too-deferential 'Squire'.

'Then undo it, Mullen,' de Calne snapped. 'Or you'll be looking for a new village to keep your sheep in.'

But then the Squire heard what he feared the most – the boy Julien gave a final gasp and the Squire eased him off his shoulder and laid him out on the ground.

He knew before he held a hand to the boy's mouth that he was dead, and so it appeared did his sister, who with a shriek of rage ran over, pushing the Squire aside and holding her brother's corpse to her, a huge sob bursting from her.

And she stared at the Squire.

And at Shepherd Mullen.

And at the two monks.

'Dominique,' cajoled the Squire, 'let him be. He's gone. I'm... I'm sorry.'

But Dominique saw only the three men before her: one scared, two arrogant.

She gently placed her brother back down and stood up. Brother Ralph went straight to the boy, and began mumbling a prayer, but it was Lucien her gaze was fixed upon.

'You,' she said out loud.

Lucien gasped. Then regained his composure. 'The spawn of the Devil speaks,' he declared, and then gasped as he fell to the ground. Dominique had wrenched Mullen's shepherd's crook from his grasp and jabbed it into Lucien's gut.

Mullen stepped forward, as if to reclaim his tool, but the girl was faster. She ensnared his neck in the crook and with almost inhuman strength, twisted. The cracking as Mullen's neck broke, echoing across the pit and into the woods above, was enough to freeze the Goodewife's blood in her veins. As Mullen fell dead, the girl swung the crook backwards with so much force that Brother Lucien's head was torn from his shoulders and it rolled further down the pit.

'Dominique! No!' cried de Calne, but it was too late. With a last look at her dead brother, the green girl tore up the opposite side of the pit, through the scared, parting crowd and into Wulpit Forest.

De Calne was on his feet, giving chase before Jude or Erwick could stop him, and despite their own cries, all they heard as the Squire was swallowed by the trees was a final yell of 'Come back! Please!'

The villagers waited nearly four hours before entering the woods, but after a good search as day gave way to night, no trace of either the green girl, nor the Squire was found. A few days later, as Headman, Erwick called a meeting of the villagers and it was decided that one final search would take place the following day. No stone would remain unturned in the woods, but if neither were found, the woods would be set alight and burned.

The Abbot reclaimed the body of Brother Lucien, and Shepherd Mullen was interred just outside the monastery. Some weeks later, the Abbot would close the monastery and with his monks retreat to an island off the coast of Anglia. None from Wulpit would ever hear from, or see, them again.

After their fruitless search, the green boy's body was taken to the very heart of the woods by Jude, the Barbers and a few other brave villagers. They covered him in twigs and branches and set the pyre ablaze.

Within hours, the whole forest was burning, and as the winter evening drew in, the darkness was lit by the golden glow of Wulpit Forest.

'It will grow back one day,' Erwick said.

'Aye,' said his wife. 'But I doubt we shall ever see it again in our lifetimes.'

'No,' added Jude. 'Nor the Squire or the green girl.'

And they never did.

Chapter Three
Something's Gone Wrong Again

'It's what friendship is all about, Mel,' said the Doctor, peevishly.

Melanie Bush sighed. This... discussion had been going around in circles for at least an hour or three by now. Mel was reasonably sure that the Doctor had forgotten exactly what the argument was about – 'it's what friendship is all about' being his catch-all answer to any argument he was in danger of losing.

'I'm not denying that,' she said reasonably. 'But it seems a pretty hostile environment to go into on the off-chance that we might possibly perhaps maybe if we're really lucky and extraordinarily fortuitous bump into some retired Time Lord who has chosen to end his days on Carsus.'

'What's wrong with Carsus?'

'I never said there was anything wrong with Carsus,' she sighed. 'Although it's probably better than Caliban.'

'And what's wrong with Caliban?'

Mel frowned. 'Doctor, where have we just been? What has just happened to us?'

'Oh. Oh yes, that Caliban. Ahh. Yes. Sorry Mel, I promise Carsus will be a nicer experience than Caliban was for you.'

'Good,' said Mel. 'Now, explain to me why we're going to

somewhere you've just described as a "big place, hard to get around" just to find one man who doesn't want to be found.'

'Who said he doesn't want to be found?'

Mel gritted her teeth. 'You did. About eighty-five minutes ago.'

The Doctor harrumphed and shoved his hands into his multicoloured pockets. 'No I didn't.'

'Yes you did.'

'Didn't'

'Did!'

'Didn't!'

'Oh for goodness' sake, Doctor, let's go to Carsus then and find him.'

The Doctor smiled widely. 'Wonderful idea, Mel. I'll set the coordinates and off we go!'

Mel breathed out. The Doctor had won. What a surprise.

It never ceased to amaze him that, no matter what was going on in the world, somehow, just by glancing up into a clear blue sky, everything seemed better. Momentary serenity, at least.

Of course, despite the blue sky, the bright sunshine and the unusually warm September breeze that was, no doubt, ebbing its way past the window on the outside, the atmosphere in this large, well-lit room was anything but serene.

Doctor Emile Schultz was facing him. Him, and the three board members – all of whom seemed to be yelling in unison, making lots of noise and achieving nothing. Which was nothing new, he had to admit. But over the last few months, it had been a different noise and type of underachieving to that which usually happened at the *Politehnica Universitatea din Bucuresti*. Of course, that was all going to change now – many of the departments were being broken up, sent to different parts of Romania; others closed down. The noise would be spread far and wide. And probably get louder. Ah well.

Noise. All his life, there had been noise. How easily he recalled the car crash of three years before, when his brakes had failed so suddenly, and that awful noise as metal was torn open by concrete as the vehicle had hit the side of the shop. Or that time during the war when a gunshot had exploded behind his right ear, and it was only by some miracle that his turning to look at a hat in a shop window saved him. On top of the sound of the gun shot (strange how no one had seen the soldier who fired it – never got to the bottom of that one), there had been the glass shattering as the bullet struck it. Then there was –

'Professor Tungard? Professor!'

His reverie broken abruptly, he glanced towards the person calling his name. It was Yurgenniev, the new administrator put in by the wave of communism that had swept over Romania during the year. A dour, rather ignorant-looking man with a large, round, fleshy face, wild eyes and wilder eyebrows, he was now squeezing those eyes tighter than a pig's and glaring in his direction.

Perhaps Yurgenniev was trying to intimidate him. He thought it might be fun to see how long a fuse Yurgenniev actually had, and imagined his head popping like a firecracker.

Instead, he just looked across at the man and said, 'I'm very sorry, I was distracted by... by the gardener outside. He was cutting the grass in a most peculiar way. Do, please, continue.' He smiled as sincerely as he could (probably not very) and waved his hand in a manner that suggested Yurgenniev should indeed continue.

Sending him a glare that probably wilted flowers in his own country, Yurgenniev turned back to his... victim.

'Doctor. My dear, dear, Doctor,' Yurgenniev said to Schultz, with a smile that could freeze water at a thousand paces. 'No one is denying that over the years, you have made an enormous contribution to the Silviculture Department. But in our assessments, we have found ourselves wondering if you are still the right person to whom we can entrust the future of Romania's glorious woodlands and forests?'

Schultz had not spoken much during the inquiry – Tungard knew that was Schultz's way. He'd always been quiet, studious and brilliant, of course. Tungard admired him tremendously – many years earlier, Tungard had let receipt of his own doctorate slip for a year because he'd taken time out to help Schultz attain his. Tungard had not the slightest interest in silviculture – to him, trees were objects one sat in the shade of to read books, they were not to be treated as a science. But Schultz was a good friend, and Tungard believed that sacrifice demonstrated the true mark of friendship.

Which was why he was sat in this room now, whilst Schultz was being interrogated – or *interviewed* as the university's new administrators termed it – regarding his exploits during the war. Tungard was determined to stand by Schultz because that was what friends did. They both knew that the communists who had taken charge of Romania during the spring would frown upon the actions taken and alliances formed by Schultz back then.

Yurgenniev was speaking again. 'Is it true, Doctor Schultz, that you aided the Nazis? That is all we need to know.'

'"Aided" is a loaded phrase,' Tungard interceded. 'No one here at the university really had much choice in the matter.'

'We all have choice,' Yurgenniev corrected him. 'That is what freedom is all about.'

Tungard shrugged and silently wondered what the chance

was that Yurgenniev was being ironic by talking about 'free-dom of choice'. Coming from a communist policeman – part of what was, in essence, an occupying force – that had to be the most outrageous thing he'd heard all day. But he said nothing. Being rude to Yurgenniev wouldn't help Schultz in any way.

Schultz finally broke his silence. 'What I did, I did because at the time it was the only action open to me.'

'Really?'

'Yes. The German military deemed what we did here of interest to their war effort. As Romania was part of their empire at that time, for the sake of my family, I did as I was asked.'

Yurgenniev pretended to consult his notes before replying – Tungard, however, was aware that the inquisitor already knew Schultz's file backwards. It was just an attempt to look officious.

'I see… family. Yes, yes a wife, Hilde, and two sons. They are here, in Bucharest?'

'Yes.'

'Safe?'

'Yes, I believe so.' The tone of Schultz's reply implied a 'for now' at the end.

Yurgenniev nodded. 'Indeed, of course they are.' Tungard was sure he could hear that silent 'for now' echoed back at the doctor.

The inquisitor then glanced at his two, until now, silent associates.

One of them, a thin-faced, fair-haired man who may have been in his early thirties or early fifties, his lined face betraying his Russian stock rather than his age, shuffled some papers. 'So, let me understand this, Comrade Schultz,' he said without meeting the doctor's eyes, 'everything you did for the Nazis, you did because you believed in their government, yes?'

'That's not what he said,' Tungard said, a little more aggressively than he intended.

'That is what we heard,' said the inconclusively-aged man.

'We were required –' Tungard started, but Yurgenniev held up his hand to quieten him.

'Comrade Professor, it is not you who are under investigation here,' he said reasonably. 'Unless you wish, of course, to volunteer?'

'No, I...'

'Precisely. I'm sure we all appreciate the fact that you are here to support your colleague and... friend.' Yurgenniev said the word 'friend' as if it were a particularly contagious disease. 'However, we would appreciate it further if you would restrict your input to playing the role of "character witness" we requested of you, and otherwise keeping quiet, yes? I'm sure you will then appreciate our continued tolerance of your presence and our decision not to investigate exactly what *you* did during the war whilst in the pay of the previous... administration.'

Tungard fell silent. He chanced a glance towards Schultz – the older man's eyes said it all. The inquisition was a sham, the communists had already decided his fate.

'I would like to request that Professor Tungard leave this enquiry and return to his wife,' Schultz said suddenly.

A look passed between Yurgenniev, the ageless man and the third member of the board.

Yurgenniev then smiled at Tungard. 'You heard the good doctor's request, Professor Tungard. Will you agree?'

Tungard breathed deeply. 'No. No, I stay to support my friend through this difficult time,' he said firmly.

Yurgenniev nodded, made a note on his papers and smiled.

Tungard was reminded of the old saying about the cat and the cream, but stayed seated and looked squarely at Schultz.

It was, after all, what friendship was all about.

A cold, grey day in a cold, grey city. Oh yes, the sun was shining; oh yes, Bucharest was a beautiful city of splendid architecture and dazzling sights; and oh yes, it was reasonably warm outside.

But to Natjya Tungard, her home had become greyer than she could ever have imagined.

She cursed as she dropped a stitch. She was knitting Joseph a sweater for the forthcoming winter (no matter how warm today was, come November, Bucharest would be freezing and damp, and the need for warm sweaters would be paramount). Many years before, she had been taught to knit by her beloved mother, in the upstairs room of their small home.

'Once you and Joseph are married,' Mother had warned, 'you will need to make him clothes to wear. His head is in the clouds, that one.'

She had been proven right, too. Joseph Tungard was always too busy to go shopping for clothes and suchlike – his classes at the university and the subsequent extracurricular activities that went with them saw to that.

By day, Joseph was a chemist, a job he neither enjoyed nor saw much point in, other than bringing in a decent wage. But in the evenings, he ran English and philosophy classes for his more intellectual, forward-thinking students. Natjya had got to know a number of these over the years. Many of them now lay beneath the soil of their homeland, victims of the war and its inevitable fallout. Joseph had become quite withdrawn over the last two or three years – Natjya knew the new communist regime that had taken control of much of Eastern Europe upset him greatly. If the Germans had been aggressive war-mongers, they at least acknowledged and admired intellectual pursuits. The communists, however, they saw no value in languages or philosophy. They had been systematically rounding up the country's thinkers and achievers under the pretence of seeking collaborators and war criminals. How long before they came looking for Joseph?

Natjya glanced up from her knitting (it was a grey sweater, naturally – any other colour of wool was very hard to come by without making huge sacrifices, both financial and moral, to the black marketeers and she would never do that) and found herself staring at a black-and-white photograph. It was mounted in a simple dark-wood frame, hung slightly crooked on the wall above the fireplace.

It showed a group of smartly dressed smiling people outside a catholic church, protecting themselves from the drizzle with big black umbrellas. In one corner, written in white ink, were the words 'The best day of my life. Thank you. J. March 28th 1937'.

Natjya stood and reached up to the photograph, running a finger across the inscription. Eleven-and-a-half years now. Eleven-and-a-half years of personal bliss amidst private tragedy. Four years after the wedding, little Luka had been born, but with the war, the hardships and the fear, their son hadn't survived to his second birthday. Natjya's mother had taught her to make clothes for the baby. These now lay, folded neatly, almost reverently, in a drawer in the bedroom she shared with her husband. Now, she just knitted clothes for Joseph. It was what she did, simple as that. Joseph worked hard at the university, Natjya worked hard in the house. What could change that perfect arrangement?

The communists, obviously. Having taken control of the country, they were conducting what Joseph, in a rare moment of angry emotion, called 'witch-hunts', finding those who had 'collaborated' with the Nazis in the early forties and sending them away.

Joseph's friend Emile was currently under such an investigation, and although she would support her husband to her dying breath, Natjya was anxious about his decision to defend Emile so publically. Who knew how these communists would react? Or treat Emile's friends? Would Joseph be next? They had already closed down the church in which the Tungards had been married, declaring organised religion to be wrong. If their souls were that hard, that blind, no one could be sure how they would take any implied criticism of their methods. And by supporting Emile Schultz, however grand and loyal a gesture, Natjya suspected that the communists would see Joseph's actions as criticism.

Her reverie was interrupted by a harsh rapping on the front door. She put down her knitting and crossed the stone floor, unlocked the latch – before the war, no one locked their houses – and cautiously pulled the door towards her.

Hilde Schultz stood there, shivering in the cold, her breath almost frozen on the air before her face.

'Natjya? May I come in?'

Natjya knew that the sensible thing to do was to say 'no', make an excuse, not let the wife of the troublemaker into her home.

But it wasn't the right thing to do and more than eleven years of life with her philosophical husband had taught Natjya that what was sensible was not always right.

'Hurry,' she said, almost dragging her neighbour inside. Without trying to seem obvious, she gave a quick glance to the left of the street, then the right, checking they weren't observed by the new state police.

Hilde shrugged at her as Natjya turned inwards once more. 'Don't worry, I made sure I wasn't followed.'

Hilde Schultz looked on the verge of tears.

'What is the matter?' asked Natjya, although she suspected that she already knew the answer.

'Emile. This... case they've brought against him.' Hilde sat in a chair while Natjya set about boiling some water on the stove. 'I think we shall have to leave the city.'

'Why?'

'Emile believes they will find him guilty of collaborating. They will exile him, probably to Russia. Or Siberia. Or Tungusta. Or –'

Natjya put a hand on Hilde's shoulder, comfortingly she hoped. 'All will be well. Joseph is with him today. As Chair of the Science Department, he still has some sway over the communists.'

Hilde shrugged. 'Oh, Natjya, I do hope so. But I also fear for Joseph.'

'Why?'

'Because his support for Emile may reflect badly upon your husband. They are an unforgiving lot, these Stalinists. Look at what they did to Trotsky. Already our neighbours are closing their shutters as we go past their houses. We are to be outcasts!'

Natjya poured hot water into a couple of mugs of dried nettle, and passed Hilde the tea. Her friend sipped at it gratefully.

'Natjya, when Joseph was at our house the other night, discussing today's meeting...'

'Yes?'

'He made an offer.'

'I see.' Natjya could imagine exactly what that would have been. How like Joseph – no consideration for the practicalities. But she liked to think that if the situation had been reversed, she would have made the same 'offer'. She sat opposite her friend, her own mug of hot tea in her hand and smiled. 'My dear, dear Hilde. We shall not allow you to vanish into the night. You and Emile and the boys, you must stay here with us if need be.'

Hilde reached out and took Natjya's hand and squeezed. 'You two are true friends. Hopefully, it will not be too long before both our husbands return, full of the fact that the communists have decided to let them go free, and life can return to normal.'

Natjya nodded, but inside she feared the worst. 'Hilde, just in case, bring the boys over now. I think you should stay here immediately. Go on, off you go.'

Without a word, but with a smile that suggested Natjya had saved her life, Hilde slipped away, back into the bustle of the streets.

Natjya quickly began tidying the house up. Four extra people in such a small home – sleeping, eating and everything else – it would be an uncomfortable few days. But she was sure it would only be a few days, then everything would sort itself out.

Joseph would see to that. That's what he did.

Sir Bertrand Lamprey finished his reading, smiled and tucked the two sheets of paper, neatly folded – he really had to make sure standards were not slipping – back inside his jacket.

Lazily, he dabbed a finger on the Hall table, and then rubbed a few motes of dust between his thumb and forefinger.

'Standards,' he muttered darkly. Then, bellowing at the top of his voice, he demanded the immediate attention of Mary.

Mary took only a few seconds to appear, framed in the doorway to the library, where she had been setting the afternoon fire. 'Sir?'

'Dust, Mary. Dust.' He wandered towards her. 'Standards, y'see. War's over, plenty to do. Don't let me tell you again.'

Mary bobbed courteously, but Sir Bertrand could see from her expression she had no idea what he was talking about. He walked away, sighing deeply.

At one time, he'd have sacked her on the spot; but these days, service, good or bad, was hard to come by. One had to make do – which was fine, so long as standards did not slip.

'Hello my darling,' said a soft voice on the stairway.

He smiled up at his wife, who was coming downstairs as if she was walking on the very air itself. He felt his chest tighten momentarily – it always did whenever he saw her.

Elspeth Lamprey was certainly a stunning woman: Sir Bertrand was aware of this not only because he thought so – and so he should, he'd married her – but because he knew what was said of her in the village. Never coarse or raucous, Lady Lamprey was held in high esteem by the working classes, probably more than he was, if he thought about it. But why not? After all, what was he but a member of the British gentry, the bearer of a title inherited through the generations? But Elspeth? Oh she seemed as if she, too, had been born into the manner, but the fact of the matter was that her father was just a civil servant from Dorset. Yet Elspeth had quickly adapted to the upper-class life and made Sir Bertrand very proud.

'I heard you screeching like a barn owl, Bertie,' she

admonished. 'Do leave Mary alone. Since Mrs Travers left us, Mary does very well to cope on her own. I don't want to lose her, too.'

Sir Bertrand nodded, mumbled an apology.

'Don't tell me you're sorry, tell Mary.'

'Can't apologise to the servants, Elspeth. Not right. Not done, y'know.'

Elspeth sighed and smiled at her husband as she reached the foot of the stairs. She traced a finger down his cheek. 'You are a silly sausage sometimes,' she said. 'One day you'll learn to appreciate their hard work and loyalty. Now, was that the postman I heard?'

Sir Bertrand nodded. 'Just some papers, you know. From Oswald. Sorting out the Union, you see. Big meeting in London tomorrow, probably be some disturbance, but I'll keep away from that.'

'I see.' Elspeth Lamprey's tone changed. 'Bertrand, dearest, you know I do wish you wouldn't stay involved with that man. He was very unpopular during the war.'

'Spoke his mind, that's all,' Sir Bertrand replied. 'Got a lot of sense in it, y'see. I just like to listen, you know. See what he has to offer us now.'

Elspeth frowned. 'I shall probably come with you, then. Helen needs to visit Doctor Maher, a check-up. Make sure she's on the mend. She so wants to be well for Christmas and her birthday.' Elspeth touched her husband's arm. 'I do think we might consider giving her an unofficial birthday in June or July. It's so unfair on children if Boxing Day and a birthday fall on the same date, don't you agree?'

'Well, never really thought about it.'

'Then perhaps you should,' smiled Elspeth.

Sir Bertrand nodded and wandered towards the dining

room. 'Fine, fine, if you promise not to refer to me as a sausage again,' he laughed, patting his waist. 'Now, tomorrow I'll get Barker to drop you off at Harley Street and pop back and collect you after he's got me to Victoria Embankment. What time do you need to be at Maher's?'

Elspeth drew a diary out of her pocket and flicked through it. 'Two o'clock,' she said finally. 'I'd like to be a little early if I can. Helen likes to see the fish.'

'Fish, eh? Right. Well, I'll get you there for one-thirty. Need to be by the Temple an hour after that – plenty of time. Will you take Helen shopping, perhaps?'

'If you think that's a good idea, dear, yes. I understand they are putting up the Christmas displays in Hamleys.'

Sir Bertrand nodded. 'Splendid idea, then. I'll just tell –'

He was cut off as the telephone rang. He picked it up. 'The Hall,' he said curtly. A beat. Then: 'Yes, rightio. See you then.' He replaced the receiver and turned to his beautiful wife. 'Change of plan, m'dear. Sorry. I have to be in London by midday.'

Elspeth shrugged. 'Well, we'll go shopping before Harley Street and...' Elspeth grimaced. 'Botheration, tomorrow morning I have the ladies coming around to discuss the village Christmas Fayre. I wonder if I can cancel –'

'Don't do that my love. Look,' Sir Bertrand took her hands in his. 'Look, you stay here, keep the ladies of the parish happy. Barker can take Helen shopping – he'll enjoy the break I imagine. He can drop me at Aldwych, then park up by Portland Square. Bit of shopping, get Helen to the doctors, and by then I'll be finished. Mosley's doing something in the House in the afternoon now, so we'll be back here a couple of hours after that.'

Elspeth relaxed. 'What a relief,' she said. 'Cancelling is not a nice option – that Mrs Shelley can be a bit frightful if her plans are changed. Now, I'll go and tell Helen, you relax and read your papers.' She kissed Sir Bertrand lightly on the forehead. 'I'll see you at dinner.'

As she swept out, Sir Bertrand could not help but smile. Elspeth and young Helen – could she really be seven already? – were his life.

Oh yes, Mosley's Union Movement was all very well, providing a good bit of subversion and danger in these post-war years, but when it came down to it, he was always happy to put away the old black shirt and enjoy family life.

The following afternoon, Barker was driving along the A140, having turned onto it just before Stowmarket, and thus up towards Eye.

Sir Bertrand was dozing slightly, aware that little Helen was sat beside him, showing her new dolly the countryside as it sped past. He was dimly aware of the lefts and rights as they came off the main road and back towards the village. The streetlights reflected occasionally on the silver cross Helen wore around her neck. Elspeth had given her that on her fifth birthday, and Sir Bertrand honestly could not remember a day when she had not worn it since.

He opened an eye casually, and was immediately enamoured of the big grin that was drawn across Helen's face. Barker had found her quite a topping doll, and Helen seemed happier than he could remember. Doctor Maher was, apparently, very pleased with Helen – her mumps had cleared up, and even the coughing had stopped. According to Barker, the doctor had given Helen Lamprey a clean bill of health.

'She's a lucky girl,' he had said apparently. 'Lots of little girls get very ill because of mumps, but you have recovered marvellously.'

And Helen had replied: 'I'm always lucky, Doctor Maher. My daddy says "lucky" is my middle name!'

Barker had been almost as excited to relay that conversation as Helen herself had been. Good man, Barker. Reliable type. Never let his standards slip. One of the very –

'Jesus Christ!'

Sir Bertrand sat up at once, ready to chastise his driver for his language, but then stopped.

He could see what had caused Barker's outburst.

So could Helen.

The late-afternoon November sky, normally so dark, was lit up with a huge orange glow. The villagers were scurrying around before them, and Barker had to stop suddenly.

'Oh Sir Bertrand,' a woman was wailing. Lamprey barely acknowledged it was the wretched Mrs Shelley. 'Oh Sir Bertrand... there's nothing we can do!'

And Sir Bertrand Lamprey grabbed at Helen, pulling her close, pushing her head down, away from the outside, trying to shield her from the flames.

The flames that had completely engulfed the Hall, the grounds and the woods at the back.

Sir Bertrand wanted to ask where Elspeth was. Why wasn't she rushing towards him? He could see Mary, huddled in a blanket, shaking, surrounded by others.

He could see Thompkin, the butler, organising everything, his face blackened by soot.

So where was Elspeth? He ought to have been asking.

But something in his chest tightened, more than ever before, and he swore he could feel it break as he knew, somehow he just knew, that right there, the very heart of the blaze had become Elspeth's funeral pyre.

* * *

Mel watched as the Doctor's hands darted expertly over the TARDIS console, flicking and pressing, twisting and turning every control possible. 'Nearly there,' he said at one point, but enough minutes had passed since then to suggest to Mel that a certain chronological exaggeration was at play here.

Mel had since had a chance to change into clothing suited to what the Doctor had assured her was Carsus's hot and humid atmosphere – a slimming pair of white trousers, with matching ankle boots, and a puff-sleeved striped blouse, which the Doctor had remarked (when they'd bought it on Kolpasha a few weeks ago) made Mel resemble a well-wrapped boiled sweet. Not rising to the bait, Mel had happily purchased it, although she did ensure that it went onto the Doctor's account and not hers. She waited for the day when the Doctor actually checked his finances and discovered her little revenge. Of course, it'd be so far off that she would have little problem convincing him that he had, in fact, purchased it for her as a gift. Or an apology. Or whatever she would come up with when it was necessary.

'Now, Mel, I'm just going to nip to the library as there's a book I want old Rummas to borrow. A collection of Herran poetry, which I just know he'll love.'

Mel frowned. It was unusual for the Doctor to leave the control room mid-flight. 'Have you programmed Carsus in, then?'

'Of course,' he tutted. 'A flicked switch here, a pushed button there, and the old girl knows exactly what to do.' With a quick wink, he opened the door to the TARDIS corridor and vanished, with a fading 'Back in a mo', leaving Mel shaking her head.

And as Mel looked back towards the scanner, she saw something weird. There, set into one of the roundels on the wall, was a picture. Clearly a photograph, black and white, and in a circular frame. Not only had it not been there before, it was of her and some other girl she didn't recognise.

There was something about the way Mel looked in the picture, something slightly off-kilter. And where had it come from?

As Mel moved to get a closer look it seemed to shimmer and fade away, leaving the more familiar, slightly back-lit roundel in its position.

'Well, that's not right,' the Doctor said, as he pored over the console. 'Have you touched anything, Mel?'

Mel stared open-mouthed at the Doctor, as he looked from the console to the scanner.

'Not right at all.'

When had he come back in?

Mel was about to answer, when the Doctor tapped her on the shoulder from behind. 'Daydreaming, Melanie? That's not like you.' And he crossed to the inner door. 'Well, there isn't much time... Oh.'

The Doctor at the console looked over at the Doctor talking and sighed. 'Not again...'

And the TARDIS exterior doors suddenly opened, followed a second later by the Doctor, taking deep breaths as if he'd been running.

'Ah yes,' he gasped. 'Of course, that would make sense.'

'Not to me it doesn't,' said Mel.

'Lucky you,' said another voice, female. It was a woman with cropped hair, apart from a length of pigtail that ran down to below her shoulders. She was dressed in a long, washed-out red dress that appeared to have been crudely torn away just below the bum, creating the illusion of a miniskirt in an outfit that was clearly more of a maxi, and was breathlessly following this latest Doctor in. 'Some of us will have to get used to it,' she said.

Mel found herself staring at the newcomers in shock. The woman was, bizarrely, herself! And this Doctor... well he was not in the same multicoloured coat as the others, more a sombre black outfit, high-collared, quite austere, topped off with a voluminous cloak. He also had a jagged, but healed gash down the left-hand side of his face, causing his left eye to be virtually sealed shut by the scar tissue. He stared at Mel through his good eye, as if not quite sure what to make of her.

'Infinite combinations, infinite alternatives,' he said quietly.

The Doctor who had initially appeared behind Mel shrugged. 'I don't think this can be right.'

The Doctor by the console shook his head. 'I'm not so sure. You see, I've been pondering –'

The scarred Doctor who had just dashed in cut across him: 'Actually I think you'll find –'

But he too was cut off as the interior door opened, and another Doctor, this one carrying a small, hard-covered poetry book, entered, stopped, looked in alarm at his duplicates and then fixed Mel with a beady glare.

'Did you touch something?'

Before she could reply, the Doctor dressed in black held up his hand. 'Listen carefully, this is very important. You need to know this.'

Mel was feeling very disturbed. A room full of, mostly colourfully costumed, identical Doctors was a little too much to bear.

The Mel with the shorn hair and torn dress looked Mel directly in the face. 'It's all to do with your friend the Lamprey.' Something in her voice implied speech marks around the word 'friend' perhaps suggesting irony. Mel wasn't sure – she'd never met her double before, let alone heard herself speak.

'Anyway,' continued the ex-exterior Doctor, 'it's important that you realise the Lamprey is controlling everything. Of course, there might be benign aftereffects but just remember this, the incidents are –'

And he and the duplicate Mel vanished. Soundlessly.

The Doctor by the scanner sighed and then sarcastically said: 'Well, that was informative but not entirely –' then stopped. After a beat, he continued. 'Oh I see. So after we left Carsus, we went to Earth. We met up at the restaurant and... oh yes of course. All of which means –'

And vanished.

'Of course!' exclaimed the former shoulder-tapper. 'I see what I meant now. Oh Mel, the Lamprey is going to –'

And he too was gone.

The Doctor with the book – Mel rather assumed this was 'her' Doctor – gently eased the interior door closed behind him.

'Well, I didn't understand a word of that. Did you, Mel?'

Mel looked at the now-closed exterior doors. How come they hadn't been sucked into the space–time vortex... oh, unless that Doctor and Mel were using TARDIS doors from the future (she assumed it was the future because she had no idea what a Lamprey was, despite her other self seemingly being very aware of this).

'Doctor, can I ask something?'

'Of course,' he replied, still staring at the various places in the control room his duplicates had stood. 'Unless you want an explanation.'

'Well, that'd be nice.'

'Can't do that.'

'Oh don't tell me. Time Lord secrets. Mustn't reveal the future to us poor mortals. Ancient Gallifreyan honour, yes?'

The Doctor shook his head. 'No, I can't give you an explanation because I haven't the foggiest idea what any of that was about.' He smiled. 'Still, shall we get to Carsus?'

'But surely...'

He held up a warning finger. 'I think, if we're going to solve this little mystery, perhaps we should play by the rules. Which means starting as we mean to go on. Carsus.'

This surprised Mel. Rulebook adherance wasn't the Doctor's finest trait. 'Why?'

The Doctor held up the poetry book. 'Because I handed this to myself in the corridor outside the library. And my other self said I should do what I was told for once.'

'Why'd you listen to him particularly?'

'You're familiar with the Time Lord ability to regenerate, yes?'

Mel nodded. Her brief time on Gallifrey had exposed her to that concept.

'Well,' the Doctor continued. 'Rather as you can remember dresses, t-shirts and coats you've owned, I remember my past bodies quite well. The one in the corridor wasn't one I knew.'

'Perhaps he wasn't you?'

'Oh, it was, definitely. We Time Lords have a feel for that sort of thing. But if he's a future me, I think he might know what he's talking about.' He breathed out slowly. 'So, Carsus, here we come!'

It was a cold, grey day on a cold, grey sea. Oh yes, the breeze was low; oh yes, the Mediterranean was a beautiful ocean of soft waves and splendid views; and oh yes, it was reasonably dry outside.

But to Natjya Tungard, her life had become greyer than she could ever have imagined.

She cursed as she dropped a stitch. She was still knitting Joseph the sweater – but whether it was the ship's motion that stopped her sleeping at night, the cold, or the tiredness and the pounding headache that had come on last evening and still not faded, Natjya could not focus on what she was doing.

'What else is there for me to do?' she mumbled to herself. 'If I cannot knit, if I cannot provide a sweater for my husband, what else am I here for?'

A small laugh came from the English woman beside her. 'Oh Natjya, what would I do without you?'

Natjya looked up sharply at her companion. 'And what do you mean by that, Monica, hmmm?'

'I mean, Natjya darling, that no matter how long this trip lasts, no matter what happens, so long as you can complain about your knitting, I know the world has not ended!'

Natjya shrugged. 'My world has.'

'No it hasn't, darling,' said Monica firmly. 'We've been through this. It's a setback, that is all.'

'Ha!' cried Natjya, putting her needles and wool back into her bag. 'A setback! Thrown out of my country, nothing to do, nowhere to go. Abandoned like a sick dog, thrown to the wolves, cast aside...'

Monica had heard it before and smiled. '"...like an unwanted bucket",' she echoed as Natjya continued her tirade. 'Dear sweet Natjya, look upon this as an opportunity.'

'An opportunity. Always you tell me to see it as an opportunity, but you do not understand. In Romania, we had opportunity. In *Bucuresti* we had opportunity. But now? Now, we go to a strange country where I can barely be understood, surrounded by strange people with their strange 'oh we won the war' ideas and we will be treated like dogs. Worse than dogs. I know how you English treat your refugees.'

Monica shook her head. 'Natjya, we've been through this before. Your English is terribly good, Joseph's more so. He has a job to go to – your wretched communists saw to that. Luscha has found you a good flat in a nice part of London and Joseph's salary will keep you in wool and needles and even buckets, should you need them. She says she'll even find you a char to come in, clean for you.'

Natjya snorted. 'I can clean! I know how to clean, I cleaned my house in *Bucuresti* every day. Why should I need this "char", hmmm? I'm not old or decrepit yet. I can still use a mop. Pah, I can still use a needle and tweezers and things. Why not just lock me away in a home, yes?'

Monica sighed and put aside the book she had failed to read over the last few days. Ever since meeting the Tungards in fact. 'I'm sorry about what happened to you, Natjya, really I am. But you have to accept that you need to move on from this. Treat it as an adventure. And in the end, the communists will, one day I'm sure, get bored with Eastern Europe, or Stalin will be toppled or maybe there'll be another war, and you'll go home eventually. But for now, try and look on the bright side. For Joseph's sake, if not your own.'

Natjya took a deep breath. She knew Monica was right. 'I just wish... I just wish we could have brought the boys. They deserved the new life, too.'

Monica nodded and touched Natjya's arm. For all the Romanian woman's yelling and moaning, Monica understood that what Natjya, and indeed dear Joseph, really felt was completely out of control. They had lost so much that night.

She thought back to the frightened little woman she had

first seen at the Black Sea docks, being 'escorted' onto the ship, her husband quietly following. Monica and her grandfather had had their attention caught by the look that Natjya had given as she stepped aboard. She had turned, looked back at what Monica had assumed were policemen, and given them a defiant toss of her head and then given her country one final, long stare. Something about her had intrigued Monica and she had made a point of seeking them out, hoping her broken Hungarian might be a common tongue. Of course, she had been delighted to discover that Joseph Tungard's English was almost flawless and although not as colloquial, Natjya had more than a grasp of the language, too.

They had explained that a friend of theirs had been in trouble with the communists and they had taken his family into their home for protection. Apparently, during the night, the authorities, tipped off by an eager neighbour, arrived and broke into their home. The other family, Schultz, Joseph had referred to them as, were taken away, screaming and crying. There had been two boys, aged about three and six, Monica believed, and Schultz's wife, Hilde. The Tungards were informed that they too were to leave Romania, although as Joseph had contacts abroad, the university at which he worked could not cover up his disappearance so easily, and as a result, they were to be exiled. Within days, Natjya had got word to a cousin of hers who had already fled to London, one Luscha Toletzky, who in turn made arrangements to receive them. The *Politehnica Universitatea* had made similar arrangements for Joseph to take up a post in London, although no longer as a chemist. Instead, he would teach philosophy, seen by the State as a wastrel's passive subject, unlikely to reveal any secrets about Romania's new sciences.

Monica and her grandfather had formed a solid friendship

with these two proud, intelligent refugees quite quickly and had already promised to help them settle in.

It was good therapy for her grandfather, Monica decided. They had been holidaying in the Carpathians after Monica's grandmother had passed away. She'd fallen ill towards the end of the war and despite his best attempts, Monica's grandfather had been unable to help her. She had died of pneumonia a few months earlier. At the age of seventeen, having herself been orphaned in 1941, Monica had been forced to grow up a little quickly and look after her maternal grandfather, who was overcoming his grief really rather well.

Monica's thoughts were interrupted by the arrival of Joseph and her grandfather.

'Good morning,' she said as Pike loomed over her.

'Read any more?' he said, in a deep but cheerful voice. 'Actually, you're looking a little green this morning. Not the seasickness I trust?'

Monica shook her head. 'No, Grandfather. I imagine I'm just a little tired.'

Doctor Pike glanced over at Natjya, then back at his granddaughter.

Monica winked at him. 'Still, this book won't finish itself.'

'I see,' he said. 'Tired, eh. Well, you remember, you promised me you'd finish it before we reached Southampton.' He picked up the book and Monica eased it away from him, hoping he wouldn't notice that her bookmark was only between pages 24 and 25. 'Dickens is so dull, Gramps,' she said, keeping his gaze. 'Can't I try something a little more... exciting.'

'Exciting?' piped up Natjya. 'Ha! She wants excitement. Try living under the communists, young Monica. That'll give you excitement.'

Joseph Tungard crouched down beside his wife and took her hand to caress it, but before he could speak, Natjya winced.

'What's the matter?' Joseph asked.

Natjya shrugged. 'I don't know. I can't concentrate and my hand is aching. So is my head.'

'Perhaps you have a chill,' said Joseph, rubbing the back of her hand gently. 'Let us ask the good doctor here, yes?'

'Oh, we shouldn't...' Natjya began, but Doctor Pike cut her off.

'Oh nonsense, Natjya. Of course I'll give you a look. Now, what seems to be the problem?'

Natjya looked at the other three. 'It's nothing. A lot of nonsense, I just have a chill I expect.'

'Headache?'

'Yes.'

'Anything else?'

'She can't knit,' Monica said quietly. 'Her hand keeps shaking. I noticed it earlier,' she added as Natjya gave her a look of surprise.

Natjya pouted. 'It's just the cold, that is all.' She smiled up at them all. 'Oh come on, I'm not used to the seas, and the wind, and it is nearly Christmas and I want to be at home. I'm feeling a little bit sad and I have a cold.' She sniffed, rather unconvincingly, Monica thought. 'That is all. We'll be in your Southampton Docks in a week or so, and Luscha has found us a nice warm flat and everything will be fine. I'll be fine,' she added, looking meaningfully at her husband. 'Now, don't fuss. Please.'

Doctor Pike stood up, and Joseph did the same. 'She's probably right, Joseph. But I think an early night tonight, Natjya, and, if you still have a headache in the morning, I'll think again. Would you like a sleeping draught for later?'

Natjya shook her head. 'The way this boat rocks around,' she said, back to her old self, 'nothing short of death itself would help me get a decent night's sleep.'

Chapter Four
Who'll Help Me Forget

Church cemeteries can be places of immense interest for those who enjoy researching such things. A fascinating record of lives and deaths, a permanent (assuming no gravestones have been kicked to pieces or daubed with graffiti) marker to celebrate the existence of a loved one, and often a sad, poignant reminder that they have gone. Some gravestones are simple affairs, a lump of chiselled granite, a name and message carved into them. Others are more expensive; marble or onyx, sometimes the headstone is joined by a flat or curved body-stone as well.

All the people commemorated have contributed to history in some way. For every famous scientist, architect or doctor, there are thousands of non-famous people who nevertheless made others happy and content, ultimately becoming the great-great-grandparents of someone who would contribute to finding a cure for syphilis, heart disease or cancer. Or maybe they were the types of people who turned left rather than right one morning and so didn't run over the five-year-old playing with his football who went on to discover the gene that causes Alzheimer's, or become a famous sports star and got his team together to raise millions for a disaster charity operating in Shanghai.

Or perhaps that little boy became a road sweeper who found a puppy abandoned in a bag, or was an accountant who learned that his boss was defrauding the banks or became a shop owner who refused to sell fireworks to a group of ten-year-olds and thus ensured they never lost eyes or limbs in a potential Fireworks Day disaster.

Such are the vagaries of the twists and turns of time; the element of chance that with each breath, with every decision taken, creates ripples that cause timelines to go left rather than right.

And thus each person who dies and is buried in one of the countless cemeteries all over the world is responsible, in theory, for birthing equally countless parallel realities, all due to them going left rather than right.

To stand in a graveyard, especially on a windy day, can be an awe-inspiring experience – a moment when you can almost feel the presence of the past surround you and envelop you with questions about who these people were, how and why they died and who was left behind who loved or respected them enough to establish these signs of remembrance. Was it illness, or accident, or murder? So many questions, almost always unanswered by the gravestones themselves.

But for some people, a visit to a graveyard isn't an excursion into facts and figures. For them it may just be a sad but necessary journey, part of a grieving process to enable healing after the trauma of losing someone close.

The man stood still, unsure if he wasn't moving through sheer inability or respect to the trembling woman at his side. He'd like to have believed it was the unrelenting cold rain making her shiver, but knew full well she was not really even aware of the weather. Her only concession to the winds had been to leave their daughter wrapped up well in the Austin, asleep and dry. Other than squeezing her hand tighter, he felt there was nothing else he could do. Of all the things life at university had taught him, grief and dealing with the effect on others of those same feelings had never been on the syllabus.

He wanted to give up, let what he really felt show through the stoic exterior he believed it was important he maintained. But that wouldn't be right. It was his wife's job to express enough emotion for the both of them.

Over to the right of the cemetery, a small café was doing its usual Thursday mid-morning business. Rather too loudly, a radiogram was blaring out the BBC's Light Programme channel. Displaying an alarming penchant for synchronicity, the disc jockey was blathering on: 'Hey pop-pickers, after just a few weeks on top, Nancy and her kinky boots have indeed walked away, leaving the top spot in the capable voices of Scott, Gary and John, who are going to tell us how the sun isn't going to shine any more. Well, with the rain coming down all over England, I can quite believe it! So here it is, this week's Number One in the record retailer charts!'

With an inward sigh at the cheerless music, the man allowed himself to kneel down and join his grieving wife over the headstone.

'Oh Anabel,' the woman was saying. 'I'm so sorry. Daddy's here, too. I promised we'd come and visit every week but I'm not sure... I'm not sure we can do that now.'

The man took a deep breath. 'We don't have to go, love. It is important that you're okay with this.'

His wife looked at him for the first time since they'd arrived. She then looked back across the cemetery, towards the car park where their green car waited. Although she couldn't see

54

their other daughter, she knew she was safely inside, snug and warm, unaware of the drama going on at the graveside.

'It's been six months,' his wife said. 'I think that while it's going to be the hardest thing I've ever done, it has to *be* done.' She smiled through her tears. 'I remember Mum saying something about it after the war. The village was full of wives, just like her in fact, whose husbands had not come back to the airfield. They sat day after day at the empty graves, never getting over it. Never moving on. I know it's been difficult since Anabel... since Anabel died, but I know that if we don't get away, don't go down South and as far away as possible from here, I'll be one of those women making pilgrimages here every day for the rest of my life.'

'We can come up once a month if you want, love.'

She laughed. It was a sound he couldn't remember hearing for such a long time now. It was a sweet, gorgeous laugh, a laugh a man could fall in love with, all over again. 'Oh yes, darling,' she said. 'I mean, it's a good salary, but it's not that good!' She squeezed his hand in return then eased it away. 'It'll be a wrench but I want to make the break.'

'Are you sure?'

'Yes. Yes, I am. I don't like it, but I know it's the right thing to do. For me. Otherwise I don't know if we'll ever forget.' She glanced back to the car. 'Or forgive. And that's the one thing we have to do.' She stood, and he followed suit.

'Besides,' she continued, not looking at him but at the fresh flowers she had laid at her feet, 'I think getting away from this place, these memories, is going to be better for both of us.' She stroked her husband's face and for what seemed like the first time in months, he believed that she was coping. And that they might have a future. 'I love you,' she added quietly.

'And I love you. So very much,' he replied, knowing he was prouder of her now than at any other time during their marriage. Just as her mother had tales about the effects of grief, so his own family had warned him that any mother who loses a daughter suffers a tragedy that few men can comprehend. Yes, they can grieve, as he had done, but a mother who has carried that child for nine months, nurtured it during the days after the birth while the husband returns to work, and watched it grow and develop almost hourly will always have a closer bond, especially to a child who died violently after only two-and-a-half years of life.

But his wife was coping, proving that, as he'd always known, Chrissie was actually stronger than he gave her credit for.

Stronger than him.

In a month they were due to head south, but he'd said he'd only go if she wanted to.

Really wanted to.

Today told him that she was ready. She might not want to, indeed, nor might he, but it was the right thing to do.

For him, for her and for their eighteen-month-old daughter, who would, hopefully, mentally cauterise this traumatic incident occurring so early in her life.

'We'll not forget her,' he promised Chrissie with a kiss.

'Of course we won't, Al,' Chrissie replied. 'But we have to move forward, embrace the pain and survive. And we will. Eventually.'

And together they headed back to the car, their surviving daughter, and their future.

And on the grave, they left a huge bouquet of flowers that got damper and damper as the sun did – as the song had promised – not shine.

Chapter Five
Are Everything

No one knows exactly who built Carsus. The Time Lords tend to think they did, but they don't know when. But then, they would. It's the kind of amazing place that they like to take the claim for. Time Lords generally act like highfaluting rag-and-bone men, dressing in poncy costumes, looking down their noses at everyone and yet actually doing little except scoop up the universe's flotsam and jetsam and – if it's of any value – claiming it as theirs. They then get some poor sod of an Archivist to write a book on the subject and nip back in time, depositing copies in various galactic libraries, and lo and behold, the eighteenth or twenty-eighth wonder of the universe was actually built/grown/uncovered by the Time Lords. No one else ever got a look in, archaeologically speaking, because they lived under the constant threat that if they argued with the Time Lords, the Time Lords would put a time bubble around them/their university/their planetary system and reverse time. Not only would they no longer exist, they never would have. Time Lords are like that. Gits. Pompous gits of the first order. No one likes them very much. Because they're gits. Big, fat, smelly ones.

* * *

'This is a very... biased view of the Time Lords,' Mel said slowly, closing the book.

'Hmm,' mumbled the Doctor. 'Picked that up a few years ago on the Braxiatel Collection, written I believe by some grumpy professor or other. Apparently she had a bit of an anti-Time Lord stance in a lot of her published works.'

'I like her already,' Mel retorted. 'Mind you, it actually says nothing about Carsus at all.'

The Doctor shrugged. 'Never mind, we'll be there in a moment or two. Then you can ask Rummas all about it. He's been living there for a few centuries.'

'How d'you know him?'

The Doctor looked up at the TARDIS ceiling. 'Oh, that's a good question. Tricky even. I mean, there are so many possible answers, where could I begin? I mean –'

'Oh never mind, I'll ask him that as well. If I can be bothered.'

The Doctor regarded Mel with an air of surprise. 'You did ask, it's not always easy to put answers in a form that your poor human mind can understand. Some questions can only be answered via pure mathematics, or quantum theory, or convoluted temporal chains of cause and effect, or –'

'It was a party, wasn't it? And you were drunk. Yes?'

The Doctor looked at his feet, wiggling his toes in his spats as if they'd suddenly become the most interesting thing in the cosmos.

'Weren't you?'

'Might have been,' the Doctor conceded, albeit very quietly.

'Can't. Hear. You,' sung Mel, enjoying herself enormously.

'It was a good party. On one of the moons of Korpal. Great parties they have there.'

'I thought he was a Time Lord?'

The Doctor beamed. 'Like me, he left his home, his peers and superiors, to see the universe. He... he collected things.'

'Things?'

'Yes. Books mostly. Loved books. Wanted to have the biggest library anywhere. Very jealous of mine, actually.'

Mel suspected the Doctor made that last bit up.

'Anyway, he was on a sojourn from somewhere or other, with some books, when we got talking at this party.'

The light then dawned. 'He nicked them, didn't he!'

'What?'

'The books. Your friend Rummas is a thief.'

'He preserves things that other people lose. Or throw away.'

Mel pointed out that, regardless of this, it was morally suspect. If not morally corrupt.

'Seriously, Mel, Rummas is a respected and responsible curator of books. He... borrowed a TARDIS once and used it to nip into burning buildings, and quake-devastated libraries and so on, saving things that would otherwise have been lost permanently. From all over the galaxies. Very responsible chap.'

'And this TARDIS he "borrowed". Had help getting that, did he?'

The Doctor activated the scanner. 'Oh look, there's Carsus now. Look at that. We're a few hundred metres above it.'

Mel was admittedly impressed. The majority of what she could see on the screen was one big construction, presumably the Library.

'Interesting design.'

'Do you think so, Mel? I always have.'

'Ever seen the Pentagon in Washington, Doctor. From above?'

The Doctor shrugged. 'Can't say that I have.'

'Looks just like that. Five sides, five points, which can imply a pentagram. An interesting symbol to find out in space.'

'Oh yes, of course. On your planet, depending on its inversion, it's either a sign of evil or pagan worship.'

'And they say that the Pentagon was built on a marsh originally called Hell's Bottom and was constructed in that shape against the wishes of President Roosevelt.'

'Your point?'

Mel shrugged. 'None really, just admiring the coincidence of finding a Masonic temple in outer space that is identical in shape and, let me count, one, two, three, four, five rings, and yes, ten spokes. Absolutely identical.'

'How do you know all this nonsense, Mel?'

'I read a lot,' she replied, throwing the biased book about the galaxy's wonders back to the Doctor. 'And far better books than that.'

The TARDIS materialised within a long, dark corridor, wood panelled and floored, giving the whole arrival an echo that all but shook those same walls.

As the doors opened and the occupants emerged, a small halogen light illuminated them from the Carsus Library's ceiling. Then another and another.

'An invite?' asked Mel.

'A path, certainly.'

'Is this one of those moments where you act obtuse, or should we follow the path?'

The Doctor breathed deeply. 'I am not obtuse. I am never obtuse. I occasionally like to take the path not indicated. However, at this time, as we're expected, I think we should follow the yellow-lit road.'

With a sigh at the bad pun, Mel followed. After a few seconds she stopped at a side turning, but the Doctor was following the lights. Mel checked her watch, then started after him.

Seven minutes later, she was at another junction. Seven more, another junction.

The Doctor finally asked what she was up to.

'Nothing,' she smiled. 'Just a theory. Now, what's in here d'you think?'

She eased open a door and looked inside. It was a series of long corridors flanked by rows upon rows, shelves upon shelves, of books. All shapes, all sizes. Hardcovers, paperbacks and leatherbounds all together.

'Impressed?' asked the Doctor.

Mel nodded. 'Brighton has a good selection in its library, but it would take up just one shelf here. Mind you,' she then remembered their earlier conversation, 'if you can pop around history, helping yourself to books – also known as stealing books where I come from, I might add – to suit yourself, no wonder it's so full.'

'In theory, the Carsus Library was designed to hold a copy of every book ever published anywhere. A sort of intergalactic Bodlien.' The Doctor smiled at Mel. 'I wrote a book once you know.'

'Did you?'

The Doctor nodded. 'Deluxe hardback, leather-bound. Wrote it on a long journey to Mars when I'd lost the TARDIS in a ga– well, in a moment of madness.'

'"In a gay"?' quoted Mel, then it hit her. '"In a game"! You gambled the TARDIS in a game and lost. Oh, I wish I could have seen that!'

'No you don't,' the Doctor said. 'You'd've hated the resultant journey. It took four months. So I amused myself by writing the history of Gumblejack fishing in the eighth galaxy. It was a bestseller.'

'Where?' challenged Mel.

The Doctor shrugged. 'Everywhere,' he said. 'All over the twelve galaxies. I did signings, spoke at dinner parties, made a fortune.'

Mel was wondering just where the line between truth and outright dishonesty was. She suspected it was getting blurrier by the second. 'And where, pray tell, is all this money now?'

The Doctor threw an arm around Mel's shoulder. 'Money! No use for the stuff. I donated it to charities the universe over. I became the Great Benefactor.'

Then it struck Mel where the money really was. 'You bought the TARDIS back, didn't you? Paid off your debts.'

The Doctor sighed. 'Trouble with you, Mel, is that you've no sense of thrill. Of adventure. Of derring-do. It's all black and white to you.'

'I just happen to value honesty over a good yarn, that's all.'

The Doctor was wandering off now, as if he hadn't heard Mel at all. 'Hundreds of thousands benefited from my financial generosity. I was the greatest anthropologist of my era!'

'I think that's "philanthropist" you'll find,' she called after him, but he just gave a dismissive 'I'm hurt' kind of wave and wandered further around the corridor.

'Wait up, Doc,' Mel called.

The Doctor stopped dead in his tracks and turned back to gaze reproachfully at his companion. '"Wait up, Doc"? When did you start channelling Peri?'

'You what?'

'Never mind.' Shaking his head in bewilderment, the Doctor pointed at a huge door that he had stopped outside. No lights were ahead, so Mel assumed this was where they were meant to be.

Indeed, on the door was a sign saying 'Head Librarian', so the Doctor knocked.

No reply.

He tapped louder. Still nothing.

He pushed on the door and it opened easily. Carefully, he put his head into the darkened room, but told Mel he couldn't see a thing. So he walked in fully and Mel followed. After three steps, a number of halogen lights in the ceiling lit up and Mel gasped.

The office was a perfect square, but with an indented roundel forming a majority of the floor, an identical indentation on the ceiling.

The walls were lined with shelves, but instead of books there were files and spiral-bound memo pads.

Every so often, a PC screen or a palm-held device was scattered round.

And dead centre of the floor was a beautiful mahogany desk, inlaid with green velvet, and a small brass lamp with a green hood. An ink blotter, an open diary and a glass of water were also taken in by Mel's quick mind.

But the most significant thing was sat in the leather office chair behind the desk. From the Doctor's intake of breath, Mel assumed this was the dead body of his friend Rummas. His eyes were wide open in shock, a trickle of dried red blood dribbling down his chin from his mouth, and what might have been a knife but may have been a letter-opener was inserted into the right-hand side of his chest, roughly below the third rib. Mel knew enough to realise that his heart had been pierced.

The Doctor walked over to the body, but touched nothing.

As he passed behind the chair, he stopped. 'Mel,' he hissed, 'I think you should see this.'

Mel hurried to join him, trying not to look too hard at Rummas's dead face, but stopped in total surprise when she saw the Doctor's discovery.

'That's not nice,' he was saying. 'Not nice at all.'

Lying on the ground was the Doctor's identical twin, big welts on his neck, eyes open and bulging.

'Caught from behind, and throttled at a guess,' he said dispassionately. In a rare moment of self-awareness, he added: 'And bearing in mind my size and shape, to take me by surprise and crush my windpipe before I could fight back means one of two things.'

'A man,' Mel said.

'Or someone you knew,' said a new voice behind them both.

Mel turned and saw Rummas stood by a small door she hadn't spotted before, positioned between two bookshelves.

'Touch your double, Doctor,' he commanded, and the Doctor did so.

'Intriguing,' said the Doctor. 'And your double, with the unfortunately positioned knife?'

'The same I should imagine. It's the third I've seen this week.'

Mel reached out to touch the dead Rummas and her hand went straight through. 'A hologram?' she asked.

'Good question Miss...?'

'Bush. Mel to my friends,' she replied.

Rummas smiled for the first time. 'I shall call you Miss Bush then until I feel it is time to presume otherwise.'

'Oh call her Mel and be done with it,' the Doctor said. 'All that "Miss Bush" stuff slows things down.'

'Please, call me Mel,' Mel added, throwing a look at the Doctor. 'And may I say I'm glad to see you alive after all.'

'Thank you, Mel. And no, it's not a hologram. It's the reason I contacted the Doctor. As I say, this is the third in a week.'

'All knifed to death?' asked the Doctor, rather indelicately, Mel thought.

'Two. The first one was just dead. Because I couldn't touch it, I have no way of knowing how, but there was no look of surprise on the face.'

'Well, I too am pleased to see you are all right my friend,' said the Doctor, crossing the room and shaking Rummas's hand. 'But I am intrigued. How many dead me's?'

'Two. Both by the knife-wounded me's. I wondered if I killed you and then you managed to stab me but both times the layout has been wrong. I suspect someone killed me, you discovered it and they killed you. After all, they used a weapon on me, but bare hands on you.'

Mel was staring at the knife, which she could now see was indeed a letter-opener. Somehow, knowing this wasn't real evaporated any nausea she felt. 'It's a convenient weapon,' she said. 'It might have been a spur of the moment attack, grabbing the nearest thing to hand.'

'She's terribly good at all this,' she heard the Doctor tell Rummas.

'Shall I tell you my theory, Doctor?' he asked.

'Go on.'

Rummas sighed. 'I think it's a time displacement thing. This area of space is legendary for space–time anomalies. Apart from Carsus itself, we have Minerva and Schyllus nearby, then, as you get closer to the edge of the system, there's Tessus, Lakertya, Molinda and, at the fringes, the lifeless gas planets of Hollus and Garrett. Both Schyllus and Minerva are known to have been affected by temporal waves at least once in the last trillion years or so, and there are reports of strange matter fragments, chronic threads and even a rumoured supernova in the distant past that didn't result in a black hole but just vanished off the cosmic map.'

The Doctor said nothing.

Mel said 'Wow', but quietly. It was quite a lot to take in, most of it would be considered impossible by the scientists on her planet.

'Wow indeed,' said the Doctor finally. 'What a lot of exciting spatial anomalies that it could be worth murdering over to control. Am I right that Carsus is at the dead centre of this system?'

Rummas shrugged. 'You know as well as I do, nothing can be dead centre of anywhere, but yes, in colloquial terms, we are equidistant from everything in this solar system.'

Mel asked whether Carsus was entirely natural or man-made.

Rummas seemed confused by the question. 'The planet is natural, as far as I know. This building was built millennia ago but no one knows who by. Why?'

The Doctor sighed. 'Careful, she'll start up about five-sided buildings and ancient Masonic rituals if you're not careful.'

'Really. Why?'

Mel smiled at Rummas's interest. 'Because going on what little knowledge I've gleaned from walking about, every junction is exactly seven minutes away from another.'

'That's true. Amazing that you should think of it, but entirely true. We discovered that a few years ago doing some rudimentary mathematical equations. What made you find out?'

'As I said to the Doctor earlier, this building is identical in size and shape to a powerful building, possibly the most powerful building in fact, on my world. And there, nowhere is more or less than seven minutes apart. Which is a big coincidence.'

Rummas looked genuinely intrigued. 'Then let me add to your wonderment. Assuming you're not from around here,' Mel nodded her assent, 'then you must be from Earth, Halos III or V, or Utopiana.'

'Why?'

The Doctor frowned. 'Yes, that's a remarkable leap of faith to choose four planets out of billions.'

'Because to my knowledge, Earth, the two Halos worlds and Utopiana are the only ones outside this system to have identical buildings. However, here you'll find one on Carsus, on Tessus, on Minerva, on Narrah, and on Garrett. And as coincidences go, those are big ones.'

'You think it's deliberate?' asked the Doctor. 'Someone designed the Pentagon on Earth to look like the Library of Carsus?'

'Or the other way around,' suggested Mel.

'Either way,' said Rummas, 'I think they are linked. And the reason I know of Earth, the Halos worlds and Utopiana is because all four planets are currently registering unusual chronon energy readings that they shouldn't be. Something strange is happening on those planets and I wondered if you two would like to help me find out what.'

Two hours later they were enjoying a rather splendid meal of lobster, a Waldorf salad and a nice Merlot that was of such a good vintage Mel didn't want to ask where it had come from. She rather suspected that Rummas wasn't averse to nipping back through time and 'helping himself' to some good food and drink as well as books. However, this time in his company had caused her to reassess her views a little. He seemed nice, if a little highly strung, but she'd almost managed to forgive his less-than-honest misuses of time travel. Almost.

Obviously she'd avoided the lobster – assuming that it wished it had avoided the pot – but the salad was nourishing and she suddenly realised that TARDIS food, whilst good and everything, often lacked taste. She was so used to it that it rarely occurred to her, but right now as she sat munching on a chunk of apple, she felt a pang for home.

A pang for Sussex and particularly a pang for her parents. For a moment she was back in that comfortable living room, at Christmas, with the tree and lights and paper chains. Presents, dates, walnuts and figgy pudding with an old sixpence in it, soaked in brandy and set alight by her proud father.

She could picture her mother, oven gloves on, bringing in plates of carved turkey (the days before Mel went to secondary school and discovered vegetarianism), brussels, crisped parsnips, roast spuds and cranberry sauce. Actually, she loathed cranberry sauce but never told anyone, believing that if she didn't eat everything, she might not be allowed to eat anything.

Funny the things we believe as a ten-year-old.

She would wolf dinner down as fast as possible, then the family would watch the Queen's Speech at three o'clock, and once that was over, she and her sister would dive into the mountain of brightly coloured presents, ripping away carefully arranged wrapping paper, ignoring tags saying 'To Mel, lots of love, Uncle John' and finding various delights inside. Never one for dolls, for Mel it was a chemistry set, or a book on wildlife in Africa or, her all-time favourite, a big book of dinosaurs, with detailed drawings of uncovered fossils and beautiful paintings of what they might have looked like. One book in particular, she recalled, came with a set of postcards that when put together created a diorama full of prehistoric creatures and birds.

One year someone had bought her a set of Letraset Action Transfers full of dinosaurs, but her stupid younger sister, arranging her dolly's tea party nearby, had spilt water onto the beautifully painted backdrop. So Melanie had gone and got her school satchel and carefully rubbed down the transfers so they formed the words M J Bush and –

Mel dropped her knife and fork with a gasp.

'Mel?' queried the Doctor.

'Are you all right?' Professor Rummas took her hand. 'You're shaking, my dear.'

Mel took a deep breath, closed her eyes and felt a shudder go through her. After a few seconds she spoke, smiling at the two men. 'Sorry, that was melodramatic of me.' She drew her hand back from Rummas and picked up her cutlery. 'Someone just walked over my grave,' she said quietly.

'What were you thinking about?' the Doctor was staring at her, curiously. 'It might be important?'

'I doubt it,' she said. 'I was thinking about...' but she couldn't remember precisely. Something to do with dinosaurs wasn't it? 'Well, it's gone. Nothing to worry about.'

But the Doctor was having none of it, it seemed. 'We're in a place where time is acting strangely, where ghosts of our dead selves crop up and –'

'They wouldn't be ghosts if they were alive, would they,' she said reasonably. Well, as reasonably as she could, desperately wanting to change tack. It worked because after one final furrowed look at her, the Doctor went back to talking to Rummas.

Try as she might, Mel couldn't bring back whatever she had just been thinking about, just jumbled images of dinosaurs, a small blob of red jam or something and... and... yes! Yes, that picture, the circular photograph she'd seen in the TARDIS earlier. The one that had disappeared. She'd forgotten to tell the Doctor about that... but he was gassing away, nineteen to the dozen again.

She finished her salad, took a sip of red wine and stood up.

'Professor,' she said, interrupting but making no apologies. 'You two seem to have much to talk about, so I thought I might go for a wander if that's okay?'

A look passed from the Doctor to Rummas, but the professor shrugged. 'I've yet to see any representations of the delightful Miss Bush garrotted, stabbed or hung from the rafters, so I think she'll be fine.'

The Doctor was clearly less convinced, but Mel cut off his protests before he could begin. 'I'll be half an hour. If I'm not back, send out the Saint Bernards.'

Rummas clearly didn't understand the analogy, but he smiled anyway. 'You'll find members of staff dotted around. Any of them will be delighted to help you with anything you may need. There are some nice reading rooms in corridor three. Big open fires, soft lighting. I try to create a "mood", I believe is the vernacular.'

'Thank you,' Mel said and headed out.

The little lights in the ceiling were forming an easy path to follow. Mel had sussed rather quickly what they meant.

'I wonder what I should do now,' she had muttered to herself, in the gloom immediately outside the Dinner Suite. 'Reading Room, I suppose.'

At which point, lights in the ceiling had flicked on. They went ahead for a bit, then veered off to the right, so she followed them as they twisted and turned.

Seven minutes later, she was standing at a huge set of oak doors, a big sign saying 'SHUSH' stencilled across them.

Gently she pushed them open and two men looked up, trying not to register surprise, but failing.

'Good evening, gentlemen,' said Mel. 'Nice fire,' she then added as she saw the logs roaring in the grate. 'So, what do you do here?'

The taller of the men, a thin-faced man with a slightly coppery hue to his skin, finally smiled. 'We are Custodians of the Glorious Library of Carsus. My name is Mr Woltas.'

The other man, shorter and fatter, didn't smile. He just turned away with a grunt of 'Mr Huu', which she assumed was his name, and picked up some books from a trolley and placed them on a small table beside a soft-looking armchair.

'The books you wanted to read, Miss Bush,' said Mr Woltas with a slightly camp flourish of his hands.

Mel said nothing, she just stared at the two men.

'Is something wrong?' asked Mr Huu, his tone bordering on bored. Rude perhaps.

Finally Mel nodded. 'Yes. I didn't ask for any books. I've only just got here.'

The two odd men passed a look to each other, then Mr Woltas produced a small black diary or notebook from a pocket Mel hadn't noticed before. He flipped through some pages, then scanned one with particular interest. 'Ah,' he said finally. 'Ah. Our mistake. You indeed haven't asked for these.'

'Yet,' said Mr Huu, as if that explained everything.

'Yet?'

'Yet. But you will.' Mr Huu hoisted the pile of books back up, but Mel stopped him. 'Well, I might as well read them if they're here.'

Another look.

'I'm not sure we can do that, miss,' said Mr Woltas. 'You see, the chronon energies that surround the Glorious Library of Carsus might be displaced should an event occur out of established time.'

'How can time be established if it hasn't happened to me yet?' Mel sat in the chair, whipping the topmost book from Mr Huu's arms.

'Time is linear,' said Mr Woltas.

'I'm not sure that's true,' said Mel. 'The Doctor told me that it's wavy and fluid. He's rarely wrong about such things.'

With a sigh, as if dealing with a particularly dim child, Mr Huu retrieved the book from her. 'Obviously it's fluid out there,' he waved in the general direction of the ceiling. 'But in the Glorious Library of Carsus, it's linear. It has to be or we couldn't select an exact moment to preview or review. Structure has to be maintained.'

'Indeed. Structure.' Mr Woltas started pushing the trolley away. 'When you do ask for these in about eight years, we'll have them for you. Sorry to have bothered you.'

Mel watched as a far door at the end of the Reading Room swung open and the two men exited.

Less than a heartbeat later, yet another door, six feet further along the wall, opened and they came back in, sans trolley.

'What now?' she asked.

'Oh, terribly sorry, miss,' said Mr Woltas, 'we didn't know the Reading Room was occupied. I'm Mr Woltas, this is Mr Huu. We're Custodians –'

'Of the Glorious Library of Carsus, yes I know.'

'You have us at a disadvantage, miss,' said Mr Huu, with his customary lack of grace and a heavy hint of annoyance.

'Look, you two just left, right?'

'Left?'

'Right?'

Mel sighed. 'No, I mean you were here. We spoke. About books. Then you went. Through there.'

The two men followed her pointing finger.

'Oh no, miss,' said Mr Woltas. 'No, we could never go through that door.'

'Why not?'

Mr Huu sighed. Of course he did. That's what he did all the time. 'Because that door leads to the new wing. Which hasn't been built yet. Not for another ten or so years. The door is purely decorative.' His tone suggested that he considered any-thing 'decorative' in life to be a waste of time and space.

Mel got out of the armchair and scampered over to the door. 'Nonsense,' she said as she did so. 'They went through it – oh.'

The door was indeed inflexible. There was no join around the edges, it was painted onto the wall.

Decorative, not practical.

'But I saw you. Spoke to you.'

Misters Woltas and Huu looked at her, then each other, then back to Mel. 'If you saw future us's, then something has gone wrong.'

'Nothing goes wrong on the Glorious...'

'Yes, yes, all right,' snapped Mel. 'But it clearly has. I definitely spoke to the two of you; you knew who I was, I didn't know you. You had books for me that I'm not due to request for another few years.'

'This is disturbing, Mr Huu.'

'Indeed. Disturbing, Mr Woltas. We cannot exist in two time zones.'

'Not in here.'

Mel anticipated the next bit. 'Because you have linear time only, here – yes?'

'Of course. Otherwise confusion would reign. No matter where or when you visit us from in the universe, any universe, here time is structured to a single path.'

'There's never flux nor can time change its state,' said Mr Huu.

'Chaos. Chaos could reign. We must tell Professor Rummas, Mr Huu.'

'Indeed, Mr Woltas. He's in the Due Back Date Room.'

'No he's not,' said Mel. 'He's in the Dinner Suite. I left him and the Doctor there less than five minutes ago. Local time,' she added, just in case it was important.

Mr Woltas crossed to a bookshelf and took down a huge clothbound book, which was clearly rather heavy. He placed it on the table next to Mel's armchair and they gathered around it.

Mr Woltas then opened it revealing not pages, as Mel had assumed, but a small silver ball, resting in a square hole cut through the leaves. Rather like those books Mel saw in Agatha Christie films that contained a key or money or another book or –

'Custodian Woltas to Professor Rummas,' he said quietly.

Instantly the ball glowed and a hologram of Rummas's head winked into existence.

'Yes?'

'Where are you sir?'

'In the Dinner Suite.'

'With the Doctor?' asked Mel.

'Is that Miss Bush with you, Mr Woltas?'

'Umm...'

Mel nodded. 'Melanie Bush,' she added helpfully.

'Yes sir, it is.'

'What is the problem?'

Mr Woltas took a deep breath. 'Miss Bush claims to have seen temporally challenged variants of myself and Mr Huu, sir.'

There was slight interference on the hologram, and Mel saw Rummas's head replaced by the Doctor's.

'Are you all right Mel?'

'Fine Doctor. It's true. I spoke to these two... Custodians, they left, then came back through another door, not knowing who I was.'

'Stay put, I'm on my way.' The Doctor's face was then replaced by Rummas's, who told his Custodians to go and check something called the Time Path Indicator. The last thing Mel heard was the Doctor's voice saying something that sounded very much like 'That's stolen Gallifreyan technology' before it was cut off and Mr Woltas shut the book.

'This is very alarming, Miss Bush,' he said.

'Very worrying,' concurred Mr Huu, not being smug at all now.

'Well, I'm fine here,' Mel said. 'So why don't you nip off and sort out this Time Path Indicator and I'll stay put.'

'You know what a Time Path Indicator is?'

'No, but the Professor just mentioned it.'

'Oh. Oh right, yes. Yes, he did.' Mr Woltas shook his head. 'I need a better memory.'

'I should have thought, working here, that might have been a prerequisite for the job,' said Mel.

With a final confused look at each other the Custodians exited. This time by the door they'd come in from.

Before Mel could sit down, she was disturbed by another door opening, this time, the double set she'd come in by.

It was Rummas and the Doctor, talking animatedly.

'You must take Melanie and see what you can find out,' Rummas said.

'Umm, Doctor...' Mel said quietly, but they ignored her.

'If there's chronon energy gone wild,' the Doctor replied, 'it may be dangerous to her.'

'She's safer with you in the TARDIS than she is here on Carsus. If the Library timeline is no longer linear, then chronon spillage is flooding the space-time vortex.'

'Chronon spillage?' asked Mel, but again, no one noticed her.

'I see,' the Doctor said, looking really quite grave. 'You're right of course. And only someone capable of withstanding chronon energy leakages can come back. If I bring her here again, she'll be torn apart if it gets out of control. I think... I'm positive Melanie was right.'

'You are?' asked Mel. 'That makes a change.'

Rummas agreed with the Doctor's assessment. 'Yes,' he said aggitatedly. 'I honestly think we're facing a pan-multiversal rip. A scratch right through the grooves of the vortex spiral, causing jumps and gashes. And if something bleeds through from one multiverse to another...'

'Or even one universe to another,' the Doctor concluded. 'That would be enough to destroy everything. Chronologically speaking.'

Rummas took something from his pocket. 'Take this. It's a locator. I need you to go to the planet Schyllus in 4387 and save the universe.'

At which point, the doors that the two Custodians had left by burst open, and Professor Rummas and the Doctor came in.

'Stupid corridors, keep changing,' said the Doctor.

'You got lost,' Rummas replied. 'And foolishly I followed you.'

'Well,' the Doctor snapped. 'We're here now. And there's Mel.'

Mel was, by now, sufficiently confused that, contrary to her normal unflappable nature, she just began muttering garbled, nonsensical phrases which included 'But you... I mean, over there... and then they...' and ended with 'oh, they've vanished'.

'Who have?' asked Rummas. 'The Custodians?'

'No,' said Mel finally. 'No, the other you two. The ones that were ignoring me.'

The Doctor and Rummas glanced at each other, then the Doctor eased Mel into the armchair by the fire and crouched down before her.

'Mel, I want... I need you to tell me everything these other us's said. Word for word.'

'Word for word, Doctor?' said Rummas. 'Don't you need to hypnotise her for that degree of clarity.'

The Doctor shook his head. 'So long as she concentrates and no one talks pointless gibberish at her,' he threw Rummas a look, 'Mel has an elephantine memory.'

'Charmed as always, thank you Doctor, by that comparison.'

And so Mel, using what she preferred to call her eidetic memory, gave them chapter and verse what she had just heard.

When she finished, Rummas took a deep breath then blew it back out slowly. 'Pretty much as I suspected. But I'm not sure about Schyllus.'

'Why?'

'Well, I can't see the point. There's not much there – it's a tourist trap. A glorified shopping centre and holiday resort. But I can't see a connection to anything else.'

The Doctor frowned. 'Well, bearing in mind what our time-lost duplicates said just now, I *do* want to get Mel away from here.'

Rummas nodded. 'I would take her back to somewhere far more appropriate if I were you, but somewhere we know that there have been temporal disturbances recently. I want you to find someone who has vanished from her own timeline, a problem I noticed a few days ago. Someone important called Helen.'

'And we find her where?' asked Mel.

'Easy,' said Rummas. 'I need you to go to the planet Earth in 1958 and save the universe.'

Chapter Six
16

The Honourable Helen 'Lucky' Lamprey smiled as she surveyed the smiling people in front of her. They were gathered there, dressed to the nines in an array of evening wear, jewellery glittering, rings polished, not a hair out of place on anyone.

The most perfect friends anyone could want, her father had said.

What Helen really wanted right now was to see everyone relaxed, wearing clothes they wanted to wear rather than what society dictated they ought to wear at such functions. She saw poor old Mr Diggle from the Post Office, representing the Rotary Club, no doubt. Where in God's name had he hired his dinner jacket from? It didn't fit, and he looked as if he was about to expire from the tightness around his neck caused by the tie he wore. Helen really wanted to just wander over to him, smile, loosen the tie and see him smile in return. See him relax.

How many of the people here came not because they wanted to see Helen per se, but because it was the 'thing' to do.

She glanced further into the crowd and could see Father's 'hired helps' sorting out drinks and food. Poor old Thompkin was still around – surely he should have retired gracefully by now. And Barker was probably outside in the cold, ferrying people from the train station in Ipswich out to the village.

For a brief moment, Helen imagined she was in the old Hall in Eye and wondered what her mother would say if she could see her now, fresh from a Swiss finishing school, ready to debut on the social circuit. Helen hoped she would be proud – she ought to have been. Daddy had done so well over the last nine years to turn his life around.

He'd dropped his political ambitions to bring up his daughter, refusing to send her to boarding school as so many others suggested. Helen knew it had been difficult – it wasn't really 'done' for a man in Sir Bertrand Lamprey's position to raise a daughter. By rights, a governess ought to have been employed, along with a variety of nannies and maids, so that he could have gone to work each day, come home, had supper with his daughter for an hour then retired to his library or bed, and have nothing further to do with her. That, according to Helen's friends from the Swiss school, is how many of them had been brought up.

But Sir Bertrand had been different. Oh yes, there'd been a governess, a lovely lady called Miss Garvey, who was proudly standing by the front door. And there had been cooks, maids and all that. But Daddy had cut down his work in London, making sure he spent three days a week here in Suffolk with his daughter, actively taking an interest in her growth. When Miss Garvey's daily work was over, he started, letting her read through his library of books, which she devoured eagerly. He took her on trips around the country and the occasional overseas jaunt, even if he was going on business.

They agreed between them that she should spend six terms in Switzerland, and although the wrench had been hard, they both knew it was a good idea. And it gave Helen a chance to ski, which was always advantageous.

Together they had mapped out a series of potential futures for Helen, with Sir Bertrand offering advice but never a firm opinion. And together they decided that Helen should go to university, study the classics and perhaps look into a job as a teacher. Money was never going to be an issue for Helen, so she could afford to take a job doing what she wanted rather than needed. Of course, there was the option to sit around the big house and do nothing, but both Helen and her father knew that would rapidly drive her potty.

Her reverie was broken by a short hand-clap – her father had reached the foot of the stairs and was beaming up at her. She descended and took his proffered hand, and bent close as he whispered to her.

'I'm sorry, darling, I had no idea all these people were coming. My fault, I left Miss Joyce at the office to send out the invites. I think she thought it ought to be a "society" event rather than a social one.'

Helen gave her father a kiss on the cheek. 'It'll be fun anyway, and remind me to send Miss Joyce a floral thank-you.'

'Well, she was just doing her job, really,' Sir Bertrand said, but Helen hushed him.

'She still did it, and did it well, if a little too well. We must always thank those that help us in life. I can't remember who taught me that, Father.'

He smiled, knowing that it was, of course, himself.

Helen pointed to the painting hung on the hall wall, amidst the portraits of men with beards and horses with long legs. It was an abstract piece, almost cubist in its extremes but clearly a five-sided shape, with concentric pentagons echoing throughout.

'You hung it!' Helen breathed. 'Oh thank you!'

'I can't let my daughter's art not take pride of place, especially on her birthday, can I? Besides,' he said conspiratorially, 'take a gander at those people looking at it. They'd scratch their heads if they'd let themselves be seen to be confused in public. I don't understand your paintings, darling, but I like the fact they upset the stuffed-shirts!'

Helen laughed lightly. 'You, Father o'mine, are normally one of those stuffed-shirts!'

He grinned back, and then went quiet, just for a second. Then he took her hand and kissed it.

'You look so like your darling mother,' he said. 'I wish she could see you now.'

Helen gently caressed the cross she wore around her neck. 'She's watching, Father. I know it. She would be so happy to see that you gave me such a glorious childhood. So on her behalf, as well as my own, thank you.' She kissed him again, then let go of his hand and loudly embraced a young woman near the steps. 'Letitia,' she said, 'how simply divine of you to be here.'

The Governess, Miss Garvey, watched with pride as her young charge worked her way through the crowd. Somehow she knew all their names, relationships and hobbies. Socialising came so easily to her, and although she clearly hadn't wanted such an extravagant birthday celebration, she adapted to it perfectly.

'Isn't she delightful,' said a voice at her ear. It was Barker, the chauffeur.

Miss Garvey agreed, and asked Barker if she could get him a drink.

'Still more driving to do, Miss Garvey,' he said. 'But thank you anyway.' He paused. 'Hard to believe nine years have passed since the accident.'

'You were there, weren't you?'

Barker nodded. 'It was a dark few weeks. We were never sure if Sir Bertrand would get over it. Apart from the Lady Lamprey, he lost everything in the Hall. Art, books, everything. Nothing was saved. He rebuilt his and Miss Helen's life from scratch.'

'And you?'

'I was lucky. I lived in the village. Thompkin and the other staff lost everything too. Thompkin's a good man, he stuck by Sir Bertrand, whereas the others took their share of the insurance and left his service. After all, he couldn't afford them.'

'You can't really blame them, I suppose,' said Miss Garvey thoughtfully. 'It's quite a wrench.'

'Oh indeed,' agreed Barker. 'Sir Bertrand was terribly good, he didn't hold it against them. Indeed, I remember poor Mary – never Sir Bertrand's favourite – being so distraught at having to leave service and begging to stay on. But he couldn't take her back, and yet he still gave her a bonus as a thank-you for the fact she looked after Helen for a few days.'

Miss Garvey sighed. 'What a wonderful advertisement for the British spirit the Lampreys are.'

Thompkin appeared behind them. 'A telephone call from Ipswich, Barker,' he said quietly.

'More guests?'

'Indeed.' Thompkin nodded politely to Miss Garvey and made his way back to the dining room where the food was spread out.

'Off I go,' said Barker with a sigh. 'See you in a while.' He doffed his head slightly to Miss Garvey and walked away.

'What a fine gentleman,' Miss Garvey said to herself. Or so she thought until she realised Helen was beside her.

'Then do something about it, woman,' Helen chided her kindly. 'He's clearly taken with you, too.'

'My lady!' Miss Garvey flushed with embarrassment. 'I had no idea... I mean...'

'Oh come on, Miss Garvey,' Helen laughed happily. 'There isn't a soul in the village who can't see it – other than each of you.'

'One cannot fraternise with other servants...'

'Servants? It's 1958, Miss Garvey, not 1908! You are our staff. And our friends. Not servants. Now, wait a moment.'

Helen waved to her father and after he made an excuse to whoever it was he was speaking to, he joined his daughter and her former governess. Miss Garvey felt as if she wanted the world to open up and swallow her whole.

'Please, my lady...' she started, but Helen held up a hand to stop her.

'Father?'

'Yes my darling?'

'Father, can you think of any reason why the delightful Miss Garvey here shouldn't "fraternise" with the lovely Mr Barker?'

Sir Bertrand laughed. 'It is a constant source of amazement to me, my dear, that Miss Garvey isn't actually Mrs Barker yet!'

Miss Garvey didn't know what to say. 'Oh sir,' she eventually muttered. 'I don't know...'

'I'll tell you what, Miss Garvey,' said Helen firmly, 'if you and Barker don't sort something out, I'll get Sir Bertrand here to make it a household rule that chauffeurs and ex-governesses have to be married by my next birthday. In fact, I think the service should be then!'

'Which birthday, my dear? Your seventeenth next Christmas, or your sixteenth-and-a-half in July?'

'Oh, sixteenth-and-a-half, Father, of course. A real thing to celebrate, I think.'

Miss Garvey just couldn't speak. She had imagined herself getting married to Mr Barker for a couple of years now, but had never dared talk to him about it.

'Father,' Helen was saying. 'Are you going to London this week?'

'Thursday, just before New Year's Eve. Why?'

'Then I shall book us railway tickets.'

'But I was going to drive...'

Helen shook her head. 'No, you were going to get Barker to drive you. That's different. But as he has just been given the holiday off by you in absentia, he and Miss Garvey can go away for a few days and enjoy the New Year together and talk. Can't they?'

'What? Oh. Oh, yes. Yes, of course.' Sir Bertrand took Miss Garvey's elbow. 'And that, by the way, is an order from the entire Lamprey family, Miss Garvey. Yes?'

Miss Garvey just bobbed and muttered some incoherent nonsense that embarrassed her further and headed off to the dining room.

As she walked away, she could hear Miss Helen laughing softly.

'I cannot think of two people I will be happier to see start a new life together, Father.'

And all Miss Garvey could wonder was what had she ever done to deserve to be employed by two such lovely people as Helen and Sir Bertrand.

It was snowing. Not a particularly heavy blizzard, indeed more of a gentle sprinkle, but it was those damp, unpleasant droplets that slowly seep into your clothes and make you feel as if you've been dipped into a rather cold bath.

Nevertheless, the Doctor was acting as if it were Antarctica, Lapland and Alaska rolled into one with a wind machine turned on full; puffing, panting and generally berating the weather for not being what he wanted, but instead being a frankly typical East Anglian winter of the late 1950s.

Mel, on the other hand, was rather enjoying the prospect of creating a snowball and dropping it down the back of his multicoloured coat.

'If we'd come in the TARDIS, I'd've had some nice cold-weather gear for you.'

Mel shrugged. Rummas had kitted her out in a big furry coat that covered her less-than-1950s outfit and she was snug as a bug in a rug, thank you very much.

She told the Doctor so.

'Oh it's all right for you humans,' he responded. 'You're used to the cold and wet. Gallifrey, I'll have you know, is like the Serengeti all year round.'

'Yes, I'm sure. Great herds of wildebeest sweeping majestically –'

The Doctor coughed loudly to cut her off. 'Leave the quotes behind Mel please,' he said waspishly. 'This is 1958 not '78.'

'I'm surprised you got the reference.'

'I'll have you know that John and Connie are good friends and we spent many hours together. I gather they based one or two characters on aspects of me, although I've never been entirely sure which ones.'

Mel snorted. 'Bet I can guess,' she muttered. 'So,' changing the subject, 'why Ipswich train station?'

The Doctor pulled a piece of card Mel had seen Rummas give him from his pocket and handed it to her.

It is the great pleasure of
Sir Bertrand Lamprey
to invite ————————
to celebrate the sixteenth birthday
of the Honourable Helen Lamprey
on Boxing Day 1958
at Wikes Manor, Wendlestead, Suffolk
Please arrive between 2pm and 4pm at
Ipswich Railway Station
and call the Manor on 2847 whereupon you
will be collected by motor car.
RSVP

Mel shrugged. 'Great. Who's she?'

'I have absolutely no idea,' the Doctor said as he began checking the timetable for trains to London. 'But if no one comes to pick us up soon, I'm taking the train back to Liverpool Street and going shopping.'

'It's Boxing Day, Doctor. In the 1950s, the shops won't be open.'

The Doctor smiled, rather smugly Mel thought. 'To some of us, certain shops are always open.'

Mel raised her eyes heavenward and wondered which foolish shop owner had given the Doctor a 365-day-per-year access card. Harrods. Liberty. Hamleys? Somehow she feared that if their lift didn't come soon, said shop owner was going to regret it considerably. She could see in her mind's eye the Doctor hammering on Harrods' doors, going in, spending eight hours wandering and finally buying a small bar of chocolate. 'Simply because one can,' he would undoubtedly say, leaving Mel to apologise profusely to whichever members of staff had been dragged in for no good reason.

Her thoughts were interrupted by the sound of a car approaching.

'Marvellous,' said the Doctor, eyes lit up like a child's. 'A Daimler. None of your Rolls rubbish here Mel, this is the car of the true gentry. I bet Sir Bertrand has a Morgan or a Bentley for casual use on Sundays, too. Perhaps I could give one a spin...'

The car pulled up and the Doctor showed the chauffeur the invitation, with THE DOCTOR and MISS MELANIE BUSH miraculously inked in where it had been blank moments before.

The driver tapped his cap, opened the rear doors and they got in.

As the Doctor settled, noisily, on the seat, Mel thanked the man.

'It's a lovely day for a party,' she said.

'Indeed, miss,' replied the driver.

'Is the Manor far?'

'No, miss.'

'Ummm. Oh, yes. Should we have brought a gift? The invitation didn't say.'

'Yes, miss.'

'Oh. Oh dear. Oh, we haven't got one have we, Doctor?'

The Doctor beamed. 'Just this, Melanie, just this.' In his hand was a little Chinese lacquer box, hand-painted and engraved with jade leaf. He flicked it open and inside were a pair of jade earrings, carved as tiny pandas.

'My mistake,' said Mel, darkly.

'Yes, miss,' agreed the driver.

The Doctor leaned forward and tugged closed the glass window separating the time travellers from the driver, so neither could hear the other.

'Well, that was embarrassing. Thank you Doctor.'

'Think nothing of it, Mel,' he laughed. 'You only had to ask.'

'So, Wendlestead. Near Ipswich. Anything else I need to know?'

The Doctor cleared his throat, signifying to Mel that, relevant or not, she was going to know something about Wendlestead now.

'I'm surprised it means nothing to you, with your enquiring mind and photographic memory.'

Mel was not in the mood for games any longer. 'Just tell me.'

'In about twenty years, the area will be different. It'll mostly be overrun by an American air base.'

'Like Greenham Common?'

'Exactly. But unlike that, Wendlestead's problems won't be sensible ladies trying to stop your governments plotting to destroy your planet, but will be possible alien sightings. Little grey men plotting to destroy your planet. An English Roswell, they'll call it.'

'And that's important in 1958 because?'

'Honestly? I've no idea. Let's wait and see, shall we.' He closed his eyes, then popped them open again. 'Oh yes, and in the twelfth century there were tales that the original inhabitants of Wikes Manor, or the Hall as it was then, took in two changeling children they found in the woods some miles away. Green children.'

'Green children?'

'Yes, lots of legends built up around that.'

'Aliens?'

'Possibly. Of course, other sources say they were a couple of wards that the local landowner needed rid of to obtain their trust money. So he poisoned them with arsenic and dumped them in a copse near Bury St Edmunds.'

'And why would people think they were green?'

'Arsenic has that effect on the skin, particularly in under-nourished children. You see, every myth has another foot in fact.'

'But no one can ever be one hundred per cent sure, can they?'

The Doctor grinned. 'Of course not. The USAF base at Wendlestead eventually "proved" their UFOs were fakes, created by a couple of youths who weren't from the area. Of course, that was after they initially blamed it on a local lighthouse. Trouble is, when it was revealed that the light from the lighthouse couldn't actually be seen, due to the excessive forests nearby and a ground fog that night, they had to find an alternative excuse. And the more alternatives you find, the more sceptical the people become. You see, you humans have a wonderful way of taking a mystery and then making it worse for yourselves by creating a hundred alternative explanations, rather than accepting the most obvious.'

Mel sighed. 'Which is, in this case?'

'As it is in most cases, Mel,' the Doctor said, closing his eyes and resting his head on the back of the seat. 'That there are some things you just cannot explain.'

Mel was shocked. 'And just how d'you know all these local stories?'

'Oh, as someone once told me, I read a lot,' was the only response she got and was the last thing the Doctor said until they arrived at Wikes Manor.

Helen Lamprey was seated on a small chair close to the door of the drawing room, sipping a glass of white wine and listening to the conversations swirling around.

To her right a couple she didn't know were discussing the snow-tipped lawns. In the centre of the room, a gaggle of rather insipid young things were gathered around a slightly older man she knew to be the Classics librarian from Bury St Edmunds. He was holding court and making jokes by punning Greek and Roman names. The dreadful caw-caws of their obsequious laughter were beginning to annoy her. By the French windows, she could see her beloved father talking to one of the stuffed-shirts who had inspected her painting earlier. And just out in the hallway, she heard poor Thompkin announcing the latest arriving guests. Which at least meant that Barker was back, which would make Miss Garvey smile.

'Ladies and gentlemen, the Doctor and Miss Bush,' came Thompkin's voice. Helen idly wondered who they might be and stuck her head out of the drawing room to take a look.

The girl seemed pleasant enough but the man! Goodness, what on earth was he wearing?

'One of your fellow artists I presume,' said a voice at her ear. It was Miss Garvey.

'I have never seen him before,' Helen replied. 'But he has a nice smile even if his fashion sense borders on disastrous. Oh look, he's seen the painting.' Helen stood up and sidled up to them, hoping to overhear their thoughts.

'Still think I'm paranoid, Doctor?' the girl was asking. Paranoia? Perhaps he truly was her doctor and it was... what was the name? Oh yes, 'Bush'... perhaps Miss Bush was the guest. Still, Helen was positive she had never seen them before.

The Doctor was pointing at the picture. 'Influenced by Braque,' he was saying, 'but there's also a good deal of Cézanne in there, which is nice. But the actual impression I'm getting is that the artist has really studied Juan Gris, as the picture has a calculated feel to it, quite, quite synthetic and yet by its essence... oh hello!'

Helen jumped as she realised the Doctor was addressing her.

'And what do you think?' he asked.

Helen shrugged. 'It's a bit abstract don't you think. Can one really call cubism art?'

'My thoughts exactly,' muttered the flame-haired Bush girl, but the Doctor shushed her.

'Oh Mel,' he scolded. 'If it's not Renaissance you get bored. Such a Philistine. Actually no, that's an insult to the Philistines.'

'Of course it is, Doctor,' sighed the girl.

Mel.

So that was her Christian name. How gauche.

'Well, I knew a lot of Philistines and they were lovely. Sea People always are, of course. Very arty themselves. Squid ink was their paint of choice. Ever used squid ink, Lady Lamprey?'

'No, I can't say that – oh. Oh, you knew it was me?' Helen was disappointed, she'd hoped to get a genuine reaction from this critic.

He beamed at her, and she felt warm and comfortable around him. 'No one other than the artist herself would use the word "cubism" to describe that masterpiece.'

Mel sighed. 'I didn't mean to appear rude, Lady Helen,' she said.

Helen laughed and shook both their hands. 'A pleasure to meet you. Who invited you?'

'An old friend of the family suggested we drop by. I'm fascinated by art such as yours,' the Doctor replied. 'He wangled us an invite.'

'"Wangled"?'

Mel butted in. 'He means, it was arranged for us. Sorry, we feel a bit like gatecrash – oh, never mind.'

'Gatecrashers,' Helen finished for her. 'I do actually know that word.' Helen was going off this Mel person. She seemed rather too quick to judge and had a superiority about her that didn't seem entirely justified. She would keep an eye on this one.

Mel was bored already. What was the Doctor doing, playing the art fan. This Helen woman seemed to have decided he was some sort of expert, and Mel hoped the Doctor would show uncommonly good sense and not go too far before he talked himself into a corner he could not extricate himself from. Then she remembered this was the Doctor. Awkward corners were his speciality.

Mel was distracted by a man walking through the crowd, clearly looking for someone. Helen then waved a hand to him.

'Oh Father, meet the Doctor.' She eased her father closer. 'Oh and his... his companion, Miss Bush. The Doctor is an art critic.'

Sir Bertrand nodded. 'Come to inspect Helen's scribbles have you? Can't get m'head around it meself,' he said, 'but can't deny it has a certain beauty and charm.'

The Doctor laughed. 'Are we discussing the pentagon in the frame or the beautiful young lady beside us?'

Mel didn't know whether to smile or throw up.

She smiled at Helen, who tossed her a haughty look, so Mel decided she didn't like this woman at all.

So why had Rummas sent them here? What was the point? Helen Lamprey was just a stuck-up member of the lower aristocracy from the 1950s, who considered herself a bit of a Picasso. Ooh. Big threat to the universe there.

Then she looked at the painting again and remembered her 'paranoid' comment earlier. Yes, it was the familiar five-sided pentagon. Just like the Library. Just like the actual building in

Washington, probably about fifteen years old in this time period. Nobility such as Lady Helen Lamprey had most likely never heard of it, after all, it didn't involve hunts, pony trekking or midnight feasts in the dorm!

'I based the shape on the Pentagon itself, in Washington, Doctor,' Helen was saying. 'It represents so much power in our world these days, especially with this so-called Cold War. I thought the juxtaposition of an image of power with the looseness of the conceit of cubist freedoms and abstractions made a nice contrast.'

Mel really, really hated her now. She was thinking about punching her.

But not quite as much as she had to stop herself punching the Doctor for what he said next.

'You know Helen – may I call you Helen rather than Lady Lamprey? Oh, thank you. Anyway, I was saying to Mel earlier, it's fascinating how the shape of the pentagon turns up in so many seats of power. The symbol itself is important to the Freemasons and with its five concentric pentagons, each traversed by ten corridor spokes, it means that nowhere in the Pentagon is more than seven minutes' walk away. Seven, of course, being a significant number to a great many cabals, sects and beliefs.'

Helen smiled at the Doctor. 'Thank you, I knew none of that.' She turned to Mel, that same smile etched onto her lips. Mel returned it, but hoped her eyes were saying 'Die Bitch Die!'

'You are so lucky, Miss Bush. To have a teacher such as the Doctor to travel with. I'm sure you must be learning so much from him.'

Mel said nothing for a second until the Doctor prompted, 'Oh you are, aren't you Mel?'

Mel nodded slowly and began imagining how much pain she

was going to inflict on the Doctor once they were back at the Library on Carsus.

That made her smile properly. And so she made her excuses and headed off to the drawing room to see if she could find a glass or three of lemonade.

The first thing she saw as she entered the dining room were the young women. Strictly speaking, that wasn't true. Mel noticed what they were wearing. Tiaras, far, far too many tiaras. And fox furs. And mink furs. And diamonds that were probably very real, very expensive and were certainly very big, screaming out 'notice me, my Daddy is richer than yours'.

Mel had to remind herself this was the post-war 1950s, where rationing still existed (she wondered how many of Sir Bertrand's ration books went on this bash) and a social conscience in young girls was still ten years away. 'Roll on Woodstock,' she muttered and whipped a glass of something that looked like fruit juice from a passing waiter, with a smile and a genuine 'thank you'. Probably the first one he'd heard all night.

God, she hated this.

It reminded her very much of her mother's 'parties' for the local women of Pease Pottage, where she spent most of her teenage years. When the family first moved there, her mother had spent an inordinate amount of time trying to fit in with the local ladies via various groups, institutes and club socials. And Mel had often come home from school to find her mother maniacally tidying up in preparation for another onslaught of towns women's guilds, friendships, leagues, etc., etc., etc.

Therefore it had been upstairs, homework, nip down for a quick tea, hi to Dad if he was mad enough to have ventured home from work instead of hiding at the pub, and back up to the TV or her books when the fearsome Mrs Carruthers led whichever army of Tupperware-loving, burberry-clad, petition-waving monsters were due that particular night.

Right now, she realised, her parents were in their late twenties, Mum having already left Durham University and got married. She would have finished her English degree and made no use of it at all. Coming from an age where girls were still rare at the big universities, her change from rebellious post-war socialite wanting equality, to stay-at-home housewife was scary – and Mel desperately hoped it wasn't a path she'd ever follow. Dad, meanwhile, would be doing his postgrad in accountancy, selling his Elvis and early rock 'n' roll 78s to get by. Neither of them would foresee that within five years they'd have a daughter.

How funny to think of them now. And to ponder for the first time in ages that they left having her till very late in life. Which was unusual in the carefree 'swinging sixties'.

Mel was suddenly aware that a man was standing beside her whom she felt she should know. There was something familiar...

'You should've asked them about your sister,' he said.

Mel ignored him. He was probably drunk, and as a non-drinker, Mel was rarely comfortable around drunks. Happy drunks. Morose drunks. Silly drunks. They all annoyed her, but it wasn't socially acceptable to tell them to bugger off, so she usually opted to ignore them.

'You'd learn so much if you just asked questions,' he said again.

'Yes, thank you,' Mel retorted and then realised she was talking to a door jamb.

'You all right, Melanie?' It was the Doctor, leaning on the door now, presumably having extricated himself from Helen

Lamprey and her father. He was looking back at them though, rather than Mel.

'Just a strange drunk man, saying something about my sister.'

The Doctor was raising a glass, toasting someone by the front door as if he'd known them for years. 'What was he saying about her?'

Mel didn't reply. That was another odd thing in a day of odd things.

'I don't have a sister, Doctor. You know that.'

At which point the Doctor sighed. 'I'm sure Anabel would be very pleased to hear you say that.'

'Who the hell's Anabel?' Mel was really quite confused now.

'Your sister,' said the Doctor with a sigh. Then he turned to look at her, ready no doubt to explain his bizarre behaviour.

And as their eyes met, he looked as if he'd been slapped across the face by a very large and wet haddock.

'I'm sorry,' he said slowly, 'I thought you were Melanie...' then he stopped. 'Only you are, aren't you?'

'Well, I'm beginning to wonder now,' Mel replied, hoping some humour would diffuse the situation, but the Doctor's face was graver than ever.

'Oh Melanie.' He stood upright, all sense of humour or relaxation gone. Instead he just stared at her, as if trying to make something square in his mind. Finally he said: 'Where was I last time we spoke?'

'At the bottom of the stairs, opposite the painting. Down there.' Mel pointed to the right.

'Am I still there?' asked the Doctor, not looking at where she pointed.

'Well, obviously not, Doctor, or you –' Mel stopped.

She could now see, chatting amiably to Helen Lamprey,

the Doctor. He hadn't budged an inch and was laughing up-roariously at something – most likely one of his own jokes.

The Doctor staring at her was now unnerving her. 'It's happened before,' she said. 'In the TARDIS.'

The new Doctor nodded. 'I came up behind you, tapped you on the shoulder and after a second or two, you vanished,' he said. 'Which is lucky as too many Doctors spoil the broth.'

'But how has this happened?'

The faux Doctor shrugged, then brightened. 'Have you, perchance, encountered a Professor Rummas on Carsus?'

Mel nodded. 'You too?'

'Oh yes,' began the Doctor. 'Yes, and that makes sense. You see he told us that time –'

And Mel was staring at empty space, the Doctor had simply vanished, just as he had in the TARDIS a while back.

Rummas hadn't prepared them for this, so Mel wandered back to 'her' Doctor and finally caught his eye.

'Excuse me,' he said to the assembled throng, and Mel all but dragged him away.

'I was doing well, there,' he said grumpily. 'Telling them all about our adventures with the Zarbi and the Proctor of Darruth!'

'Yes, and they believed you.'

'Of course they did.'

Mel sighed. 'Sometimes you can be infuriating.'

'Only sometimes? I'm slipping.'

'You're not the only thing.'

The Doctor frowned at this. 'Whatever do you mean.'

'I just spoke to you.'

'I know. Quite abruptly, and yanked me away from my adoring audience.'

'No not you you, another you. By the entrance to the dining

room. He was quite surprised to see me. And you.'

'Me?'

'Yes, you. He saw you. Then he vanished mid-sentence, which was probably the only good thing about it really.'

The Doctor beeped Mel's nose. 'It's a good thing I know you love me really.'

Mel sighed. There were days... 'Anyway,' she said firmly. 'That's the second time that's happened. He mentioned that Rummas had sent him.'

'Multiple Rummases as well as multiple Doctors.'

'And Mels.'

'Oh indeed, and Mels. Where would all we Doctors be without our Mels. Did you see her, by the way?'

'No! And I'm quite glad frankly. Two of you is bad enough, two of me is freaky.'

'Freaky?'

'Yes, freaky. As in weird, bizarre and rather disquieting.'

'Ah. Freaky. Right.' The Doctor shrugged. 'If he's gone now, there's not much we can do is there.' Then he stiffened and took a deep breath. 'Mel,' he commanded, all frivolity gone. 'Mel, grab both my hands. Now!'

Without questioning, Mel did so. 'What's happening?'

'I'm not sure but the hairs on my neck just stood up and my hair curled tighter. Something's going on here. Look!'

Mel tried to turn her head to follow his gaze, but it was difficult. It felt like she was pushing her face against invisible treacle. She wanted to speak but was aware that even her breath was moving in slow motion. If she hadn't been holding the Doctor tightly, she guessed that, like everyone else at the party who had seen what had so alarmed the Doctor, she too would have been frozen like a statue.

Frozen that is, all bar two others.

Clearly facing the same treacle effect, Helen Lamprey was trying to push through her immobile guests, obviously terrified by what she was seeing – people still; a glass that had been tipped, frozen in mid-drop, globules of golden liquid oozing out but now caught in mid-air.

She was trying to reach her father, but that was scarier still.

Sir Bertrand Lamprey was, like the Doctor, totally unaffected by the time freeze and instead was moving at normal pace, trying to get people out of the way so that he could reach his slo-mo daughter.

'Sir Bertrand!' yelled the Doctor, and the other man stopped.

As if the sound were only just catching up with her, Helen began to move in the direction of his voice.

'Sir Bertrand,' said the Doctor again. 'I can explain the time freeze, but can you explain why you're not affected and Helen is only slightly?'

Mel gripped the Doctor tighter, aware that it was his Time Lord energy that surrounded his immediate body that was taking care of her. So what was the Lamprey family's excuse for still moving, however slowly.

'I don't understand, man,' Sir Bertrand yelled back. 'What's happening?'

As if in answer, Helen pointed, slowly, upwards. It was a strain for Mel to match her direction, but both the Doctor and Sir Bertrand were able to look straight upwards. When her eyes caught up, Mel realised the top half of the building was gone, almost as if it had never been there. No ruins, no damage, it was simply gone.

Maybe it was an effect of the time distillation, but Mel felt no wind, no cold. And all she could see were a few clouds gathering in the night sky, blotting out the stars.

'That's no cloud,' the Doctor said suddenly.

And indeed it wasn't, it was something that parted, and revealed a huge alien creature, like a giant snake slinking across the sky. It had a suckered, tendrilled, hollow head, yet it seemed to be looking for something, despite no evidence of eyes.

A word came into Mel's mind, unbidden. 'Lamprey,' she murmured.

'Yes?' said Sir Bertrand.

'Yes!' smiled the Doctor. 'Well done Mel! It must be a real Lamprey.'

Sir Bertrand had reached the Doctor and Mel, the slow-running Helen was just a few paces behind.

'What's that noise?' Sir Bertrand shouted.

And sure enough, Mel could now hear what seemed to be a heartbeat, terrifyingly loud.

'A pulsebeat,' the Doctor murmured. And then he pulled away from Mel and she felt...

... everything moving as normal. The party guests around her were laughing again, drinking and eating. The ceiling was back, and music was playing.

It was as if nothing had happened.

Then she saw the Doctor, seated on the stairs, a distraught-looking Sir Bertrand beside him.

'Helen,' she thought. Didn't like her much, but she couldn't see her.

'Ah Mel, sorry I let you go,' the Doctor said as she sat beside them. 'But I needed to try and get to Helen.'

'Where is she?'

'Gone.' Sir Bertrand was shaking slightly, clearly bewildered if not really rather distressed. 'The snake thing just... just took her.'

'Temporal transmission of matter,' the Doctor failed to clarify, but thought he did. 'It drew her away second by second, using time as a method. That's why it let her move, so it could draw her away.'

Mel looked around. No one else at the party seemed aware that the focus of the party had gone.

So she said so.

The Doctor looked at her as though the thought had only just occurred. 'Yes, now that is weird,' he agreed. 'Sir Bertrand. Look around you.'

'Why?'

'Just do it man,' snapped the Doctor. Mel was going to caution him for being abrupt, but checked herself. She understood that if the Doctor allowed Sir Bertrand Lamprey to wallow, he'd get no sense from him.

Indeed reacting to the barked order, Sir Bertrand looked around him.

'That wallpaper... it's wrong.'

The Doctor grimaced. 'Got to be more than that. These people are at a sixteenth birthday party and their hostess has vanished in front of them, yet no one's batting a well-mannered eyelid.'

'Oh my god,' breathed Sir Bertrand darkly.

Mel meanwhile was distracted by something else odd and yanked the Doctor's arm. 'The painting. It's still there. Helen's gone but her painting is hanging by that group examining it. Why aren't they curious?'

'Possibly because of that lady there, Mel,' said the Doctor. 'She's acting as if she is the one who painted it. Time has made an adjustment, installed a new artist. Who is she, Sir Bertrand?'

'My wife.'

'Ah. Hadn't spotted her before.'

'There's a reason for that, Doctor,' Sir Bertrand said. 'She died nearly ten years ago. Burnt to death in a fire at our old home. She's never been here before.'

'Well, if she's dead, that's not too surprising.' The Doctor stood up. 'I'll have a word.'

'My wife... Elspeth... it can't be...'

Mel sat closer to the shocked Sir Bertrand, as confused as he was, and watched the Doctor.

'Lady Lamprey?' the Doctor was enquiring. 'May I ask where you...'

He was interrupted as Lady Lamprey grabbed his arm. 'Oh Doctor,' she said. 'Just the person. I was telling Lady Joyce here about your comments when you came in.' She looked to another lady. 'He recognised the influence of Gris immediately. Such an expert,' she said proudly.

The Doctor opened his mouth to speak but then seemed to relax. 'You're absolutely right, Elspeth,' he said. 'What inspired you?'

Lady Lamprey stared at her feet momentarily. 'I lost my husband and daughter in a fire some years ago, Doctor.'

'I'm so sorry.'

'So I used my grief, turned it into something positive. Hence my interest in cubism.'

Mel suddenly realised that the Doctor was completely absorbed by this new scenario and she jumped up, pushed past some outraged guests and yanked on the Doctor's arm.

Angrily he swung around on her but she pulled harder, almost pulling him over.

But it was enough to get him out of Lady Lamprey's immediate presence.

'Thank you Mel,' he said quietly. 'I was nearly absorbed by the temporal rupture that has been created here.' He looked across to the steps. 'And Sir Bertrand has gone, thus fitting in with the new existence Lady Lamprey is part of.'

'Why was he able to move through that time disturbance caused by the creature?'

'The Lamprey, as you called it, Mel.'

'All right, the Lam... and their name is Lamprey. Oh, I'm thick.'

'No you're not,' the Doctor reassured her. 'Because beyond the name, I can't see a connection. And it could be a coincidence that the creature looked like a Lamprey.'

'I could do with some air,' Mel said quietly. 'Whatever Rummas wanted us to find out here, I think we've failed. We lost both Helen and her father.'

The Doctor nodded, and they made their way to the front door where a man, the same one who had announced their arrival, opened the front door for them.

'Good night, sir, miss,' he said politely.

Mel felt the cold winter air on her face and breathed it in deeply. Cold it might be, but out here in the country, it reminded her of home. She looked up at the stars, unmarred by writhing serpentine creatures now, and smiled. Then a thought hit her.

'Doctor, have I ever told you I had a sister?'

The Doctor thought for a second then shook his head. 'As I remember from spending time with your delightful parents, I believed you were an only child.'

'Me too,' Mel said. 'So why did the other you seem to think I had a sister called Anabel?'

The Doctor had no answer for that and instead suggested they find the chauffeur and get him to drive them back to Ipswich.

'No need,' Mel said quietly, and indicated he look behind them.

Wikes Manor was gone.

And in its place was a dome of swirling blue light that dimmed as the dome shrunk away until there was nothing there at all.

And they were back at Ipswich railway station. The TARDIS would be standing a few minutes' walk away, tucked into an alleyway off the main street, where they had left it earlier, discreetly behind the Corn Exchange.

It took them ten minutes to reach it. Soon Mel was kicking snow off her boots at the doorway as, without saying a word, the Doctor unlocked the doors, and led her inside.

Seconds later, the cold night of Suffolk was briefly disturbed as yet another solid object vanished and that same air rushed to fill the vacuum it left behind.

Chapter Seven
Moving Away from the Pulsebeat

It was the brightest, most cheerful day of the season. DiVotow Nek was smiling happily at his tiny baby brother. DiVotow was already twelve years old, and he thought it was about time his parents had another child, especially after... well, after what happened.

In a few more years, DiVotow would finish his studies and would join his father and uncles in Utopiana City. He sat in the park, letting his toes curl around the long grasses, watching a tiny bug crawl over his left foot, doing whatever it was that bugs needed to do in their busy lives.

And who was DiVotow to interfere.

'Don't let it bite you,' called his mother as she laid out the food, but DiVotow understood the bugs. He knew that so long as he didn't make any sudden movements, it would just treat his warm fleshy foot the same way it treated rocks, mud or concrete. An obstacle to be circumnavigated, climbed over or ignored.

It tickled slightly, but he didn't mind that. He flopped gently onto his back, feeling the grass against his naked skin, wriggling slightly to make himself comfortable, but not enough to frighten the bug.

'You'll get burned,' warned his mother, and he lazily reached out and felt around for his shirt, and enjoyed the texture as his fingers found it.

The bug had dropped off now, so he rolled over and pulled the shirt towards him. This now gave him a perfect view of Utopiana City.

Gleaming glass and chrome towers stabbed into the blue sky – each connected to another by a series of what looked like tiny needles. In fact, these were quite long and were large glass pathways, moving floors carrying people from office to office, shop to shop, home to home.

Somewhere up there, in the tallest one, whose spire he couldn't even see, his father was finishing his morning chores and would take a fly-car down to the park, ready to join his loving family in their first day out together in, oh, weeks now.

He smiled as he brought a picture of his father to mind. A wonderful man, one of the science ministry. Like everyone on the planet, DiVotow's family benefited from the work his father did, just as his father had before him. As a result of their endeavours, planet Earth had no crime, no illness, no pollution. DiVotow had heard of other planets that lived in the most terrible conditions, and DiVotow was keen to help them better themselves. Utopiana City was respected the Solar System over for its advances, and DiVotow hoped that after serving his apprenticeship, he could join Uncle Kori and go out to the other worlds, helping them solve their awful problems and showing them how to make their homes like his, so that their children could enjoy park lunches under beautiful blues skies, with beautiful families, and know that their babies could be born with healthy bones, intelligent brains and all the fantastic opportunities that he had had as a youngster.

DiVotow rolled onto his back again and closed his eyes. He began daydreaming, thinking of the day when his mother had announced that any day now, DiVotow was to gain a baby brother, called Toli Nek. The joy he felt at this wonderful news!

He screwed his eyes tighter – he could feel the hot sun on them – perhaps he should get his visor?

DiVotow tried to open his eyes, but couldn't. He wanted to reach out for his mother and Toli, tell them there was a problem with his eyes – but couldn't move.

He couldn't open his eyes.

Instead, the images in his head of his happy family were suddenly disrupted.

The sky was black; really, really black. The tall Utopiana City was wrecked, the linking tubes broken and drooping, people falling from them, dying as they hit the concrete thousands of feet below.

DiVotow tried to call out, tried to scream.

Instead, he saw in his mind's eye his mother and baby brother trying to scream, fighting off... something and DiVotow couldn't touch them. Couldn't discover exactly what was wrong.

He wanted to cry, to fight back.

His dream was becoming... becoming... what was that old word? Uncle Kori had used it once... explained it to him years ago...

Nightmare!

This was a nightmare. A nightmare in which his whole life had turned upside down, become everything the other planets were in reality.

It was DiVotow's worst fear.

The broken buildings and walkways were everywhere now; Mother, Father, Toli, gone, crushed by concrete.

DiVotow finally managed to scream and, in doing so, his eyes opened and he saw the sky forming into shapes.

A massive, green, twisting snake-creature, faceless, covered in pulsating suckers, breathing long tendrils of rubbery flesh. The noise that accompanied it was like a giant heartbeat, but not beating with the rhythm DiVotow would normally attribute to hearts – it was more like a laugh. A deep, booming laugh.

Laughing at his torment, his torture.

'People of Utopiana City,' screamed out an amused voice, dripping with evil. 'Welcome to the only future you have now. Welcome to the pulsebeat!'

DiVotow gasped, joining in as every single inhabitant of Utopiana City stared up in fear at this new invader. And, just like him, their continued existence was now a whim of the strange creature with the massive heartbeat.

'Can't... move...' he wanted to say. 'Got to get away... away from the beat of that heart... that pulse...'

But it was all to no avail. And deep, deep down, DiVotow knew that if he was to ever escape this particular nightmare, the likelihood of seeing his uncle, his father, maybe even his mother was slim.

'We are the Lamprey,' the voice from the skies boomed. 'We are your new master. Be aware that we are power immortal and power absolute.'

And behind every breath, every plosive sound, that pulsebeat continued, filling DiVotow's ears, drowning out the sounds from his own panicked heart.

And he was still wondering when it would cease – if it would ever cease – when he slipped into the darkness of unconsciousness.

* * *

The Praetorian Guardsman was desperately bored. Nothing ever happened in Brighthelmston. Nothing had happened for at least two hundred years, it seemed pretty unlikely that anything was likely to happen today, so why was so much time being spent guarding the seaside from invaders. Seemed a bit daft, especially as the Empire controlled Europa entirely, most of Macedonia and the Far East. Only the New World offered any real opposition and their technology was so far behind the Empire's that it seemed fairly unlikely that a threat would come from there.

He looked out toward the horizon, where the sky met the sea in a dazzling display of, well, bugger all really.

'Let's face it,' he said aloud to no one, but preferring the sound of his own voice to the silence. 'We've eighteen nuclear submarines out there, no one's going to get past that lot. So why am I here?'

'Because it's a pretty pier?' asked a new voice behind his shoulder.

The Guard's laser sword was lit and up before he'd finished turning, but the speaker had already moved out of the way. The stranger was a large man in all respects, but clad in a loose black outfit, tightened at the neck due to a billowing, jet-black cloak, attached by a silver clasp. The Guard was immediately suspicious – this was not regulation Empire clothing; the style, colour and texture seemed wrong. A barbarian from across the seas perhaps? From the New World? No, the accent was wrong, that was Britannian certainly. Of course, he might be a spy.

The man/spy/whatever ran a hand lazily through a head of tightly curled blond locks. 'Brought me back here again, old girl? Why is it always Earth?'

The Guard realised the stranger wasn't talking to a person, but to a white coffin, standing upright beside him. The Stranger followed his look and seemed almost as surprised as the Guard.

'That can't be right. You're supposed to blend in you stupid machine,' he said and gave the coffin a swift kick.

The Guard stared in astonishment, aware his sword was limply drooping beside him now, but too amazed to bring it to bear. With a slight groaning sound, the coffin shimmered and changed, now resembling one of the many canvas guard tents that dotted the shoreline.

'Six bodies she's lasted me,' said the stranger. 'And now she starts playing up. Still, she's in better shape than me, eh? At least she can change her shape easily.' He was pointing to the scar that disfigured his face, which caused one of his eyes to be seared closed.

But the other eye seemed to be staring with enough intensity for both and the stranger smiled.

'So, you on duty then?'

The Guard nodded dumbly, then remembered his voice. 'Halt. Stranger. State your name and business here in Brighthelmston?'

'I'm the Doctor and I'm a visitor to this part of the Empire. May I enquire what the year is?'

'Day 156,0037 of the forty-eighth Julian calendar,' the Guard replied without thinking.

The stranger frowned. 'That late, eh?' Then he began mumbling quietly to himself. 'So, the Empire is at its strongest, Caesar must be the Empress Margarita and it's about eighty years since that meteorite struck Tunguska. Near Subartu. Marvellous, a little over ten years till the next millennium begins, so I'm not too far out.' He looked back towards the Guard and smiled.

'Any chance you might take me to your leader?'

* * *

Praetor Linus took another gulp of wine and placed the goblet back on the tray. With a nod, the taster backed away, and Linus allowed himself a moment of relief that both he and the taster were alive for another few hours. Of course, it was unlikely that if anyone wanted to depose Linus they'd be clumsy enough to poison him – the Praetorian Guard's science section was good and would identify any killer within hours. But, frankly, that wouldn't be too much comfort if Linus were already dead.

But no, he was in far more danger from one of his subordinates – direct assassination was a long-accepted method of promotion, the men and women of the Guard being far more likely to follow a killer who let it be known they were killing their predecessor than someone using subterfuge. Praise the Gods that anyone in the Empire be allowed to use guile and cunning where good old-fashioned brutality and blatant attention-seeking would do.

Linus hated his job, and not just because he had to watch his back all the time.

Sussex was a dull, dull garrison to have been placed in charge of. Clearly he'd offended someone in Camulodunum and thus the decree had come from the Capital City that he was assigned this region. Nothing ever happened, no one invaded (how could they – everything in the immediate proximity was part of the Empire anyway) and the people were dreary merchants and craftsmen always eager to serve the Empire.

What Britannia needed, what the Empire needed, was a good old-fashioned war. A campaign against the New World or one of the Oceania countries. Something that would make the men and women of the army proud again, instead of docile. Although he'd never say it aloud, Linus often wondered if it were time for a new Emperor, someone less consumed with their own power and more interested in her people.

A door slid open with a quiet electronic sigh and Captain Rovia marched in. She was a tall, imposing woman, from a long line of Praetorian Guards. She was also fiercely loyal to Linus and had said on more than one occasion that any assassin that wanted Linus's job would need to go through her first. That alone, Linus half believed, was the main reason no one had yet attempted to kill him. Getting past Rovia wasn't everyone's idea of fun.

'Two things, Praetor,' she said crisply. 'The magii are marching from Regnum to Brighthelmston. Again.'

Linus sighed. 'Oh great, the backward-brigade. Yes, Magii, let's throw away all our technology and live like our forebears did. Bet they still wear synthetic clothes and read their books of nonsense through prescription glasses though. Well, we can't stop 'em. They have a right...'

'Right?'

'Yes, Rovia, they have the right to demonstrate. Even in an Empirical nation, everyone still has the right to complain. Set aside the beach area for their tents and horses but have the Guards watch them carefully. Last time they turned up, we had three deaths in "unusual circumstances". I don't want a repeat of that.'

'Yes, Praetor.'

'And the other matter?'

Rovia paused and chewed her bottom lip, as if she was trying to work out how best to say something. Linus opted to put her out of her misery.

'Can't be that bad, Rovia. What is it?'

Rovia exhaled slowly. 'Well, it seems one of the Guards, near the west pier, has found a stranger.'

'Oh how thrilling. It's not like – having nice hot beaches and cottage industries making homemade ice creams – we ever get strangers down on the South Coast.'

'Not quite what I meant. The Guard says... the Guard says that this stranger just appeared from nowhere and has a coffin that changed shape and became a tent.'

Linus said nothing. He just looked at Rovia. She returned his stare for a full thirty seconds, before adding, 'He swears he's not been drinking.'

Linus smiled slightly. 'No. No I'm sure he hasn't. Well, I suggest you have this stranger brought here because if it's who you and I think it is...'

'He's already here, Praetor. The Guard had the sense to bring him and –'

Rovia was cut off as the door slid open again and the stranger from the seashore strode in. His face was beaming a huge smile and he held his hands out, palms up, in the traditional greeting of peace.

'Praetor Linus, how are you?' he said. 'And, no don't tell me, it's Rovia isn't it?'

Linus couldn't help but smile. 'Doctor! It's been a long time.'

'Linus you haven't changed a bit.'

Linus tilted his head in acknowledgement of the compliment. 'Nonsense, Doctor, I'm older and greyer. You, however, genuinely haven't. And my offer still stands, we have experienced laser surgeons who could repair your scar in an instant. A new eye as well?'

The Doctor looked at his feet. 'It's a badge, Linus. One I feel I must wear at all times.'

Linus nodded. 'Absolutely, old friend. I understand. You were fond of her, weren't you?'

The Doctor smiled and Linus was aware that Rovia was frowning.

'Of course, you never met the Doctor's friend from the New World. A charming savage whom the Doctor tried to educate in our ways, to raise her from the dark to the civilised world.'

'One tried,' the Doctor agreed. 'But I realise now, there are just some people you cannot change. She was born an ignorant savage and thus she died.'

Rovia shrugged. 'An accident?'

The Doctor shook his head. 'No. No Brown Perpugilliam – that was her tribal name, and nothing I could do would convince her to take an Empirical one – well, she died saving me. A noble sacrifice, made during the battle that scarred my face, with an enemy of the Empire, Dominicus.'

Rovia nodded. 'I remember him. Pure evil.'

Linus held a hand up. 'And gone now, apparently all thanks to Brown Perpugilliam. Alas that she fell taking him down.' Linus decided to change the subject. 'Anyway, what brings you back from the stars and planets to our humble sphere, Doctor?'

The Doctor cast a quick look to Rovia but Linus shook his head. 'It's all right, Rovia has my complete confidence in all matters. She is well aware of your true origins.'

'And the Empress?'

Linus laughed. 'Oh rest assured, Caesar only knows you as a traveller from a far island as yet unconquered by the Empire. And after you did us that service with the reptile monsters, she has enquired no further as to where your isle may be. I told her that in return for your services, I promised to keep its location secret. She has, amazingly enough, respected that bargain.'

Rovia, however, was less happy. 'It might not have been wise to reveal your TARDIS's camouflage technique in front of a Praetorian Guardsman, however.'

'Ah. Yes. Well, I thought if he saw that, it would expedite my arrival in your fair palace that much sooner.'

Rovia shrugged. 'Well, it worked, but I can only hope that the extra money I gave him pays for his mouth to stay closed.'

Linus shrugged. 'It may be easier to have him killed on his way back to barracks.'

'No!' The Doctor looked shocked. 'Expedient as that may sound, I'm not sure I want a man's death on my conscience.'

Linus shrugged. 'Fair enough. Now, Doctor, to what do we actually owe the pleasure?'

The Doctor shoved his hands into pockets that had, previously, been all but invisible on his silken black suit, and brought out a tiny microcircuit board. 'I need some help with this,' he said simply. 'It's the masterboard for the image translator in the TARDIS. It's broken and needs some reprogrammed chips.'

'And how can I help you with that?'

The Doctor laughed. 'Oh my dear Praetor, because I know from past experience that your Empire has at its disposal some of the best computer technology in this arm of the galaxy. And I know that you, personally, have an IT department even Caesar herself cannot equal.'

Linus nodded and smiled. 'Devious as ever, Doctor. But of course I shall help you.'

Rovia snapped to attention as the Praetor began escorting the Doctor towards the door.

'Stay with us, Rovia,' Linus said quietly. 'Nothing must happen to our guest.' And as the Doctor moved slightly out of earshot, and couldn't hear him over the sound of the door swishing open, he added, 'And make sure that guard is dead within five minutes. All right?'

'Absolutely, Praetor. I shall see to it at once.' And as Linus led the Doctor forward, the Praetor caught a glimpse of Rovia getting out her cellphone and placing a call...

The celebrations were in full swing, across every continent on every planet in the Milky Way. Jubilant peoples rejoiced in their freedom from oppression, their survival from the onslaught. Such was the joy felt by everyone that crimes were forgotten, collaborators freed and readmitted into society – yes, life had been that hard, that dangerous that in the spirit of willingness to move on, every transgression, every betrayal was forgiven without remorse.

This was a galaxy on the threshold of a new beginning. The Earth Empire, the evil Nazis and their space-conquering *Führer* were finally destroyed. Five hundred years after first emerging on Earth, their vile evil was destroyed forever. Thousands of worlds – previously hostile at best, openly at war at worst – had banded together to make one final fight-back possible, brought into brotherhood by the overwhelming need to face and destroy the galaxy's one true foe.

Of course, no one was sure how long this fragile euphoria could last: cynics and historians alike agreed that peace was dubious at best and despite the utter annihilation of Earth, now just a thermo-nuclear lifeless asteroid floating uselessly around its own solar system, how long would it take for the old enmities to re-emerge. But for now, everyone hoped that this galactic street party would serve as a reminder in the future that they had, once, all been unified; and maybe, just maybe, that peace could be kept up after all.

Optimism was rare in the cosmos – Earth had seen to that

– but perhaps there was a chance the peoples of this quadrant of space could find something to keep them whole and happy.

Haema Smith was one such person. As an Earth evacuee, expelled by the Nazi Party because of her familial heritage, she had been dumped on Halos V and brought up by a caring family there. Haema knew when she'd been unceremoniously deposited there that her own parents, and thus her unborn sister, must be dead – the Nazis had seen to that. And if she'd kept even the tiniest flicker of hope alive in her heart, as she watched the trillions of tonnes of cobalt being smashed into Earth and the Mars colonies on the video screens, that flicker went out. Because she was now a rarity in the galaxy: a living human, probably one of a million, two million at best, scattered across myriad worlds and star systems, fleeing the Nazi persecution but now accepted – at least, she hoped the others were as accepted as she had been – into whichever society they found themselves in.

Haema ducked as Marlern Jarl, a cute boy from across the street, chucked some streamers over her head. Marlern had lost his mother and two brothers very early on in the battle for Halos V, but was as happy as the next person right now. Haema couldn't begrudge Marlern nor any of his people their joy at the utter destruction of her homeworld. She knew it had been the right thing to do. Marlern was really rather adorable – he'd been protective towards her when she'd first arrived, and they'd been out to the shops a few times and even worked side by side in a munitions factory a few months ago when the final push was approaching. He had nice eyes, a cheerful smile and although her upbringing forbade cross-cultural liaisons, Haema could see that such traditions were irrelevant now. She liked Marlern and wondered if they might have a future together? Hell, the galaxy needed a bit of a population boom right now, and whilst it was the biological norm on Halos V for the male to bear the children, as a human she could as well. That had to be a good thing, surely.

Haema's somewhat cheeky thoughts about a naked Marlern evaporated quickly – her attention was drawn to a strange, rhythmic throbbing sound that had started to drown out the party. Gradually, bands stopped, cheering subsided and celebratory bangs and flashes died down as the pulsebeat took over. One or two of the elders began clapping their hands over their ears – it really was a noise that penetrated your very being and vibrated enough that Haema imagined her heart literally bouncing around in time.

By now everyone's attention had been drawn to the sound, but no one could tell where it came from. Was this something to do with the celebrations, which had got out of hand? Surely not a new invasion – the Nazis were destroyed, everyone knew that! Of course there were rumours that the *Führer* had been cloned many times – perhaps he'd regrouped and reformed the Socialist Party elsewhere and was choosing a moment, a really good moment in fact when everyone's guard was down, to strike back?

As Marlern dashed over to Haema, concern in his beautiful blue eyes, the answer came from above.

Haema gasped as the sky seemed to be pulled back, like a set of curtains being parted and... and something was there, bearing down on the people of Halos V as Haema might look at a hill of ants. The thing was like a vast jade snake, but in place of a serpentine head was a blossom of tendrils and a gaping maw that might have been a mouth. From out of that space, the throbbing pulsebeat became a laugh – the most evil, darkest sound Haema had ever heard.

She felt Marlern holding her arm, gasping. 'Look,' he hissed at her.

And Haema saw that everyone around them was frozen, like some tableau or painting. No one was moving. It was as if Halos V had been simply switched off and no one but she and Marlern could still move.

'I don't understand...' she began, but was interrupted by a mocking laugh from the entity in the sky.

'Yes,' it boomed. 'You two will do nicely.'

And for Haema everything went cold. And black.

'And in Ship 567 we have that enigmatic superstar The Human Bullet, competing in his eighteenth race this season, and looking to keep his position as the number-one stardragster in the quadrant. Place your bets now as to who will win this, the most exciting race possible. The course is set up and ready – the stardragsters start from just beyond the moon, and speed off towards Mars, onto the rings of Saturn, where they'll skate across those beautiful works of natural art and slingshot back around Titan and head back towards Earth. Oh, if only there was other life in the solar system, I'm sure the little green Martians from Mars and those jovial Jovians – and whatever else God might have seen fit to create – would be cheering as loudly as we will be from down here in Europa's capital city, Tallin. Already thousands of drag fans are gathered in the skies above the Wastelands, or North America as the old sportsmen used to know it. This landing strip is appropriate – the stardragsters will land in the southeastern corner of the Wastelands in an area that used to be called Texas. In the pioneering days of space exploration, Texas, and in particular a region called Houston, was the site of many exciting scenes when those first Apollo and Gemini missions took off. Of course, such a momentous occasion couldn't pass without a brief mention of the true home of man's early space travel, the infamous Cape Canaveral on the peninsula that used to be Florida, but is now sadly no more, as it sunk beneath the waves at the same time as the old Californian peninsula when the terrible hydrogen accident devastated millions upon millions of lost souls in North America. Indeed, should The Human Bullet win today, he has pledged a percentage of his winners' credits to create a permanent memorial in the Wastelands, to honour his ancestors – apparently he can trace his lineage right back to the late 2130s, and a family living in a city called Kissimmee on that Florida peninsula. He says the memorial will recreate the moment when... wait... I'm sorry, I have to stop now. The race is about to begin, they're under starters' orders and we're crossing straight over to the EUBC Network's satellites around the moon for the start. And... and yes! There they are, all twenty-six magnificent one-man ships, preparing to speed off into the lifeless backwaters of the solar system. What an exciting day for sports fans this is.'

Going by that hype, the occupant of ship 567, aka The Human Bullet, ought to have been some square-jawed, blond, blue-eyed heroic type, with rippling muscles and the kind of perfect, whiter-than-white toothy grin that says 'Hey girls, I'm just the man for you'.

Certainly that was how he was portrayed in the media, and websites were littered with photos of him all over the world, a different swooning girl on each arm.

The truth, as these things often are, was as far from that ideal as humanly possible. The real Human Bullet, as opposed to the well-paid supermodel stand-in, was a twenty-eight-year-old man, prematurely balding, with a huge gap in his front teeth and a belly for whom the name 'pot' may well have been invented. His name was Kevin Dorking, and although he did have ancient American ancestry, his forebears were from Carnfield, Illinois, before they were fried to atoms 165 years previously in the hydrogen 'incident'. Kevin's more recent family were from Bridlington, Humberside, in the Euro State of England, and his manager, the stand-in, Kevin's mother and Felix, her cat, were the only people who actually knew the truth about The Human Bullet.

Kevin had spent much of his childhood fiddling with trucks and aircars at his dad's garage. When his father passed away, Kevin's inability to get his head around facts and figures meant the business went under in less than two years and he found himself doing dodgy jobs for dodgy people on the Euro-mainland and the Balearics. However, whilst his credit dealings were shaky, his expertise in mechanics bordered on genius and thus he began entering races, eventually building up a mystique when he began stardragracing. Because of the sunshields and polarised helmets necessary on stardragsters, no one ever actually saw the pilots once they'd blasted off from wherever on Earth they blasted off from. Thus it was incredibly easy for The Human Bullet to be marketed by his manager as a drop-dead-gorgeous hunk, rather than a weedy unmarried nerd who hadn't quite mastered the art of a daily shower and deodorant use.

The result of this was that his manager scooped millions of credits and gave Kevin enough to keep the stardragsters running, his mum with a roof over her head and enough Cattychunks for Felix. The rest went on hiring the model and buying a range of properties on the Côte d'Azur.

However, unknown to Kevin, his manager, Kevin's poor old mum or Felix, today's race was going to take an unplanned turn.

Kevin was, as expected, well in the lead and was just careering around Phobos on his way back to Earth when he happened to glance into the monitor screen in his cockpit to see the state of the other ships... all of which seemed to have stopped moving. And whilst Kevin would never consider himself greatly endowed with brains, he knew that ships don't just come to a stop in space, otherwise they get caught in orbits and, if they're not careful, dashed to pieces on the surface of whichever lifeless planet, moon or asteroid they make the mistake of conking out near to. For all twenty-five other stardragsters to do this simultaneously was, well, statistically impossible. Or, at the very least, highly unlikely.

Then Kevin heard a sound over his headphones... no *not* over the headphones. It was coming through the whole ship, vibrating everything with a rhythmic pounding. Like a heartbeat. Kevin's first thought was that he was having a heart attack, that he would in fact be last seen plummeting downwards onto Phobos and being vaporised. He thought of his mother, bereft of a son and income, of Felix bereft of Cattychunks. And of that poor model, whatever his name was, who would have to 'die' as well.

Then across the pulsing heartbeat, he heard a voice, speaking to him.

'Yes. Yes, you'll do. You're the best this existence has to offer me.'

It occurred to Kevin that he was definitely dying. After all, if anyone had really believed he was the best on offer, that had to be delusion talking.

'No, this is quite real. You're not dying.' The heartbeat had spoken, the voice now attuned to the rhythm. 'This is far worse.'

Kevin then blacked out and, sure enough, his stardragster

plummeted onto Phobos and disintegrated. But no one on Earth saw this happen as they were all frozen. Just like the Utopiana that DiVotow Nek was from. And the Halos V Haema Smith and Marlern Jarl had been from. And indeed countless other planets across countless other realities and histories.

Frozen in a millisecond of time for all eternity.

'So, apart from utilising my science division, Doctor, why are you here on Earth? I hardly imagine a casual visit to the Empire is high on your list of priorities, and frankly I'm sure any number of aliens in outer space could serve your IT needs better than us.'

The Doctor, Linus and Rovia were walking down a long, sterile corridor, their feet echoing slightly on the concrete floor. As with everything regarding the officialdom of the Empire, sterility and functionality was paramount.

It crossed Linus's mind now and again that a painting of a tree or some animals in a jungle might brighten the place up but Caesar wouldn't approve. The Empress wasn't known for her appreciation of such things. She didn't appreciate much except a lack of invasions, dissent and poverty. At least, in her direct view. Linus doubted she gave two figs what happened away from Camulodunum these days.

The Doctor was apparently admiring a concrete pillar that was identical to all the other concrete pillars that guarded the room into which they were heading. 'Very nice,' he muttered, patting it grandly, as if it were the finest piece of architecture in the Empire.

Linus mentally shrugged – that was the Doctor all over. A good man who had saved this planet a number of times, not that he ever told anyone. Indeed, as far as Linus knew, only about six other people on the planet knew of his true origins.

Linus considered himself both flattered and honoured that he was one of them. The Doctor had once given him a tiny green ball that, he had said, was to be used in emergencies. Linus gathered it was some kind of alert beacon, which would draw the Doctor back to Earth if used. The Praetor made sure no one in the science division ever became aware of its existence or only the gods knew what trouble that would land the Doctor in.

Thus Linus and the Doctor entered the science division, Rovia making her farewells and heading back to the operations area.

The Doctor kissed her hand and watched as she walked away.

'You're safe with that one, Praetor,' he said. 'She wouldn't harm a hair on your head.'

'I know,' Linus said. 'That's why she's still alive and working for me.' He smiled at the Doctor's look of surprise. 'Honesty, Doctor, is something you told me you appreciated. I can afford a degree of sentiment but, on the whole, I have to be practical and surround myself with people I trust because they'll keep me alive, not because I like them.'

'Which camp is Rovia in?'

'Both,' Linus said simply, then changed the subject quickly. 'So, what kind of person are you looking for?'

The Doctor was gazing at the ten or so people working at PCs ranged around the room. The quiet hum of computers, the tapping of keys and the occasional buzz of an internet connection were the only sounds. No one talked. No one even looked at their co-workers.

'A collective or a sweat shop?'

Linus felt as if he'd been struck. The last thing he'd expected from the Doctor was criticism and this one stung. Probably because, as the outraged denial died in his throat, Linus knew it was an accurate description. He answered as best he could.

'They and their families are well catered for.'

'But they're slaves. After centuries, the Roman Empire is still built on slavery.'

'Not slaves,' Linus began. 'Willing participants in –'

'Oh spare me the semantics, Praetor,' snapped the Doctor. 'Slaves, good old-fashioned indigenous people, forced to work for their masters.'

This was too much for Linus – although the Doctor had been waspish, he'd remained quiet so no one else could hear. But Linus couldn't stop himself. 'That's not fair, Doctor! I'm as Britannian as any of these people. Generations have passed since the Empire first invaded this island and now we all consider ourselves part of one people.'

The Doctor remained quiet. 'Glad to hear it, Praetor. So. Why the slaves? I mean, if you're all one big happy family...'

Linus took a deep breath. One or two of the IT workers actually looked over but a swift glare from their Praetor made them resume work. He stared at the Doctor, hard. Instead of the usual turned-away gaze he got from most, the Doctor's one eye stared back. Not with malice or even severity, just... Linus could only call it quizzical. Genuine puzzlement perhaps?

The Doctor continued. 'You see, the Roman Empire rules three-fifths of your planet. The other two-fifths aren't, frankly, worth you ruling – Oceania is too far away to cause you problems, the New World is still savage. So why, when you have medicines that can prolong life far beyond the norm, and you have a technology that, applied properly, could send you to the stars, and art and literature that museums and libraries the universe over would die to possess, do you still build your society on slavery?'

Linus opened his mouth to speak. To offer the usual retort as when so-called 'civil liberties' groups asked the same basic question (although the 'the universe over' bit rarely cropped up, to be honest). To imply that it was ludicrous to suggest slavery still existed. To be affronted at such an accusation, that Caesar herself would be appalled to discover that any of her people believed such nonsense and that everyone who worked did so freely, with full benefits and free will. To then proudly point to the Praetorian Guard's record on civil liberties and policing of demonstrations and to point out that were the Empire so tyrannical, demonstrations would be banned.

But Linus knew he was facing the Doctor. He also knew that demonstrators *were* barely tolerated, that a lot of activists either had 'accidents' or found themselves new 'jobs' on patrol boats heading to the New World, which rarely returned or... oh what was the point?

'We are all slaves, Doctor. Slaves to the good of the Empire, slaves to the doctrine that has kept this planet free of war, famine and poverty.'

He wondered if it sounded as hollow to the Doctor as it did to himself.

The look the Doctor gave him suggested it did. But he said nothing, just walked towards the sla... towards the technicians operating the PCs, monitoring whatever it was they were monitoring. CCTV, financial transactions. Private cellphone or landline calls.

Not for nothing was the Praetorian Guard called the eyes and ears of the Empire. And while Linus's division wasn't the biggest or most well-equipped Guardhouse, it was good enough for the southern part of Britannia.

The Doctor was standing beside a young woman in a pale-red work dress. Linus briefly tried to bring her name to mind, but realised he couldn't. His first instinct was to shrug and remind himself she was only a worker girl. But then he realised that, in fact, the word he wanted to say was 'slave'. And he felt a pang of conscience that he could barely name all his guards, let alone any of the slaves, male or female, in the Guardhouse. Damn the Doctor, he always brought his guilt to mind.

'Hello,' the Doctor was saying cheerfully to the girl. 'What are you working on?'

'A project to enhance society and enable the Empire to function satisfactorily,' the girl replied, and Linus winced. Of course she would say that, it was drilled into them in the first week of their appointments.

If the Doctor doubted her sincerity, he didn't let it show. Instead he leant toward her screen and pointed at something – Linus couldn't see what and in fact had no idea what this girl was working on. It wasn't his job to know. He looked toward the technical supervisor who was quite wisely avoiding his, or anyone else's gaze whilst the Praetor was in the room.

Didn't help Linus though. He might've been able to get a clue out of him.

'I think, young lady, you'll find that if you move that equation to this column and bring that into the preliminary column and transpose x for y, you'll increase the efficiency by some quite considerable way.' The Doctor beamed down at the girl as at first indignation, then realisation and finally what might also have been admiration crossed her face. 'My name is the Doctor,' he said to her. 'And you are?'

The girl opened her mouth to answer then closed it again.

'Go on,' the Doctor encouraged.

'I am Technician 38, designated Terminal H as my workstation.'

'Yes, very good,' said the Doctor. 'But what is your name?'

The girl swallowed and reached back to her shoulder, twiddling absently with the long, thin pigtail of hair that ran from the back of her otherwise almost shaved head. Linus noted it was red and it crossed his mind that if she'd not had the regulation slave... regulation *worker* haircut, she might have quite an attractive look about her.

'My name is Melina,' she said.

'Hello Melina.' The Doctor offered her his hand and Melina took it and they shook. 'You don't like it much here, do you? Bit of a waste of your talents.'

Linus was looking at the Doctor and the girl.

Except, for just a split second he wasn't. Not quite.

Instead, he was in a wholly different room, surrounded by wholly different people. The only constant was the Doctor and the girl. Except the Doctor was in a ridiculously colourful coat and trousers. His smiling face was unscarred, and he seemed to have a somewhat healthier glow to his skin.

The girl had a mass of tight, curled red hair, and was wearing a pale green top and strawberry trousers, with small towelling things around her ankles.

The girl was Melina, Linus was sure of that. They were smiling at each other. The Doctor turned and looked at Linus and started to say something.

'I'd like to borrow Melina, Praetor,' the Doctor said. His one good eye twinkled slightly as he straightened up, adjusting the black cloak clasp around his neck.

'Why?'

'I'm not really sure,' the Doctor replied. 'She just feels... right.'

The shaven-headed technician looked at her Praetor, but he couldn't tell whether she was alarmed or amused.

Linus closed his eyes and re-opened them. Nope, the Doctor was still in black, the girl still in her red dress. Whatever he'd just seen was obviously a hallucination of some sort. Overwork, stress, that sort of thing.

'Yes, of course,' he heard himself saying. 'I'm sure the supervisor won't mind.'

If the supervisor did mind, he had the good sense not to contradict his Praetor and so seconds later, the Doctor offered his hand to Melina, who took it and stood up. 'This way, my dear.'

The Doctor turned to look at Linus as he and Melina passed by, and leaned his head towards him, and spoke softly. Conspiratorially.

'Yes, Linus, I felt it too. And you looked a lot happier and more relaxed in the alternate reality.'

And then he and Melina were gone, leaving Linus feeling, as he often did when the Doctor turned up, totally out of his depth.

Chapter Eight
Whatever Happened To?

Joseph Tungard paused just before inserting the key into the door. Slightly, and ludicrously, breathless after climbing the few steps leading up from the pavement, he stared through the glass of the door and into the gloom of the hallway. Mrs Jones still hadn't picked up her daily post, and a newspaper was propped up against her front door. Opposite, in number two, Joseph could imagine he was hearing the constant arguments that went on between the strange couple who lived there.

And upstairs would be Natjya.

With a deep breath he turned the key and nearly jumped out of his skin as a car horn tooted behind him. Looking back down and onto the road, he saw the green Wolsey belonging to Doctor Pike. Putting a cheerful grin on his face, he waved and started down the steps as Pike got out of the car.

'Did you get the message, Joe?' Pike yelled as he hurried over.

Joseph was instantly alarmed. Not only had he not received a message, but Pike was carrying his medical bag.

'No,' he said simply. 'I have just come home early from work.'

Pike was at his side now, not breathless at all. 'All right old man, no need to panic. Natjya may have taken a turn for the worse. Monica was with her anyway and she called me straight away. Let's go on up.'

The two men quickly ascended the two floors to Flat 6 and entered (Joseph still out of breath by the time they arrived, Doctor Pike acting as if he'd casually mounted two steps rather than two flights).

Monica Pike was sat on the sofa, smoking a Turkish and placing a three of diamonds on the table before her.

Natjya, seated in her wheelchair, a blanket over her legs, ignored the new arrivals. She reached forward and scooped up the discarded card and four previous ones, slotted them into the hand fanned before her and then placed two tricks down onto the table: a run in spades from four to eight and three threes in various suits.

'She's picked this up too well,' Monica said without actually addressing the men.

'It's easy,' Natjya said. 'Better than your bridge with all its strange combinations. This is a proper game, invented by Romanian gypsies hundreds of years ago.'

Monica smiled. 'I think you'll find that gin was invented about a hundred years ago in the courts of Queen Victoria, my dearest,' she said and took a blind card, adding it to her fan and discarding a five of clubs.

'How are you feeling, Mrs Tungard?' said Doctor Pike, crouching beside her.

'Oh I am fine, Doctor. Your granddaughter worries over the slightest thing, fusses over nothing.'

'Monica?'

Monica carried on playing cards as she spoke. 'Oh, Natjya felt a bit ill and was sick in the sink and has been complaining of headaches.'

'Always I have the headaches,' Natjya said tersely. 'I do not know why you all worry so.' She wheeled herself away from the card table fractionally and tried to readjust her blanket.

Joseph automatically moved over, took it off, refolded it and laid it back, adding a peck on her forehead for luck.

Joseph then sat on the arm of the settee, opposite his wife, and stared into her eyes. Her sad, slightly watery eyes. 'Because my darling, we are concerned.'

'Ah yes, so concerned that you work all the hours the Lord gave you in your university, meaning poor Monica here has to come and waste her pretty young life looking after an invalid.'

Monica took another card. 'You are not an invalid, my darling, you are a friend, and I have very little else to do these days. Oh, and I've just won.' She placed down a run from ten to King of hearts and three sevens, leaving her with an empty hand. 'That's twenty, thirty, sixty, eighty-five to me and...' she flicked through Natjya's tricks, 'seventy minus whatever is in your hand.' Natjya placed her remaining cards face up. 'Ten, twenty, twenty-five, thirty, thirty-five. Take from seventy gives you a total of thirty-five.' Monica beamed at the men. 'My first win in eight games, gentlemen.'

'I was distracted by these brutes bursting through the door as if there was a fire or something,' said Natjya. Joseph gave her a hug and she whispered in his ear, very quietly: 'Ask them to leave, Joe, please?'

Joseph stood up. 'Can I make you a cup of tea, Doctor Pike? Monica?'

Monica shook her head – she'd had about six already. 'No, we should be leaving. Come along, Gramps.'

Doctor Pike stood up. 'If you are sure, Mrs Tungard?'

'Oh I am quite well, Doctor. Your granddaughter is the best medicine I could ever want.'

Pike nodded. 'If I may wash my hands before we go?'

Joseph nodded. 'You know where the bathroom is.'

As Pike wandered further into the flat, Joseph moved to the kitchenette, followed by Monica.

As soon as they were out of sight of the living room, they embraced and kissed passionately. After a moment, Joseph drew back.

'I cannot carry on, my darling. You do understand that, don't you?'

Monica looked at him stoney-faced. 'If your wife were to find out...'

'She mustn't!'

'... it would kill her. Possibly quite literally.' Monica smiled. 'Which would make life easier all round, don't you think?'

'According to your grandfather, she should have died three years ago.'

Monica shrugged. 'Medicine isn't all it's cracked up to be. Even doctors make mistakes.'

'I'm sorry, Monica, but when we began this, it was in the knowledge that my Natjya would die and never find out. Three years on, it's becoming a bigger and bigger risk. I won't hurt her!'

'Hurt her! For God's sake, Joe, when you're in my bed, do you worry about hurting her? When we meet in cafés and restaurants, while you're "working late", do you worry about hurting her? Do you hell!'

Joseph looked at his feet. 'That's different.'

'Different in what way? Oh, I see. Out of sight, out of mind. Well, blow that darling. I want you. You want me. And one way or another we'll be together.'

'Well, you may have to wait a while before you see me again. The department's main benefactor is heading up to London and I have to wine and dine him for a couple of days.'

Monica grinned. 'Is he rich darling? I mean, I love you dearly, but you're not exactly rolling in spare cash.'

Joseph wasn't sure whether to be genuinely affronted or just feign it. Was this British humour or a real comment? 'He is rich, that's why he's a benefactor. Sir Bertrand is generous but careful. I have to prove to him that the department is still worth his investment. Over the last five years I've built it up, but we still need Sir Bertrand's capital to compete with Queen Mary's and Imperial.'

Monica sighed. 'Whatever you need to do, my darling, you do it. Just make sure I get a chance to see you before too long.' And she kissed him, savagely, on the mouth again.

He eased her away, almost fighting for breath, trying to ignore the familiar, but odd, coppery taste she left in his mouth. Like blood, but there was no sign of bleeding.

There was a cough at the door and Joseph was aghast to see Monica's grandfather stood there. Did he see? Would he say anything to his patient?

He just pointed to the door back to the hallway and both Joseph and Monica headed that way, Monica pausing to give Natjya a quick peck on the cheek. 'Take care,' she murmured.

Natjya took Monica's hand in her own. 'I don't know what I'd do without you. You are my lifeline.'

Monica smiled. 'I'll always be here for you, dearest. Never doubt that.'

And she followed Joseph and her grandfather out of the flat and into the hall.

'I'll cut straight to the point, my boy,' Doctor Pike said.

Joseph wanted to laugh at being called a 'boy' by a man only fifteen years older than he, but didn't. 'Tell me everything,' he said.

'Well, thinking back over the tests of the last few years, ever since that wretched boat trip, she's been in decline. It's been nearly two years since she became dependent on the wheelchair, and not because her legs don't work but because she tires too easily.'

'That I know,' said Joseph, a bit more tersely than he meant.

'And you also know my diagnosis has always been that she has a touch of pleurisy.'

Joseph nodded.

'Something's changed, hasn't it Gramps,' said Monica, frowning.

Doctor Pike bit his lip before answering. 'You did the right thing, my dear, in not washing away the vomit in the sink. I got a good look at it.'

'I thought that's what you were up to,' Monica said.

'And?' Joseph had a bad feeling where this was going.

'Blood. Spots rather than a stream, going by the sink. I'm sorry Joseph, I think we're looking at consumption.'

Joseph frowned. He didn't know the term.

Monica took his hand. 'Tuberculosis,' she said.

Joseph felt like he'd been hit with a rock. He almost staggered.

'But that... that's slow. And painful, isn't it?' He didn't want that for her. She deserved better.

Doctor Pike nodded. 'And she probably hasn't got long.'

'Should I tell her?'

'I don't see what that would gain at this stage. Natjya's not daft, Joe. As she gets weaker and iller, she'll begin to realise that she's getting worse not better. I suggest that if you tell her now, she'll begin to look for evidence and that more often than not leads to a decline. She may have another few months yet. Better not to let her fret.'

Joseph could swear he saw a flash of something go across

Monica's eyes at the 'few months' bit. Anger? No, he would have expected that. Disappointment? Possibly, but no. It was more akin to bewilderment, or surprise.

'Listen Joe, I'll take Monica home and dig you out some essays and journals on TB, and you give them a read. Ultimately if you tell Natjya, that's up to you. It's your life, both your lives and you must lead them as you see fit. But I think TB can be scary and, as we all know, Natjya's bark is worse than her bite.'

'You mean, she'll cover it up, but this'll scare her?'

Pike nodded. He then shook Joseph by the hand and led Monica down the stairs to the entrance hall.

Monica gave Joseph a look back over her shoulder, but his mind was too preoccupied to really acknowledge it.

But one day, he'd remember it.

He'd remember that it was a look of pure hatred.

It was raining. Not a particularly huge downpour, indeed more of a gentle drizzle, but it was that shivery, unpleasant drizzle that slowly seeps into your clothes and makes you feel as if you've been dipped into a rather cold bath.

And it isn't just clothes that become wet and unmanageable.

'Look at my hair,' the Doctor moaned as he stared into the shop window, his multicoloured reflection staring grumpily back. 'Frizzled.'

'Frizzled?' repeated Melanie, fairly certain it wasn't a word she recognised. 'Is that Gallifreyan for "a mess"? perchance?' she teased.

'Frizzled is a perfectly accurate and recognised scientific term for slightly wavy hair that goes dramatically tight and curled when damp. My hair is frizzled.'

Melanie shrugged. 'You look like Diana Ross,' she said.

The Doctor stopped staring at himself and gave Melanie

what she called his Tigger look – as if he couldn't quite comprehend whether he'd been insulted or complimented.

'Early eighties Ross,' Melanie helpfully added. 'Not the Supremes heyday.'

Apparently understanding that he'd now definitely been insulted, the Doctor turned away from Melanie and walked into the shop.

'I'd like an umbrella please,' he bellowed, and with a sigh Melanie followed him in, preparing to apologise, as usual, for his demanding rather than requesting nature.

Instead she found the Doctor stood alone inside a shop positively brimming with umbrellas, mackintoshes (or the local equivalent thereof), hats and other wet-weather gear.

'A plentiful supply,' he said quietly. 'Just no one to supply us.'

Melanie decided to rap on the counter but no response was forthcoming, so she instead reached over and took a large green golfing umbrella. 'This'll do,' she said.

The Doctor reached from behind her and took it out of her hand, replacing it in the stand.

'Melanie! I'm shocked at you.'

'Eh?'

'You can't go around stealing things just because no one is here to receive our custom.' He looked back out through the door and onto the deserted streets. 'Or indeed anywhere at all.'

'Precisely,' responded Melanie, taking the umbrella up again. 'And I don't need my clothes, notoriously shrinkable in the rain, becoming all clingy and see-through. And if,' she added quickly, forestalling his response, 'anyone does turn up, I'll happily pay them.'

The Doctor harrumphed something about dubious morality,

but didn't take the umbrella away again and instead held the door open so she could exit. As she did so, he once again swiped it from her grasp, this time unfurling it and holding it above his head.

'Hey,' she said, ready for an argument.

'Taller than you,' he said simply. 'You carry it and I'll just get a poke in the eye. I carry it, we're both dry.'

Melanie was going to mutter something about poking him somewhere closer but thought better of it. Instead she tried to draw his attention back to the empty street. 'This is freaky.'

'"Freaky"? "Freaky"?' the Doctor snorted. 'And what, pray tell, does "freaky" mean in this context?'

'"Freaky" as in they told us that Schyllus was a good world for shopping, business and picnics. "Freaky" as in where are the people to buy from and have picnics with. That "freaky".'

'Oh. Oh that "freaky". Right. Yes, I concede, it's indeed "freaky". And not good weather for picnics, although I am a little peckish and –'

'I mean,' continued Melanie hurriedly, 'if they need umbrellas and shops and roads and pubs, then they must be pretty much like you and me. Basically.'

'Basically?'

Melanie sighed. 'I mean they're not going to be inch-high ant people or sixty-foot giant jellyfish. Everything about this street, this area, suggests two arms, two legs and creatures about our height. So it's not like we can't see them or risk treading on them.'

'Perhaps they're invisible,' the Doctor suggested.

'Then how come we're not walking into them and no one stopped us pinching the brolly.'

'Borrowing.'

'All right "borrowing". Either way, I think this place is like the *Mary Celeste*.'

The Doctor held his hand out from under the umbrella, testing the rain. It was really pouring now. He then licked his hand. 'Basic H_2O, a bit saltier than the rain you're used to, but harmless. You may be right.'

'About what?'

'The people. Not invisible. Not here. Freaky.'

'So why did Rummas suggest we come here? He seemed quite insistent about it.'

The Doctor wandered away from Melanie, leaving her in the rain. She was going to complain but instead just sighed. 'Why do I bother?' she muttered, then she called out: 'Excuse me? What have you seen now?'

The Doctor yelled back, 'Don't just stand there, you'll get wet. Come here.'

Blowing air – and another deep sigh – out of her lungs, Melanie strode off to where he stood now.

'Sorry Melanie,' he said. 'I thought you had an umbrella.'

Without speaking, Melanie eased the umbrella out of his grasp and covered herself. Despite the rain, the Doctor seemed oblivious to the fact he was getting drenched. He crouched down in front of a storm drain built into the pavement. 'Listen,' he said.

Melanie frowned, trying to concentrate over the pounding rain. Nothing... no, there. Yes, there was a sound. A rhythmic breathing. Melanie had been in enough tight situations with the Doctor since their first meeting in Derby to know the sound of panic. Of fear.

She crouched down beside the Doctor and leaned slightly forward, ignoring the rain that hit the back of her neck and trickled down her spine; it just rolled off her skin. But she was too intent on trying to see who was inside the drain, hiding from them.

'Hello,' she called softly. 'Hello, we're not going to hurt you. The Doctor and I have just arrived and we wondered where everyone was. Can you get out?'

For a moment there was no response, but then a small girl's voice spoke. 'Has the pulsebeat gone?'

'Pulsebeat?' repeated the Doctor. 'What's that?'

'I... I don't know,' said the girl, still hidden. 'It was the word that came into my mind when it arrived. It stopped Mummy. Everyone stopped moving. I hid here.'

'Very sensible,' said the Doctor. He looked upwards. 'It seems to have stopped raining now. You can come out if you want.'

'Everyone's stopped,' the girl repeated quietly.

'When?' asked Melanie. 'I mean, when did this happen?'

'This morning,' came the response.

The Doctor stood up. 'Well, we're nothing to do with any "pulsebeat", we're travellers. We're looking for your friends and family. Can you get out so we can talk properly?' He looked up into the sky, then ran a hand through his hair.

Dried, by the scorching sun that had been hidden by storm clouds seconds earlier. 'Odd,' he murmured.

Melanie glanced towards him and grimaced. 'That is weird isn't it.' She shook the umbrella but no water came away. It was bone dry. 'Seattle to the Sahara in one minute.'

The Doctor just smiled at Melanie. 'I think the word is "freaky".'

They were disturbed by some scrabbling from within the storm drain and Melanie watched as a young girl, about eight or nine, dirty and wide-eyed, crawled out.

She looked at the Doctor, then at Melanie and gasped.

'I get that a lot,' said Melanie. 'This is the Doctor, he's from a planet called Gallifrey. I'm from Earth. My name is Mel Baal, but my friends call me Melanie. I'd like you to, if that's okay.'

The little girl nodded, a bit shaken and trying to take in everything, Melanie guessed.

'I'm Kina,' she said. 'They made my mummy stop.'

The Doctor gently scooped her up and, taking the umbrella from Melanie, rested it on the ground, then placed Kina under it, to keep cool.

'There, is that better?'

Kina nodded. 'Thank you,' she said politely.

Melanie smiled. 'Where has everyone gone, Kina?'

Kina was staring at Melanie, but she was used to that. 'Where are you from?' asked the girl.

'I'm from Earth,' Melanie said.

'Do they all look like you there?'

Melanie laughed lightly. 'No. No, many of the people on Earth look just like you. And the Doctor here. But I'm a bit special, a bit unusual.'

'You see Kina,' said the Doctor, 'my friend Melanie has a mummy just like yours I expect. But her daddy is one of a magnificent race of reptile people who'd lived on the Earth millions of years before Melanie's mummy's race evolved properly.'

'Is that why she's weird? And got funny skin?'

'Out of the mouths of babes,' muttered the Doctor, but Melanie shrugged.

'She's probably never seen anyone other than people like her.' She looked at the poor frightened youngster. 'Yes Kina, that's why my skin is green and these are called my scales.' She wanted to give this poor girl a comforting hug, but thought if she was that freaked out by seeing the way she looked, it might be misinterpreted. Melanie was used to that reaction. 'But inside, I'm just like you and want to be your friend. May I be?'

Kina didn't look convinced.

'And,' added the Doctor reassuringly, 'if you'll let us, we'll try to help you find your mummy.'

The black Wolsey was being driven carefully along the A5 towards the Pike family home in West Hampstead. Inside, the two occupants were engaged in a heated discussion. Not a row per se, but loud enough.

To most observers, it might have seemed a bit odd, a bit non de rigeur on late 1950s Earth, for a debutante and her grand-father to get quite so heated, but, nevertheless, the discussion was blistering indeed.

'You were supposed to have killed her by now! I need Joe left without any distractions!'

Doctor Pike was concentrating on driving while listening to Monica's admonishments. All he said in reply, through tight lips, was: 'You won't get him if the old woman catches you two at it. In her own blasted kitchen! For goodness' sake, girl, what were you thinking?'

'I was thinking "Gramps", that we've been trailing this man for ten years now and I'm getting fed up playing the part of dozy social whirlwind trying to seduce him. Have you any idea how repulsive it is sleeping with a man old enough to be my father?'

'If your wretched father were still alive, Monica, this wouldn't be our problem.'

Monica said nothing as the car made a couple of right turns into West Hampstead, but as Pike slowed down outside their home, she finally let it out.

'If the two of you had used your brains instead of brawn, you might have realised that blowing up a communist supply train might just take my so-called Daddy down with it! The plan is being made up as we go along!'

As the car rattled to a halt and Pike switched off the engine, Monica opened the door, got out and slammed it shut. Pike was emerging on the opposite side, reaching back for his bag of tricks.

'Oh and who the hell is "Sir Bertrand Lamprey"?'

Pike stared at her in bemusement. 'Who?'

'I asked you that. He's Joseph's money-man at the university. Apparently Joe is babysitting him for the next few days. I assumed that, as he shares my real name, we might be related. After all, we're not exactly common, are we?'

Pike frowned. 'I genuinely don't know a Bertrand Lamprey. In theory, you're the last. There shouldn't be another. It might be a coincidence.'

Monica snorted and went to the front door, getting her key out and opening it. As they went in, she flicked a light on in the hallway and began scooping up the post. 'In our line, coincidences shouldn't occur. Either you and Daddy made a big mistake or Sir Bertrand is trouble.'

'He can't be from here,' Pike said. 'Not from this timeline anyway.'

Monica stopped at that and slowly placed the unopened mail on the hall table. 'Are you saying one of the alternate Lampreys has crossed over? To here? Why?'

Pike shrugged. 'I rather think "how?" is the more appropriate question.' He hung his coat up and held up a hand as a voice could be heard coming from the back of the house:

'Is that you, Doctor?'

'Hello Mrs Philips,' called out Monica.

A door opened, revealing a small kitchen. 'Oh hello miss,

Doctor Pike. Dinner will be about fifteen minutes if that is all right?'

'Perfect Mrs Philips,' Pike said, opening the door of the living room and easing Monica through. 'See you then.'

Mrs Philips smiled once and went back to her kitchen, closing the door behind her. Checking that she was out of earshot, Pike closed the living-room door behind him.

'I rather think that, despite our good Mr Tungard's plea for you to stay away, you need to escort him on at least one dinner date and see if Sir Bertrand is a true Lamprey or if it's just some horrible coincidence.'

'And if he is one?'

Pike sat in an armchair and scooped up a newspaper, unfurled it and began to read.

'Then, my dear girl, you have a problem.'

'So what d'you think's happened to everyone, Doctor?'

Melanie was stood atop a transparent see-through plastic canopy that shielded a cake shop from Schyllus's strong sun.

It was about fifteen minutes since the rain had been evaporated by a dry heat that caused the horizon to shimmer. Every so often a gust of wind would disturb dust and dirt from roofs and deckings, but those brief breezes were the only respite from the scorching heat.

Below Melanie, shaded by the same canopy, the Doctor was wiping sweat from his brow, little Kina hugging his left leg. 'I have no idea,' he panted. 'But it's certainly strange. As is this climate change.'

Melanie smiled. Most people from Earth would, like the Doctor, be sweltering, but for Melanie, as a hybrid human/ reptile, she was literally basking in the heat. Her unique scaled skin almost imperceptibly rising and falling as she breathed, acting as an autonomic air-conditioning system for her body, she licked her lips with a 'slightly-indented-but-not-forked' tongue (it was an old school joke) before agreeing with him. 'I can't see anything. As I said, it's like the *Mary Celeste* – everything perfectly arranged, cars in car parks, washing on washing lines.' A third eyelid briefly nictitated across each of her eyes, clearing the dust. 'But nothing alive. Not people, not animals, not birds. I can't even see any insects.'

The Doctor was focusing his attention on Kina, asking for not the first time whether she could explain what happened and why she was still there. The Time Lord had quietly suggested to Melanie that her hiding place of a storm drain was unlikely to be the cause of her saving. 'After all, I can't believe everyone was outside. Some would have been under the cover of houses, working in basements or some such. Yet we've seen no one else.'

Kina was still being less than helpful, however, although Melanie suspected this was from a mix of fear and confusion rather than deliberate obtuseness.

That was more the Doctor's bag.

'The pulsebeat came. Everyone stopped 'cept me. I hid.'

The Doctor nodded. 'And did you see where everyone went?'

Kina looked confused. She stared around her, behind the Doctor, then upwards, towards Melanie. Seeing that look made Melanie decide to clamber down and join them on the ground.

Kina was still saying nothing.

'We want to help you, Kina,' Melanie said quietly. 'Just tell us as much as you can remember.'

'Snake,' the little girl finally said.

'Snake,' repeated the Doctor in a voice that failed completely to disguise his frustration. 'That helps,' he added, quietly enough that only Melanie would hear.

'What sort of snake?' Melanie coaxed Kina, chucking the Doctor a look that said: 'Shut up and let me deal with this.'

'Big snake. In the sky. No teeth. Suckers and flippity-floppity bits.'

'"Flippity" –' started the Doctor, but a ferocious look from Melanie stopped him. 'Well, it still doesn't help, does it?' he muttered.

'And then what happened. Did the snake scare everyone away. Did it frighten your mummy? Make her go away?'

Kina shook her head. 'Not gone away.'

The Doctor was beside them both in an instant, all trace of tetchiness gone. 'Hello again, Kina.' He smiled his bestest smile, designed to gain the trust of frightened little girls the universe over in a wholly non-threatening away. Melanie was always jealous of that smile.

It had worked on her a few times, too.

'Can you see your mummy now?'

Melanie was confused by this, but confused further when Kina pointed behind them both.

'Is she all right?' said the Doctor.

Kina shrugged, but stayed focused on what was, as far as Melanie was concerned, a shop doorway.

'If they've disappeared, Doctor,' Melanie asked, 'how can she see her mother?'

Without taking his smiling face away from Kina's line of vision, the Doctor spoke softly to his companion. 'What did Kina say when we first asked about her mother?'

Melanie closed her eyes, using her memory to bring the phrase back. 'She said: "They made my mummy vanish."'

The Doctor shook his head. 'Your mind's going Melanie,

you're mixing it up with what we assumed to be the case. Think harder.'

'Got it: "They made my Mummy stop."'

'Spot on. We thought they'd vanished, but they haven't. They've stopped. Literally. Time has stopped for these people, but not their surroundings. So the rain, the sun, the wind, it carries on. We carry on. But Kina's friends and family stopped while everything around them carried on.'

Melanie frowned. 'Some kind of time manipulation?'

'A clever interstitial trap.' The Doctor stood up and moved away from Kina, a few feet back. Then he stopped. 'Kina. Kina, I'm going to reach out and I'd like you to tell me when I'm touching your mummy. Is that okay? And I promise you that by touching her, I'm not hurting her in any way. Is that all right with you?'

Kina looked between the Doctor and Melanie, who smiled reassuringly at her, hoping that would be enough to swing things in their favour.

It worked. Kina looked at the Doctor and nodded.

'Thank you, Kina,' he said. 'Now you just raise your hand like this when I'm very close but not touching her, yes?'

Again Kina nodded her understanding. Her acceptance.

As the Doctor took a few tentative steps to his left, Kina shot her arm into the air. The Doctor smiled at her. 'That's very good, Kina. Very helpful indeed. You're doing very well with this. Are you okay to continue?'

Kina nodded. It seemed to be her favoured form of communication, really.

The Doctor reached gently forward, wiggling his fingers slightly. 'Just tell me as soon as I touch her, yes?'

'Yes,' said Kina, breaking her silence. A second later, she said quietly: 'Stop. That's Mummy.'

'Is your daddy there, too?' asked Melanie.

Kina pointed slightly further to the Doctor's left and Melanie slowly made her way to the approximate area indicated. 'Stop,' Kina said to her after a few seconds.

The Doctor smiled at Melanie this time. 'Can you feel him?'

Melanie said not.

'Me neither,' said the Time Lord. 'Yet I can sense there's something here. Something slightly...'

'Out of phase?'

'Very good. Yes, call it Time Lord intuition, but there's definitely some kind of time distillation around here.'

'So how can we bring these people back into step with reality?'

The Doctor shrugged and moved both himself and Melanie further away, hopefully out of Kina's earshot. 'I honestly have no idea. I'm more concerned as to what kind of power can do this and why it didn't do it to Kina if it selected everything else alive.'

Melanie looked around her, shielding her eyes from the sun. 'Not wishing to cast aspersions, but we only have her word that she's the only one. We've only seen this one town.'

The Doctor agreed. 'And of course, only her word that her parents were standing where she said they were. But as I said, I can tell there's something weird going on here.'

'Time Lord gift? A sixth sense?'

'As automatic to me as breathing is to you.'

Melanie chewed her lip. 'I don't see what else we can do here. Whatever Rummas wanted us to track down isn't obvious and I think that a scared little girl trapped, effectively alone is more important anyway.'

The Doctor raised an eyebrow at her as he bent down,

sifting sand through his fingers. 'Are you saying we take Kina aboard the TARDIS?'

Melanie said that was exactly what she meant.

'And,' continued the Doctor, 'what then? Leave her alone with Rummas at the Library? Without her parents?'

'Well, I'm not sure...'

The Doctor stood up again, watching as a few last grains of sand dropped to the ground. 'My TARDIS isn't a number nine bus, Melanie. I can't just take people away from their homes because I think it might be best for them. It's a short-term solution, surely. After all, whatever she ends up doing on Carsus, we're no closer to finding a way of returning her parents and the rest of Schyllus's inhabitants to normal time... normal time...'

Melanie recognised that look. The Doctor's brain was suddenly kicking off on a new thought path, and no doubt leaving her far behind. After a few moments, she prompted him. 'Well?'

'What if, Melanie Baal, we've got it all wrong?'

'Wouldn't be the first time,' she joked.

'Seriously, what if we have. What if it's not the inhabitants here who are out of time, caught in some interstitial break between now and now, but it's us?'

Melanie wasn't sure she could follow this. 'Are you saying that it's you and me that are wrong?'

The Doctor smiled. 'I'm thinking of the weather. It started raining and instantly went to a hot summer's day. The ground is dry, no evidence it has rained here for ages, but we know it has. Suppose, just suppose, that we were crossing through interstitial time ourselves, that the rain was months ago and as we adjusted to the new time frame, so time caught up with us, hence the good sunshine now. We were settling in, if you like, to the time flow here. Hang around long enough and our bodies will catch up with Kina's friends and family. They're not out of kilter, we are.'

Melanie shrugged. 'Either way, it doesn't help us, we don't know how long it's going to take.'

The Doctor glanced back at Kina, now sat in the road, drawing circular patterns in the sand with a stick. 'She's not dressed for wet weather is she? She's in a small summer dress. The change in weather seemed as much a surprise to her as it did to us, but for different reasons. We wondered where the rain had gone, she wondered where it had come from.'

Melanie slipped her arm under his, easing him closer. 'There is another possibility,' she whispered.

The Doctor grimaced. 'That what we see as a bewildered little girl missing her mummy is in fact a ravenous evil monster, setting a trap for us?'

Melanie considered this. 'That wasn't what I was thinking at all, but actually seems more likely than my idea.'

'Which was?'

'That this is all an illusion and we're still on Carsus, still in the Library.'

The Doctor patted her hand. 'Whilst I prefer your version, I'm beginning to suspect mine may be closer to the truth.' He pulled away from Melanie and went back to Kina, kneeling down before her. He looked at the pattern she had created in the sand.

'That's pretty, Kina. What is it?'

'Spiral scratch,' she said.

The Doctor could see the concentric circles that created a spiral effect. 'And the scratch?'

Kina drew a line heavily through the circular motif, breaking every circle.

'Ah. A scratch.'

'It's what must be done,' Kina said simply.

And Melanie watched as the Doctor all but jumped backwards. In fact he may well have done, but Melanie was, like the Doctor, startled by Kina's voice. It was no longer that of a little girl. It was a male voice, older than Kina. Kina herself just looked up at them both as Melanie crouched down next to the Doctor.

Melanie had heard the expression that the eyes are the gateway to the soul. If that were true, Kina was suddenly a very different, and deeply troubled, soul to the one who'd been with them previously.

Her eyes were bloodshot, the pupils dilated so that the iris was now just a dark red spot.

'I've seen enough Stephen King films to be alarmed by this,' Melanie breathed.

'Fascinating,' the Doctor said. 'Complete personality transference, resulting in the contraction of the ocular –'

Melanie shushed him. 'Don't need the science, Doctor, just the reason.'

Kina smiled at her, but Melanie wasn't convinced this wasn't the rictus grin of some demon-spawn ready to devour her!

'Sorry to alarm you both,' said Kina in the man's voice. 'I'm channelling through our daughter as she seems to be the only one who escaped the attack. My name is Hemp, Kina is my daughter. Please do not be alarmed by this process, it is quite a natural one for our species, but I understand from your reactions that you are unfamiliar with it. Kina is unharmed. Indeed, if it makes you more comfortable, please be assured that she is now in my mind, talking with Marka, her mother. My wife.'

The Doctor sat crosslegged, as if talking to possessed kiddies was an every day occurrence.

'What happened Hemp? How can we help?'

'I'm not sure, Doctor. Our world was attacked, exactly as Kina described it to you. I'm guessing that we move at a faster rate than you – if we are invisible to you, let me explain that to me, each time we speak, I'm waiting thirty minutes for your response and using software to speed up your words so I can understand them.'

'Oh.'

Hemp laughed. 'That wasn't worth waiting for! Seriously, thank you for finding Kina, I'm not sure how we can go about bringing her, and maybe you and Melanie Baal, back into our physical world but we are trying.'

The Doctor nodded. 'Understood. Can you offer any thoughts as to why Kina was affected in this way? Has she ever shown any chronological manipulative powers? Any signs that she can operate on altered states or planes?'

There was a long pause, and Melanie wondered if the question had thrown their voice-recognition programs, but the Doctor shushed her.

After a bit longer, Hemp spoke through Kina again. 'No, Doctor. None of us have ever registered anything like this before.'

'What invaded you, then? Let's look to that and see if we can draw any conclusions.'

Kina suddenly gasped, her eyes widening, and Melanie had time to note that they were back to Kina's normal shape and colour. Then she fell forward.

'Kina!' yelled the Doctor, scrabbling forward to scoop her up. 'Hemp?'

As Kina hit the ground, Melanie was transfixed on what was

now behind her. It hadn't been there before, she was sure of that, but it was there now. At first she thought it was small but as she watched, it reared up, stopping at about six feet high. Long, slender, snake-like green body, but no face. Instead, just a gaping maw, with tendrils and stalked suckers. If it had eyes, Melanie couldn't see them, but from the serpentine way the head darted from side to side, it could clearly see, as it was apparently sizing up both her and the Doctor.

The Time Lord had scooped up Kina's unconscious form, her head lolling back slightly in his arms.

'A Lamprey,' he breathed.

'A Time Lord,' the Lamprey hissed back, although the voice seemed to come from all around.

'A what?' Melanie thought she might as well join in.

The Doctor never took his eye off the creature in front of them as it rocked from side to side, drinking in the air. 'A Lamprey. Creatures that exist within the space–time vortex, able to co-exist in multiple locations at once but feeding off chronon energy.' He hugged Kina tighter, addressing the Lamprey. 'How did you get onto a three-dimensional world?'

'My secret. Our secret. But we're here now, all across all time and space.'

'All of time and space,' corrected Melanie, hoping humour was a useful defence. 'You aliens can never quite master syntax.'

The Doctor shook his head. 'Sadly, it's probably telling the truth Melanie. All time and all space. All universes, parallel realities, everything. Back home, my people spent millennia studying these creatures, trying to find a way to keep them locked away from pure existence.'

'Why? What do they do?'

'Devour time. There's nothing they like more than to

completely extinguish an entire multiverse of realities just to feed.'

Melanie took a step backwards. 'Nice.'

'And I want the girl,' the Lamprey spat. 'Now!'

'No chance,' said the Doctor.

He went into action instantly, lowering Kina to the ground and wrapping her inside his huge coat, completely enveloping her.

And the Lamprey vanished.

The Doctor smiled grimly. 'Melanie, we need the TARDIS. Now. Don't stop for anything.' Then he looked into the distance. 'Hemp, if you are still able to hear any of this, I'm taking Kina to safety. Trust me, please!'

They started hurrying back towards the shopping street where the TARDIS was parked. 'Why the wrapping up?' Melanie asked, pointing at Kina's muffled form.

As they ran, the Doctor was getting puffed. 'Because the Lamprey needs a focus, someone's unique mental waves. It can then home in on them, and break through into their reality. That's why Kina was in the drain when we found her. It couldn't reach her down there – it must need plain sight. When that pulsebeat she mentioned occurred, it didn't affect her people. It affected her. She must be some kind of time-sensitive, a mutation in her people's natural development.'

'I know the feeling,' said Melanie, rubbing her scaled arm.

'The Lampreys always seek out time-sensitives on any given world, use them as an anchor and then arrive. My coat is thick enough to protect her from the Lamprey's mental probing until we're safely aboard my ship.'

The TARDIS was in clear view now. Melanie had her key out and ready, and she reached it first – being somewhat smaller and less heavy than the Doctor. She slid the key into the lock and pushed the door open, reaching back for the bundle that was Kina.

The Doctor stumbled at the last minute and Melanie had to dash back to catch Kina, as she toppled out of the coat. And safety.

The Lamprey reappeared instantly, swooping down towards the exposed child, but Melanie was quicker, throwing herself straight into its path.

The Lamprey swerved off at the last moment, its maw spitting tiny flecks of blue electricity at her, but they missed completely.

This gave the Doctor time to scoop up Kina's unconscious form and push straight into the TARDIS.

Melanie twirled around, grabbed the dropped coat and threw it around herself.

The Lamprey went left, then right, left again, Melanie mirroring its movements.

With a final defiant hiss, it vanished again.

Melanie could faintly hear a sound like a heartbeat but it soon faded. And after getting her breath back, she followed her friend into the TARDIS.

The Doctor was sitting crosslegged in the TARDIS control room, trying to cajole Kina into wakefulness. 'It's not working, she's comatose,' he said quietly.

Melanie activated the door control and said nothing as the doors closed silently behind her. The Doctor looked up at her and pointed to the red-handled lever on the console. 'Activate that please,' he said.

Melanie did as bidden, and seconds later the TARDIS dematerialised from Schyllus, on its way back to the Library on Carsus.

The Doctor stood up, carrying Kina, whom he placed into Melanie's waiting arms. 'Take her to a bedroom, please. Stay with her.'

'And you?'

'I need to contact Rummas. If the Lampreys are crossing through realities, there may be any number of alternative me's and you's out there, coming into contact with Lampreys. They need to be warned.'

'Putting aside the headache that I'm getting thinking about what you just said oh-so-casually, how can Rummas do that?'

The Doctor took a deep breath as he slipped his coat back on. Then he looked gravely at Melanie. 'As you pointed out when we left Ariel, he's a thief as well as a librarian. And he has in his keeping an ancient Gallifreyan power that should never have left home. He has the Spiral Chamber. And it may fall to you and I to destroy it.'

Melanie sighed deeply. 'Of course it will,' she said. 'It always does.'

The Doctor watched sadly as she and Kina went through the inner door and off to a safe, warm room somewhere.

It didn't seem fair. Poor Melanie had had a rough enough life already as a hybrid of two life forms. Did he have the right to put her through more trauma? Perhaps it was time to send her home. Rummas would be able to do that, he was sure.

He was about to follow Melanie out into the TARDIS interior when he found himself bumping into her, stood by the console. Which was strange as he was sure she hadn't come back in. Her back was to him as she stared at a roundel on the wall opposite. He tapped her on the shoulder.

'Daydreaming, Melanie? That's not like you.' And he crossed to the inner door. 'Well, there isn't much time... Oh.'

He had turned to speak again and realised the Melanie he was facing wasn't Melanie Baal at all.

It was still Melanie, but a wholly human Melanie. She seemed as alarmed to see him as he was her.

She was saying something, looking around, and the Doctor followed her glance. This Melanie seemed to be talking wordlessly, as if there were other people in the control room, and the Doctor began to wonder if this was connected with what had happened outside.

'I don't think this can be right,' he said, choosing to ignore her now and cross to the console. Still on course for Carsus, so nothing had changed.

Then he remembered his words to Melanie, his Melanie, about parallel realities. This human Melanie could be from one of those and might be seeing a number of other alternate Melanies or Doctors.

Which offered up another, less pleasing possibility. Why was she seeing the multitude rather than him.

Of course, the theory of parallel universes, multiverses and even an omniverse was nothing new. Theories had abounded ever since work into the origins of the Lampreys had begun thousands of years ago back home. Of course, it was a chicken-and-egg situation – did the Lampreys exist because of the multiverses or did the multiverses come into existence because the Time Lords accidentally created them whilst meddling with the Lampreys' unique existence within the spirals of the vortex.

This didn't make it any easier though. Because if this new Melanie was seeing others and he wasn't, it implied that she was Melanie-Prime if you like. The real Melanie and he and his Melanie were the alternates.

'Not a happy thought,' he mused, 'but shouldn't stop us

finding out the truth.' He watched this pink-skinned Melanie for a couple more moments, silently having conversations – something or someone had clearly come in from outside the/her TARDIS, which was distracting her.

'Of course!' he said, more to himself as she probably couldn't hear him. 'I see what I meant now. Oh Melanie,' he tried to say to her, 'the Lamprey is going to force a confrontation, use all our multitudinous chronon energies to feed. Kina is a trap, it didn't want her at all. It wanted us. Me. My TARDIS. All over the realities, loads of time-sensitives are going to have shared Kina's experiences and loads of do-gooding Doctors like me are going to try and help them.'

And he was alone, the alternative Melanie having winked out of existence.

He wondered what to do next. If he took Kina to Carsus, was she safe or was he further playing into the Lamprey's plan? And what could he tell Melanie?

He stared at the console and then made a decision.

Chapter Nine
Nostalgia

Imagine, if you will, a vortex. A really powerful vortex that drags into itself anything that comes into its trajectory. A vortex made up of an infinite number of, well, levels for want of a better description. And if they seem to diminish as they get towards the bottom of the vortex, rest assured, it's an illusion. For this vortex has no bottom. It is, being constructed of chronon energy, and thus temporal in nature, endless. Eternal. Bottomless, topless, middleless. It is neither linear not multifaceted in existence. It is completely unique and is, theoretically, situated at the centre of creation. Of course, in a multiverse that expands exponentially and is unfixed and infinite in nature, a 'centre' is a theoretical and practical impossibility. For millennia, scholars have tried to fathom the true nature of what they have come to refer to as 'The Spiral'. They have failed because, of course, they cannot tell whether each time they examine the Spiral they are seeing it exponentially or randomly.

It is theorised that creatures live within the confines of the Spiral, creatures that have access to multiple dimensions and realities. Although these theories cannot be disproved, nor can they be proven, as no acceptable method of determination can be found. No one can ever be sure, if these creatures do indeed exist, whether due to their crossing of the timelines they are actually temporal duplicates of just one original creature or whether they really are legion.

If, however, these creatures, which have reportedly been observed and described as Lampreys due to their appearance, do exist, the theoretical power they must possess is beyond measure as well. Some theories suggest that these Lampreys can cross from one plane of existence, or reality even, at will. If one accepts the existence of parallel realities, and there is sufficient proof of this in a number of field researches found in the APC Network records, then the fact that these creatures can cross in and out is both exciting and worrying. For if breaches were to occur, if the Spiral were to become damaged in some way and allow leakage between these realities, all of creation could descend into chaos and ultimately only the Lampreys would survive. If they feed, as hypothesised above, on temporal energy, then the energy accessible to them within the myriad realities created every nanosecond by chaos and chance would supply them with nourishment for, in theory, eternity.

Amongst the other, possibly apocryphal, myths evolving around these Lampreys is that they have been spotted by time-sensitives existing an almost corporeal existence on some planets, disguised as natives. Some tales say they are there to wait for an opportunity to absorb the chronon energy of a planet should it suffer a temporal mishap, other stories tell of Lampreys opting to leave their nomadic existence in the Vortex behind and actually just live on a chosen planet as one of the natives, but for eternity, seeking nothing but peace and quiet.

None of these legends have been substantiated.

These creatures are therefore to be studied at every

opportunity and, if need be, a way found to harness or destroy them.

For the sake of creation.

Coordinator Rellox, Arcalian Council for Temporal Research.
Report acknowledged but suppressed by order
of President Pandak III.

Mel deactivated the monitor, and the TARDIS data bank whirred and sunk back into its recess on the console.

'Wow,' she said. 'Your people know how to take a hundred words to say something simple.'

'Simple? Simple? Those researches took thousands of decades.'

'Oh I know,' Mel said. 'But all they needed to say was: Spiral. Keep Away. Dangerous Creatures At Large. May Threaten Creation If Allowed To Escape.' She beamed at the Doctor. 'There, much simpler.'

The Doctor flicked some switches and turned a dial or two, as if trying to convince her he was doing important work.

Mel wasn't fooled for a moment. 'Besides, how did you get that information if President Panda Bear the Third suppressed it?'

The Doctor ignored her, pretending now to examine some complicated ticker-tape read-out spewing from a slot on the console that Mel was sure hadn't been there before. 'Interesting,' he murmured. 'Interesting.'

'What is it?'

'This? Oh, nothing,' he said, as if hiding a big secret.

Mel sighed. He could be such a big baby sometimes. She tried a different tack. 'All right, Doctor, I'm impressed.

Impressed that the Time Lords could discover the Spiral, the Lampreys and the threat they present. I'm impressed that Time Lords invented TARDISes, transcendental engineering and a machine that can turn jelly babies into licorice allsorts and back again. Satisfied?'

Her companion shrugged. 'Don't know what you mean. Wasn't wanting you to be "impressed". Just thought it might interest you to learn everything known about our enemy, that's all.'

Mel wanted to kick him – she positively hated it when he got into one of these moods. She resisted. 'And I've memorised it. Well, precised it anyway. But it's not going to bring Helen back, is it?'

'Interesting name.'

'What, "Helen"? Comes from the Greek, means "Bright One". Probably a derivative of Helios.' Mel caught his eye. 'See, I can be smug and irritating, too!'

The Doctor just gave her that 'look' and said quietly: 'I don't believe it's a coincidence that her surname is Lamprey.'

Mel took the hint and decided to play it seriously. 'But what can the connection be? Both Helen and her father looked as shocked as us to see that creature.'

'Yet neither of them were affected by the time distillation. Nor was Sir Bertrand's mind readjusted after Helen was abducted, suggesting he is a time-sensitive of some kind.'

'So what now?'

The Doctor flicked some switches with a rather OTT flourish and smiled at Mel. 'Back to Carsus, find out what Rummas has been up to and and see what happens next?'

If he opened his eyes, he might die. Or see something horrible. Or be forced to see that creature again. Or...

If he kept his eyes screwed tightly closed, fighting to keep the outside world from breaking in, he could be safe. Safe from snakes with no heads.

'Hello?'

It was a voice. A girl's voice. He could hear it clearly so she had to be nearby.

Damn.

He opened his eyes.

No snake. No horrors. Nothing. Absolutely nothing at all.

'Hello?' he replied, alarmed at how hoarse he sounded. He cleared his throat and tried again.

A response.

'Who's there?' came the girl's voice. 'I can't see anyone. It's dark.'

That was true. It had crossed his mind that he hadn't opened his eyes at all, but by staring down he could see his fingers flexing, very dimly, so his eyes were open.

'I don't know where I am. Or where you are,' he called back. 'Sorry, not much help am I?'

'Marlern, is that you?'

'Nope. Sorry, I'm DiVotow Nek. What's your name?'

The voice had come from his left, quite some way off, so he turned his head in that direction. He tried to go forward and that was when he realised he was... well, he couldn't move his legs. Or bend. Indeed, only his left arm was free and the darkness wasn't getting brighter. That was alarming. 'And I can't move,' DiVotow added ruefully. 'Which is a bit of a problem.'

'Me neither,' the girl called back. 'I'm Haema Smith. Did the creature get you too?'

'Snake thing?'

'Yup. No head. Marlern was with me, but he's not now.'

'How can you tell?'

There was a moment of silence, then: 'Good point. Okay, I can't see him.'

'Can you see anything?'

DiVotow's head jerked to the right. A new voice, male, had asked that.

'Nope,' he said cautiously. 'And you are?'

'My name is Kevin Dorking. I was in my dragster one minute, then I found myself here, listening to you two.'

'Dragster?'

'Never mind. I can't move either, but I can see someone on the floor, Haema. Could that be your friend? He's out of it, I think.' Perhaps recognising his tactlessness, the newcomer quickly changed the subject. 'So, anyone got any idea how long we've been here?'

'Or where we are?' added Haema.

A shaft of very bright light erupted ahead of DiVotow, illuminating everything around him, but making him blink for quite a few seconds.

Writhing at the centre of the light was the creature he'd seen in the skies above Utopiana, albeit smaller now. But no less impressive. Or downright terrifying.

It was accompanied by the throbbing noise he'd heard last time as well, the rhythmic pulsebeat that threatened to both overpower yet relax his senses. It was almost hypnotic...

Hypnotic! He had to shake that off. This monster meant him harm, of that he was convinced.

He curled his right hand into a ball, letting his fingernails dig into his palm, acting as a small but noticeable and slightly painful distraction. Which was what he needed.

He turned his head left and right, now able to see the shadowy forms of Haema and Kevin. He could also see the other guy slumped forward in a bizarre manner near to Haema, Marlern presumably.

DiVotow realised that his legs, up to just above his knees, were embedded in mud or some other substance. That was why he couldn't move – Haema and Kevin were similarly encased. Marlern, therefore, was hanging forward, but stuck upright due to the same process.

'Haema,' DiVotow yelled. 'Try to wake your friend up. But very gently.'

'Why?'

'Because he'll break his neck if he wakes too suddenly.'

Haema was looking at Marlern, at least DiVotow thought she was. It was difficult to be sure in this murk.

The creature in the light was gyrating from side to side, its whole head jerking back and forth, as if sizing up its captives.

It stopped suddenly, the tendrils in its face area vibrating as it spoke. 'Welcome to the Spiral, my time-sensitives. Each of you are, it seems, the best your realities have to offer.' It turned to face the unconscious Marlern. 'Except him.'

'What's wrong with him?' Haema asked shakily.

'He's useless. No chronon energy at all. A waste.'

'He's not a waste,' Haema yelled back. 'He's my friend!'

DiVotow didn't understand all this 'time-sensitives' crap, but he could see it meant something to the monster. And if Marlern wasn't one, then Haema had just made a mistake, albeit an understandable one, by protecting him. It would give the creature leverage over her. Hell, over DiVotow, too, because although he didn't know any of these people, it was clearly a case of them against the creature.

'So you want him to remain alive?' the creature asked.

Haema said she did and, as DiVotow suspected, it was exactly what the creature wanted her to say.

'Then you will do what is asked of you, or he dies. Slowly and painfully,' it added. Unnecessarily, DiVotow thought. Somehow the threat was already implicit in its tone of voice.

'What are we to do?' asked Kevin.

'Simple.' Another beam of light, behind the creature, blazed into existence. Motionless and seemingly unconscious within it was a girl. Tall, nice cheekbones, classy-looking. 'This creature embodies chronon energy. It is your job to keep it alive by letting it absorb the chronon energy that courses through your bodies.'

'And how exactly won't that hurt us?' asked Kevin.

Good question, DiVotow thought. I'm going to like this guy, he thinks on his feet.

The creature gave a laugh. It wasn't a nice sound.

'You'd be no use to me... us... dead. Observe.'

And DiVotow felt his head flung backwards, his eyes closed instinctively. And he felt as if he was on some kind of fairground rollercoaster, dropping without a safety bar. He wanted to cry out, but Haema was doing enough yelling for all of them.

Then it stopped and he felt his lungs fill with air again. Panting, he opened his eyes and he was now looking downwards, the pretty girl from the light lying spread-eagled directly below him. He turned his head – Haema and Kevin were in the same position, and he realised he was, too. His hands and legs encased in solid metallic glove-like clamps, his body in a coffin-like device. A series of clear tubes ran from each of his clamps and down into the star-shaped coffin-device the girl was in. Marlern, however, lying on the ground far below, still looked as if he were asleep. Or dead. No tubes linked him to the girl.

There was a fourth coffin, unoccupied, slightly to DiVotow's left, and much smaller than his or the others'.

A child. The creature was waiting for a child.

The throbbing started up again and after a few moments the creature appeared, hovering in space between them and the unconscious girl. It looked towards the empty coffin device. 'Sadly, there has been a delay in obtaining Kina of Schyllus, so the three of you will have to donate more than your fair share. You should hope she turns up soon.'

And it vanished.

'What now?' wondered Haema.

As if in reply, DiVotow felt something flowing through his body, snatching his answer away, and the tubes linking him to the girl began to glow slightly.

Within a few seconds, DiVotow wanted nothing more than to sleep. He felt as if all the energy was being drained out of his body.

The Doctor and Mel were wandering the endless corridors of the Carsus Library once more. They'd seen no sign of Rummas, nor Misters Woltas or Huu. Which was odd as they'd called ahead from the TARDIS and Rummas had promised to meet them in the corridor outside the Reading Room where Mel had encountered the strange Custodians earlier.

'What is it about Time Lords and time,' Mel asked innocently, 'that the one thing they can't do is actually tell it?'

The Doctor hurrumphed and pushed open the Reading Room door.

Mel wanted to be surprised – but actually wasn't – that despite having come through this door before, it allowed entry to a different end of the Reading Room than she'd been expecting.

What did cause her eyebrows to rise though, were the three people in the room.

One was Professor Rummas, dead, she assumed due to the large knitting needle protruding from the base of his skull. He was lying face down on the rug before the fireplace.

Crouched over him, hand still on the weapon, was a man Mel had never seen before, dressed in a brown sports coat with leather-patched elbows and navy slacks. He wore a small pair of glasses, and was running a hand through thinning silver hair.

Stood further back, arms folded, a disdainful look on her face as though she were watching a dull TV show rather than a murder, was a younger woman. Late twenties, her hair and make-up instantly told Mel she was from her world, circa the 1950s.

Neither person acknowledged the Doctor or Mel, and Mel guessed why.

'Another time spill?'

The Doctor confirmed this and walked straight to Rummas's body, kneeling down, ignoring the now-straightening-up killer who was speaking, sadly silently, to the woman. Mel noticed, however, that he wasn't looking at her – indeed, his focus was still on the dead professor.

'Probability or certainty?' Mel wondered allowed, trying to remain dispassionate.

'Good question, Mel,' the Doctor replied, now looking up at the perpetrators of this heinous crime. 'I hope "probability".'

'So do I,' said Rummas, from behind them.

Again, Mel was surprised she wasn't surprised at his arrival.

'I wonder what the point of that was.' He crossed past her and knelt beside the Doctor, trying to touch the needle, but his hand went straight through it.

Mel noticed him wince. He was sensitive to time spillage? But as a Time Lord, he should be exactly the opposite – it should have no effect at all. Why did it hurt him?

'I'm not sure you should do that, Professor,' the Doctor was saying.

'It's all right,' the professor replied. 'I always get a twinge when I discover myself dead. I think it's Time's way of telling me to watch myself.'

The Doctor stood up, regarding the now arguing couple, their mouths moving furiously in silent anger. 'At least we have a view of our murderers.'

'Suspects,' corrected Rummas, and the Doctor waved a hand as if, begrudgingly, accepting the chastisement. 'And assuming it's been them every time,' Rummas continued, 'I would like to believe, if it is, they must be getting very fed up with killing me.'

'Not you this time,' Mel said, pointing at the Doctor.

'I suspected before that the Doctor was an innocent by-stander that got in the way,' Rummas reminded her. 'I wonder who they are.'

'Or where they're from.'

The Doctor was now stood next to the woman. 'Earth at a guess,' he said.

Mel nodded. 'Yes, 1950s again,' she said. 'Same era as Helen Lamprey.'

The Doctor was trying to inspect the woman's handbag, clutched to her thigh. Being insubstantial, he could not move it, so he was trying his best to gaze at it from every angle. 'There's a monogram on the clasp,' he eventually explained. 'One initial is an M, but I can't see the other.'

Rummas brought something out of his pocket. 'I wonder if this'll work,' he muttered and held it before him.

'What's that?' asked Mel.

'Digital camera, linked to the central library's records. If either of them are famous in any way it should be able to match them, given the parameters. Limited as they are.'

He took a picture and as he did so they winked out of existence.

'Interesting,' the Doctor murmured.

'Annoying,' Mel replied.

'No, not really, I expected it. But was it a coincidence or did something, somewhere want to stop us getting a picture of them and whisk them away?'

Rummas shrugged, rubbing the back of his neck as if subconsciously feeling the wound of his now faded dopplegänger.

Mel realised the Doctor was eying him curiously. 'I wonder if that's where the idea of someone walking over your grave comes from?'

'I'm sorry?'

'It's a phrase back home,' Mel explained. 'When you shiver involuntarily.' She looked at the Doctor. 'Are you suggesting that what it really is, is some time-displaced alternate person walking over one's future grave?'

'Could be. Ripples in time and all that.' The Doctor smiled suddenly. 'Did you get a picture, Professor?'

Rummas crossed to one of the tables strewn with books, cleared them aside and tapped something on its side. The tan-leathered top rose upwards revealing a screen, some controls and switches on its underside.

'Now that's what I call desktop publishing,' Mel said. Rummas placed his camera on a small area beneath the screen and immediately the screen displayed the images he'd taken.

Sure enough there were five photos of the room, two of

which clearly showed the perpetrators of the crime before they vanished into the ether.

'So, you have a database here that can help us identify these two?' asked the Doctor. 'After all, with the acquired knowledge of a trillion civilisations, they might be in here somewhere.'

'How many hours will that take?' Mel asked.

'Not many, theoretically,' said Rummas, assuming they're from a still-existing timeline or universe. But if they're chrono-escapees, time-riders or vortex-joysters...'

Mel sighed, not wanting to ask what that meant. 'If it helps, I reckon they're human, from sometime between 1930 and 1965, going by the woman's clothes.'

The Doctor smiled at Mel then back at Rummas. 'There you are, a timeframe to narrow it down.' He looked back over his shoulder at his companion and winked. 'Good call, Mel.'

Mel beamed happily and wandered over to look closer at the images. 'L,' she said quietly.

'Sorry?'

'It's an "L" on the handbag. Her initials are "ML", I think. I bet it's Lamprey!'

Both Time Lords looked at her bemusedly. 'That's a leap of faith,' Rummas said quietly.

'It's intuition,' Mel responded quickly. 'Women's intuition. Rarely wrong.'

After a brief moment Rummas coughed. 'I've got a possible ID on the man, look.'

'That's him,' Mel concurred. 'Look at the nose. Our killer has more hair, but that's definitely him.'

'It might be him,' the Doctor said more evenly, 'but we can't be sure. That said, it's a place to start. Who is he?'

'A fairly nondescript scientist and researcher called Joseph Tungard.'

Mel sighed. 'And? I mean, what else does it tell you?'

'Nothing. Beyond the usual stuff of birth and death.' Rummas read on, and then hurriedly added: 'He achieved nothing much really.'

'When did he die?'

Rummas shook his head. 'I can't divulge that information I'm afraid, Miss Bush.'

'Why not?'

'Because it's privileged information.'

Mel thought this was daft and said so. 'It's not like I'm taking a trip to Earth and can tell him is it? Doctor?' No response. 'Doctor?'

The Doctor smiled weakly. 'I rather think that's where the professor wants us to go next, am I right?'

'I think it's essential, Doctor. And if your friend is right and the woman with him is a member of Helen Lamprey's family, who knows what you might find out.'

Mel knew she was beaten. 'Oh all right then, let's go Tungard hunting.'

The Doctor beamed. 'That's the spirit. A quick bite to eat first and then we'll be off.'

'Great idea, Doctor. I'm starved. Can I get a Waldorf salad up here, Professor?'

Rummas nodded happily. 'Nothing the cafeteria can't rustle up. Shall we go?'

And the three of them headed out of the room towards, presumably, the café when Mel suddenly stopped and cursed herself.

'What's the matter?'

'Sorry, Doctor. I left my watch on one of the bookshelves, I'll catch you up.' And she darted away before either Time Lord could respond.

'Well, that's Mel for you,' explained the Doctor as she hurried away. 'Scatterbrained to the end.'

'Hmmmm,' Mel muttered. She'd sort him out for that one later.

Once they were out of earshot, Mel hurried her pace and quickly retraced her steps to the Reading Room, slipping in quietly.

Rummas had left the computer screen illuminated, and after a few seconds Mel got the hang of the lack of keyboard. Everything seemed to be controlled by gently waving a finger a few millimetres above a small trackpad.

And she was going to find out as much as she could about Joseph Tungard until she recalled something else Rummas had said.

And so she inputted a search parameter for herself.

SEARCH RESULTS: 117,863 results match MELANIE JANE BUSH. ORIGIN WORLD: EARTH. BIRTHDATE 22/07/64.

'That's not exactly one per alternative timeline,' said a familiar voice behind her. 'But it's still quite a lot.'

She turned sheepishly as the Doctor frowned at her. 'You should never want to know your own future, Melanie.'

'Why not?'

'Because the temptation to change it will be too strong. What if you found out you died in a car crash next week? You'd stay away from roads that day and the timelines of hundreds of other people would be affected by the ripples.'

Mel was aghast. 'You do things like that all the time!'

'I'm a Time Lord, and if I know the past, present or future, I know how to manipulate around it. If I told you that in three years' time, we'll be trapped on an ice planet called Quaeter and you'll fall to your death down an icecanoe, what would you do?'

'Stay away from Quaeter, obviously.'

The Doctor frowned. 'And if our being there saved millions of people because we were guests at an intergalactic peace conference?'

'We'd find a way around it. Surely it's better to know and to avoid such things?'

'Our lives have so many advantages, Melanie. We see myriad things we'd otherwise be denied. But there's a price to pay. Your price is not knowing. Mine is knowing.'

Mel took a moment to digest this. 'You know when you're going to die?'

The Doctor smiled sadly. 'Not to the minute, but as that time approaches, one has... twinges. A certain preternatural instinct. But we go ahead anyway because what will be, must be.'

'*Que sera, sera*,' said a new, but familiar voice, from behind them.

Mel turned and found herself facing herself. Sort of. Herself apart from the green skin, a puckered mouth and webbed hands. Apart from that, it was like facing a mirror. Even the clothes were the same.

'Melanie – I'm sorry, I don't know your surname – Melanie, meet Melanie Baal.'

'What do you mean you don't know my na– oh. Oh, I see. You're not my Doctor.'

The Doctor shook his head. 'Different universe. Sorry.'

Mel turned back to her almost-dopplegänger and held out her hand. Melanie Baal shook it. 'Hiya. I'm Mel. Mel Bush.'

'Hi yourself, Mel.'

Mel opted not to be too phased by this. 'So, if there are a hundred and seventeen thousand, eight hundred and sixty-three Melanie Bush's in the universe, how many more are there with different surnames yet all, basically, the same person?' She looked at Mel Baal. 'Aesthetic differences aside.' Then she decided that being phased was indeed inevitable. 'Phew. I can't comprehend this.'

'Me neither,' said the green Melanie. 'But I never understand what he goes on about anyway. I just pretend.'

'You too?' said Mel, realising she liked her duplicate enormously. 'It's so annoying when he assumes I do.'

'And you have to pretend so often,' Melanie Baal agreed, 'or he goes into too much detail and leaves you none the wiser.'

'And he shouts a lot.'

'All the time.'

'Louder and louder.'

'All right,' the alternative Doctor said. 'That's quite enough out of you two. Frankly one Melanie is more than a handful. Two of you is undeniably devastating.'

A door slid open to reveal Rummas, who took in the scene in a moment.

'So that's what you were up to last week, Miss Bush,' he said.

'"Last..." Oh. Oh I see. You're from their timeline, not mine.'

'Indeed. Off you go, Miss Bush. If I remember correctly, there's a Savoy salad waiting for you.'

'Waldorf.'

'Whichever. Bye.' Dismissing her, Rummas turned to face the other two. 'Now, I need you to go to a party...'

Mel smiled again at her quasi-reptilian double, nodded at the other Doctor and hurried out.

The restaurant was tucked away behind the Charing Cross Road, known mostly to theatre goers and stars. It had not exactly an exclusive door policy, but one needed to be connected to be assured of a seat.

When Sir Bertrand Lamprey had called ahead to reserve

a quiet table for three, he had assumed his wishes would be carried out without too much problem.

So he was somewhat flustered to discover that instead his table was on a raised area, overlooked by a huge gilt-edged mirror that reflected the entire restaurant. It was like sitting at the High Table at a university.

Sir Bertrand was not comfortable in social occasions at the best of times, but after the death of his wife and the more recent strange disappearance of his daughter, he was uncomforted terribly easily now.

He was also concerned that the table was set for five, not three. Indeed, had he desired, another four people could have been added. Comfortably.

The maitre d' who showed him to the table assured him that the orders for the change had come from his household, but Sir Bertrand was sure they hadn't, and told him so.

He stared at his guests. Joe Tungard and, going by the wheelchair, his wife were who he had expected. The older man and young woman to the left, however, were not.

'I fear I am at a disadvantage,' he said as he prepared to sit.

Tungard smiled weakly, and immediately Sir Bertrand knew his discomfort was shared by the Romanian.

'Pike,' said the older man, offering his hand. 'Doctor Stephen Pike and may I present my granddaughter, Monica.'

Monica also shook Sir Bertrand's hand, and it crossed his mind it was like holding alabaster, it was so cold and pale.

As if reading his mind, Monica laughed lightly. 'It is an unusually cold night, Sir Bertrand. For May.'

Sir Bertrand harrumphed an acknowledgment and sat.

Joe Tungard indicated a Moët unopened in a bucket. 'I took the opportunity,' he said quietly. 'I do hope it was not presumptuous.'

'You are not a presumptuous man,' said Natjya Tungard just as quietly.

That told Sir Bertrand all he needed to know. He'd met Joe some weeks earlier and found him very likable, driven and intelligent. He had opted to fund his work at the university almost immediately – tonight's dinner was just to seal the deal, as it were. He had hoped that Joe was not the kind of man to 'invite' additional guests to another man's dinner party, and that had been Natjya's way of telling him that this was indeed the case.

'So,' he said to Pike. 'So tell me, how do you know these fine friends of mine?'

'We met on the boat from Romania,' Pike explained, and droned on for a few moments, but Sir Bertrand quickly filtered him out and concentrated on Monica, who was saying nothing, just sipping water and staring at him. No matter what Sir Bertrand did, which direction he faced or who he spoke to over the next few moments, he was aware that Monica's eyes followed his every movement, in the way a leopard watches an antelope in total stillness. Taking that analogy further, Sir Bertrand decided that if Monica saw him wriggle ever so slightly, she'd pounce.

He had taken an instant dislike to her, yet the dratted woman had spoken barely more than her greeting.

Much small talk ensued, with Joe eager to talk about the funding deal, almost as if he was trying to stop any other subject being brought up.

By the time a waiter offered the brandy, Joe Tungard was exhausted and Natjya more shrivelled and shrunken than Sir Bertrand had seen a human being before.

That was when Monica pounced.

'Interesting name, Sir Bertrand.'

'My grandfather's,' he said quickly. 'Died at Ingogo you know. Terrible business.'

'Yes,' Monica said. 'I remember.'

'Ah, you've read about it in history books,' Sir Bertrand nodded. 'Of course.'

'Of course,' smiled Monica and for a tiny moment, Sir Bertrand wondered... no, that was impossible. But there was something in the way she had responded, a condescending touch, as if she'd not read about it at all. As if she'd... but to experience it, to remember it, she'd have to be getting on for her eighties at least. And she was thirty if she was a day.

'Now I apologise for... disturbing you this evening, Sir Bertrand,' she continued, 'but it was your surname I was interested in.'

'Lamprey?'

'Absolutely.' And Monica produced her handbag – crocodile skin by the look of it. Her finger pointed to the clasp, silver letters reading 'ML'. Sir Bertrand frowned.

'This delightful gentleman is not really my grandfather,' she said of Doctor Pike.

Sir Bertrand didn't know whether to be more surprised at the irrelevance of her statement, or the pure shock that went across the two Romanian's faces.

Joe took it especially badly, it appeared. And suddenly Sir Bertrand knew why.

He was in love with her – having an affair perhaps? The way he had sat awkwardly away from her, too close to his ill wife, but was now leaning toward Monica, eyes wide in confusion.

'You... you're not?' Joe asked.

'My dear friends,' Monica said, 'it was not a deliberate attempt to defraud you. The good doctor has indeed brought me up as his granddaughter, as his son and daughter-in-law brought me up as their offspring but in truth I was adopted.'

'Adopted?' That was Natjya.

'I don't remember my own parents very well. My brother and I... were separated from them when we were terribly young.'

'You have a brother?' Joe looked like one more revelation would floor him.

'Alas no longer; he died, oh...' Monica gave a little laugh as if she were discussing a book or play, not a deceased sibling, 'it seems like centuries ago now.'

'And what has this to do with me?' Sir Bertrand realised someone needed to take charge of the situation quickly.

'The "L" in my name stands for Lamprey, Sir Bertrand. I've never encountered anyone else with that name that I shared any... common heritage with. I hoped maybe if we met we might shed some light on my early life. Discover if it is a coincidence, or we have a shared past.'

Sir Bertrand was about to ask, possibly unchivalrously, but he believed in honesty more, if she was after money. Of course there were many other Lampreys – a glance at the telephone directories in Westminster Library could have told her that much. However, in his particular branch of the family, he was the last. So she could not have been related to him – he knew his family tree too well.

Unfortunately, he never got to explain that, because the wine waiter arrived with a folded sheet of paper.

'Sir Bertrand Lamprey?'

Sir Bertrand took the proffered paper, opened it to find a note.

LOOK INTO THE MIRROR.

DO NOT TRUST ANY OF THEM.

MAY WE JOIN YOU.

He crumpled the paper into a ball and placed it in his pocket. 'Just a note from my broker,' he said apologetically. 'I need to make a telephone call. Please excuse me, I shall return forthwith.' And he stood up, turning to face Monica. 'And we shall continue this most... interesting discussion Miss Pike... no, sorry, Miss Lamprey.'

And he stood up, nodded a 'Mrs Tungard' at the other lady and turned to walk away, to a discreet alcove where he knew the telephones were situated.

He glanced up in the mirror, looking for anyone familiar, and tried to hide his shock as he did. They had conveniently sat themselves at a table for two in the path to the telephones so it would not look contrived as he passed them.

'Doctor! Miss Bush!' he declared loudly enough for everyone in the restaurant to hear. 'What a delightful surprise. What brings you to London, all the way from Suffolk?' He then hissed through gritted teeth: 'I'm on my way to the telephones. Get over to my table with pleasure, I shall be back shortly.' And he continued walking, snuck into the alcove and lifted a receiver. Hoping no one could see him, he held it to his ear, pretended to dial a number and talked nonsense into the receiver for a few moments. He then slammed it down as if angry (just in case anyone was watching) and stomped back to his table, by which time he was pleased to note, he now had six guests.

'My friends,' he said jovially, 'may I introduce –'

'Already done,' said Doctor Pike, with a touch of ice in his voice. 'The Doctor here has been... entertaining us with his fictions.'

'Fictions?'

'Yes,' Natjya said. 'He was telling us about a new murder mystery he's writing.' She leaned closer to Sir Bertrand as he sat. 'I do hope it's as good as Miss Christie's works. I have just finished her latest book; so enjoyable. I never got the fact there were two murderers, though. She's so clever.'

Sir Bertrand smiled at Natjya and patted her hand in a far more patronising way than he intended. 'Doctor? Your... novel?'

'Yes, I thought I'd ask the good medical doctor here a little question about murder.'

Doctor Pike looked uncomfortable, and the Doctor seemed to smile at him more.

'Yes, you see in my latest book I've set a murder in a library.' The Doctor looked over to Natjya Tungard. 'I'm calling it *Another Body in the Library* as an homage to dear Agatha's works.'

Natjya laughed politely. 'One of my favourites,' she said, then took Sir Bertrand's hand. 'That one wasn't even the right body!'

'Anyway,' said Melanie Bush sharply, as if trying to drag them all back to the topic – although Sir Bertrand wasn't entirely sure what the topic was right now. 'As the Doctor's typist, I need to know whether he has the specifics of the murder correct,' she continued. 'Our killer goes into the library and murders a nice, sweet old professor.'

For some reason, Joe Tungard was looking very pale and his brandy glass was shaking slightly. He was staring at Monica, who, Sir Bertrand noted with interest, was avoiding catching his eye and instead was staring intently at the Doctor. Not her grandfather, but the one from Helen's sixteenth birthday party last Christmas.

The one who saw that creature. Who remembered while everyone else had forgotten.

The one who promised to get Helen back, and who Sir Bertrand had given up hoping to ever see again.

So if this charade would somehow help find his darling daughter, he'd go along with anything, everything in fact, that the Doctor said.

Miss Bush continued. 'So, anyway, our killer uses his...' and Sir Bertrand was sure Miss Bush glanced at Natjya Tungard for the tiniest of moments, 'his wife's knitting needle. The killer jabs it through the base of the neck and upwards, through the soft tissue and directly into the brain, killing the professor instantly. Is that possible, Doctor Pike?'

Doctor Pike shrugged. 'Pretty much, yes. You'd need some strength to do it though. Nasty mind you've got, Doctor,' he added. 'That's a painful way to kill someone.'

'Really?'

'And not too efficient either. A knitting needle into the heart would be better. Less force, less chance of just doing your professor an injury. Although, have to say, he'd be pretty scrambled afterwards.'

'So,' mused the Doctor, 'if you were trying to put someone out of action, but didn't care if they lived or died, it'd do, yes?'

Pike nodded sagely. 'Yes, their brain would be severely damaged. They might survive but much of their cognitive abilities would be gone. Memory, speech, probably sight as well. In fact, it's a pretty horrible way to do someone in without actually killing them. Would avoid the death penalty because it wouldn't be murder.'

The Doctor clapped his hands. 'Excellent.' Then he turned to Natjya Tungard. 'And you, Mrs Tungard? When did you notice one of your needles was missing?'

And everyone at the table went quiet.

Eventually Natjya frowned. 'How did you know I'd lost...'

'Oh it wasn't lost,' the Doctor continued, as if describing a holiday in Wales rather than what appeared to be an actual murder, 'it was stolen by your husband. Used to kill Professor Rummas at the Carsus Library.'

Joe was silent, and without taking his eyes off Natjya and still beaming at her, the Doctor eased the brandy glass from the distraught professor's hand.

Monica broke the tension by laughing. 'Oh Doctor, this is marvellous. A kind of acting class, yes? Seeing how dear Natjya would respond in a similar situation.'

But no one else was laughing.

Instead the Doctor, still smiling at Natjya but clearly addressing Monica, spoke quietly. 'How did you do it Monica? I mean, as a Lamprey, I can see how you went into a multitude of timelines, killing as many Professor Rummases as you could – and a couple of me's, which is truly unforgivable –' and at this he turned to face her. 'But please, how did you take a mortal human with you. How did you bring Professor Tungard here. And why?'

If Sir Bertrand was expecting Monica to pooh-pooh all this, he was sadly disappointed. Instead, she just shrugged. 'Why? I needed a scapegoat and someone with access to the right chemicals. It's taken this backward little race of apes this long to get there. And by becoming romantically involved with him, he would do exactly what I wanted to ensure I never told that crippled cretin sat there.'

Unsurprisingly she was pointing at a shocked Natjya.

Joe Tungard said nothing. He just stared at the tablecloth.

'So I could access the right materials to create a tiny rift that I could then enhance, open and use to access subspace. For the first time in, well if you'll excuse the pun amongst time travellers, literal centuries!' Monica laughed. 'And it felt fantastic. But then I discovered Rummas was trying to stop me, all the Lampreys throughout the multiverse, and so I opted to stop him.'

'An infinite number of Rummases in an infinite number of universes,' the Doctor said (not that Sir Bertrand understood a word, and yet there was something...). 'You do realise that's an impossible mission, don't you?'

'Not at all, Time Lord. All I have to do is break the Vortex, scratch through the chronon walls and seal thousands of universes at a time in a millisecond time loop. I've lost count of how many I've done so far, but quite a few trillion. Every so often, a Rummas catches up with me, so I have to stop him. Easy.'

The Doctor stood up. 'Madam, every time you seal off a universe, that chronon energy has to bleed somewhere. You are creating unbridled chaos power, unlimited temporal spillage. What are you doing with... oh no.'

'Yes that's right Doctor. All that spillage, all that chaos energy, all that redundant is/was/maybe is sustenance to me. I'm absorbing it, growing stronger and stronger. Another few centuries and nothing will stop me. I can break out of the confines of the Vortex and swim in my natural form throughout the multiverse, feeding. I already have a limited ability to do that.'

'I know. We've seen past, or maybe future, versions of you ourselves.'

'Really? What was I doing?'

'Kidnapping Sir Bertrand's poor daughter,' said Mel.

And then Sir Bertrand knew.

And with a terribly primal scream that made everyone in the

restaurant turn and look at their table, a millennia or ten's worth of memories flowed back into his head.

He remembered pursuing the two young Lampreys out of the Vortex onto a lush green world; the boy, the healer, the perfect counterbalance to the destructive force that was the girl.

He remembered seeing them create a portal to another world and another and another, and he remembered chasing them through each one until a collapsing tunnel under a hill stopped him. Just for a moment. Just long enough for him to think about riding a time wind back a few seconds, to try and find an alternative route through.

He remembered doing this maybe a hundred times but to no avail.

So he went forward, to a period where the hill simply didn't exist any longer and found himself in a flat field by some forest or other. The hill had gone and he was on a planet called Earth, but could find no trace of his quarry.

Quickly adapting his form to that of an inhabitant of this strange new world, he tried making enquiries but had no idea whether a day, a second, a century or an entire millennium had passed.

He remembered using his knowledge, his experience to create a financial empire in this pathetic place, hoping to build some kind of trap, to draw the two Lampreys to him.

And he remembered meeting a native human woman. He remembered her falling in love with him.

He remembered their lives together and his mission, his old existence fading from memory.

And he remembered deliberately putting chronon blocks into his own mind, deliberately shutting off his knowledge of who he had been, why he was there. Because he had found love.

And he remembered having a daughter. And a fire. And pain and grief and anger, and with each year of pain, he remembered burying his real self further and further down until nothing would ever dredge it up again.

Even seeing the Lamprey last Christmas that stole his beloved Helen away couldn't break the conditioning.

But this evening had finally done it.

And with no regard for anything, Sir Bertrand Lamprey changed his physical state for the first time in... well, aeons.

And facing the others, ignoring the fear, the terror or fascination on their faces, he stood before them as a Lamprey.

And planet Earth stood still, frozen in a moment in time.

Everywhere except at that dinner table.

There, he deliberately let his five 'guests' remain alive and aware.

'Where's your brother? Your balance? The good to your evil?'

Monica smiled. 'He... he died. A long, long time ago.'

'So it was just you I was chasing through history,' he said to Monica.

And in the blink of an eye, Monica, too, was in her Lamprey form. 'That's right. And now you've caught up with me. What are you going to do?'

'Destroy you. Annihilate you. Utterly obliterate you.'

'Oh dear,' the Doctor said to Mel. 'I didn't mean for this to happen here. I think we have a problem.'

Chapter Ten
Sixteen Again

The Honourable Helen 'Lucky' Lamprey smiled as she surveyed the smiling people in front of her. They were gathered there, dressed to the nines in an array of smart party wear, jewellery glittering, rings polished, not a hair out of place on anyone.

Well, those that had hair, of course. The ones with scales tended not to have hair, and then there was that very odd couple in the corner. Helen initially thought they were some strange sculpture until one of them spoke with multiple voices that sounded like someone had tipped a ton of stones into a heavy-duty rock-crushing machine going rather fast.

All he/she/it had said was 'Hello', but Helen wasn't used to seeing eyes blinking with molten rock behind them and had gasped rather loudly. Neither of the rock people had spoken since. Neither of them had hair anyway. Or clothes.

What Helen really wanted right now was to see everyone relaxed, wearing things they wanted to wear rather than what society dictated they ought to wear at such functions. She saw poor old Mr Xxerxezz from the Spaceport Office, representing the Narrahans no doubt. Where in God's name had he hired his dinner jacket from? It didn't fit, and he looked as if he was about to expire from the tightness around his neck caused by the tie he wore. What was the point of a people whose skin

188

was mostly matted fur wearing tight suits? Helen really wanted to just wander over to him, smile and loosen the tie and see him smile in return. See him relax.

How many of the people here came not because they wanted to see Helen per se, but because it was what they had been ordered to do.

She glanced further into the crowd and for a brief moment Helen imagined she was somewhere else entirely. She had an image of an old building, warm and soothing. A house she knew. And there was a man, a human, beside her.

Still, no matter, that was clearly tiredness talking and now she had a job to do.

Her reverie was broken by a short hand-clap – one of the arthropod-guards was beaming up at her. She took his proffered claw, and bent close as he whispered to her.

'I'm sorry, madam, I had no idea those two were coming. My fault, I left others to send out the invites. I should have made it clear that no half-breeds were to be –'

'It's all right, Chakiss,' Helen said firmly. 'I'm glad they're showing an interest in something other than making trouble. And I don't like the term "half-breeds". You make Miss Baal sound inferior. I may not like her but she is still welcome in my dome.'

Chakiss nodded in subservience. 'My apologies madam.'

Helen pointed to the painting hung on the hallway wall, amidst the portraits of men with beards and horses with long legs. It was an abstract piece, almost cubist in its extremes, but clearly a five-sided shape, with concentric pentagons echoing throughout.

'I like where you hung it! Thank you!'

'I can't let my mistress's art not take pride of place, especially on her sixteenth birthday, can I?'

And again, Helen Lamprey had the strangest feeling of *déjà vu*, although something wasn't right about the surroundings.

To distract herself, Helen gently caressed the cross she wore around her neck. 'Father's watching, I know it,' she murmured to herself.

'Father?' chittered Chakiss. 'I didn't know you remem... knew your father, madam.'

Helen frowned. 'I think some of the atmosphere is getting to me. Maybe it's the fumes from the punch.' She thanked Chakiss again, then let go of his claw and loudly embraced a young woman near the steps. 'Letitia,' she said, 'how simply divine of you to be here.'

She moved on to the next guest and the next, sipping a glass of white wine and listening to the conversations swirling around.

To her right, a couple she didn't know were discussing the snow-capped mountains. In the centre of the room, a gaggle of rather insipid young furry things were gathered around a slightly older human she knew to be the curator from the Assembled Images Museum on Garrett. He was making jokes by punning Garrettian and Lakertyan names. The dreadful caw-caws of the obsequious laughter of his audience were beginning to annoy her. By the French windows, she could see Miss Baal talking to a dreary arthropod who had dismissed her painting earlier. And just out in the hallway, she heard Miss Baal's travelling companion holding court on the merits of the painting itself.

Helen had never seen him before, but thought he had a nice smile, even if his fashion sense bordered on disastrous.

'Influenced by Braque,' he was saying, 'but there's also a good deal of Cézanne in there, which is nice. But the actual impression I'm getting is that the artist has really studied Juan

Gris, as the picture has a calculated feel to it, quite, quite synthetic and yet by its essence... oh hello!'

Helen jumped as she realised the Doctor was addressing her.

'And what do you think?' he asked.

Helen shrugged. 'It's a bit abstract don't you think? Can one really call cubism art?'

'My thoughts exactly,' muttered a haughty old humanoid woman, gazing at it through pince-nez, but the Doctor shushed her.

The Doctor was bored with the party, but particularly with this old dowager who had attached herself to him the moment she had hobbled through the dome's porch. Perhaps if he tried a bit of rudeness, she might get the hint and skedaddle. 'Oh you colonists,' he scolded. 'If it's not Renaissance you get bored. Such a Philistine. Actually, no, that's an insult to the Philistines. No, I take that back, because I knew a lot of Philistines and they were lovely. Sea People always are, of course. Very arty themselves. Squid ink was their paint of choice.' He turned to look at his hostess. 'Ever used squid ink, Lady Lamprey?'

'No, I can't say that I have,' Helen replied with a laugh as she shook his hand. 'A pleasure to meet you. You came with Miss Baal, yes?'

Then she seemed distracted by someone walking purposefully through the crowd, and waved a hand to him.

'Oh Chakiss, meet the Doctor. He is an art critic.'

So this was Chakiss. This should be interesting.

Chakiss nodded. 'Of course you are, Doctor. Professor Rummas warned me you'd be coming.'

The Doctor laughed. 'Warned? Am I a threat or something?'

Chakiss paused before replying. 'Warned is indeed the wrong

word. Please forgive me, my grasp of the human tongue isn't as good as it ought to be whilst I am in Lady Lamprey's service.'

The Doctor nodded and then spoke fluently in Chakiss's own language, keeping a huge smile on his face. 'Unlucky for you, then, that I can speak your tongue very well, and while our birthday host no doubt thinks we're exchanging pleasantries and jokes, allow me to assure you Chakiss that I know exactly what you're up to.' He then dropped back into English. 'And so they both fell into the water,' he finished laughing uproariously.

After a beat, Chakiss also laughed. 'You translate your wit very... accurately, Doctor.' He glanced back at Helen, flexed his wings under his dinner jacket and chittered as he made his excuses and moved into the drawing room.

'He doesn't like me much,' said the Doctor.

'Chakiss is very loyal to me,' replied Helen. 'And he doesn't like anyone much.'

The Doctor bowed slightly. 'My lady, I fear I have taken up much of your time and should allow your other guests to share you.' He leaned closer. 'Although I'd stay away from the old dowager over there. She doesn't actually like any art, your cubism or otherwise.'

Helen laughed, and the Doctor headed towards the dining room after Chakiss. He stopped by the door as he caught a glimpse of Melanie, but determined not to make eye contact. He wasn't sure if Chakiss knew they were connected.

'Yes, thank you,' Melanie was saying to someone, but the Doctor hadn't noticed her companion. He was keeping an eye on Helen, seeing who else she spoke to.

'You all right, Melanie?' he asked, leaning on the door jamb.

'Just a strange drunk man, saying something about my sister.'

The Doctor raised his glass, as an ironic toast to Chakiss, who was now heading back out, carrying an empty tray, probably off to yell at some poor serf who'd forgotten to keep the drinks flowing.

'Your sister? What was he saying about her?'

Melanie didn't reply immediately, but finally said: 'I don't have a sister, Doctor. You know that.'

The Doctor thought that was slightly odd. 'I'm sure Anabel would be very pleased to hear you say that.'

'Who the hell's Anabel?'

'Your sister,' said the Doctor with a sigh. Then he turned to look at her, hoping she would be ready to explain her bizarre behaviour.

And as their eyes met, he felt as if he'd been slapped across the face by a very large and wet haddock.

'I'm sorry,' he said slowly, 'I thought you were Melanie...' then he stopped. 'Only you are, aren't you?'

'Well, I'm beginning to wonder now,' Mel replied.

'Oh. Mel.' He stared at the human girl in front of him. A pure human, not a hybrid, so her father was unlikely to be a reptilian scientist called Baal. This was clearly prior to their meeting in the Reading Room on Carsus. 'Where was I last time we spoke?' he asked her finally.

This strange non-green version of Melanie was eyeing him up, and he felt sorry for her. His behaviour must seem insane.

'At the bottom of the stairs,' she said after a beat. 'Opposite the painting. Down there.' She pointed to the left.

'Am I still there?' the Doctor asked her, not wanting to look in the direction she had pointed. In case another him was there. Which would not be a good thing.

'Well, obviously not, Doctor, or you –' Mel stopped.

Clearly she could see another Doctor, her widened eyes told him that. Poor girl.

This Mel regarded him again, the confusion in her face evident. And a small amount of hostility perhaps? 'It's happened before,' she said quietly. 'In the TARDIS.'

The Doctor nodded. He remembered being in the TARDIS, just after they came back with Kina. 'I came up behind you,' he said slowly, recalling his own confusion. 'I tapped you on the shoulder and after a second or two, you vanished,' he said. 'Which is lucky as too many Doctors spoil the broth.'

'But how has this happened?'

The Doctor wasn't sure. Twice in one lifetime was bad enough, but time playing tricks twice in one day... Then a thought struck him. 'Have you, perchance, encountered a Professor Rummas on Carsus yet?'

Melanie nodded. 'You too?'

'Oh yes,' began the Doctor, realisation dawning. Silly of him not to have realised earlier. 'Yes, and that makes sense. You see he told us that time that leakages were occurring from alternative universes. A case of maybes and could-bes and –' He stopped. He was now addressing a door jamb, the human Melanie having vanished again mid-sentence, just as she had in the TARDIS. 'Question is,' he said to himself, 'whose reality are we in now – mine, hers or no one's?' He cursed himself – the first thing he should have asked the other Mel was where she thought she was. If she'd said this space station, that would've been a good answer. But suppose Helen's birthday party was taking place on another planet for her? What if Helen were a Martian, a Sontaran or a Pakhar? Anything was possible.

That said, Rummas hadn't prepared either Melanie – his Melanie – or him for this, he'd just given them that vague suggestion that 'things might get complicated'.

Useful warning, that.

So the Doctor wandered back to 'his' Melanie, who was chatting amiably with a few of Chakiss's friends and managed to catch her eye.

'Excuse me,' she said to the assembled throng, and he all but dragged Melanie away.

'I was doing well, there,' she said grumpily. 'Telling them all about our adventures with the Zarbi and the Proctor of Darruth!'

'We have a problem.'

Melanie sighed. 'Well, you have one, certainly. You're going to get a piece of my mind. The one in the red top was rather sweet.'

'I just spoke to you.' The Doctor was hoping she'd see how serious this was.

'I know. Quite abruptly, and yanked me away from my adoring audience.'

'No not you you, another you. By the entrance to the dining room. She was quite surprised to see me.'

'Another me?'

'Yes, you. She vanished whilst I was waxing lyrical about why I thought this had happened, which was probably the only good thing about it really.'

'I can believe that, she must've been overjoyed!'

The Doctor sighed. There were days... 'Anyway,' he said firmly. 'That's the second time that's happened. She mentioned that Rummas had sent her... Multiple Rummases as well as multiple Melanies.'

'And Doctors. One of *you* is bad enough, two of *me* is odd. Freaky.'

'Freaky?'

'Oh not again. Yes, freaky. As in weird, bizarre and rather

disquieting.' Melanie then smiled and gave his arm a reassuring squeeze. 'Let's not start that conversation again?'

'Ah. Right.' The Doctor shrugged. 'As she's gone now, there's not much we can do is there.' Then he stiffened and took a deep breath. 'Melanie,' he commanded, all frivolity gone. 'Mel, grab both my hands. Now!'

Without questioning, Melanie did so. 'What's happening?'

'I'm not sure but the hairs on my neck just stood up and my hair curled tighter. I knew after Schyllus we shouldn't have gone back to Carsus.'

'And maybe we shouldn't have accepted Mission Number Two of the day to come here?'

The Doctor smiled weakly. 'You may be right. My need for adventure appears to be overriding my need for self-protection these days. Sorry.'

'Accepted. Now, you said something's going on here?'

The Doctor pointed over her shoulder. 'Look!'

Melanie was trying to turn her head to follow his gaze, but he could see she was finding it difficult. Within a second or two, she was frozen like a statue.

He looked at the party guests. It was the same all over.

Bar two people.

Clearly facing the same treacle effect, Helen Lamprey was trying to push through her immobile guests, obviously terrified by what she was seeing – people still; a glass that had been tipped, frozen in mid-drop, globules of golden liquid oozing out but now caught in mid-air.

She was trying to reach Chakiss, but that was weirder still.

Chakiss was, like the Doctor, totally unaffected by the time freeze and instead was moving at a normal pace, trying to get people out of the way so that he could reach Helen.

'Chakiss!' yelled the Doctor, and the arthropod stopped.

He looked at the Doctor, then pointed upwards.

It was becoming a strain for even the Doctor to fight this strange time disturbance, it felt like he was swimming through treacle, but he managed to look straight up. The top half of the building was gone, almost as if it had never been there. No ruins, no damage, it was simply gone.

Maybe it was an effect of the time distillation, but the Doctor felt no wind, no cold. And all he could see were a few clouds gathering in the night sky, blotting out the stars.

'That's no cloud,' the Doctor muttered.

And indeed it wasn't, it was something that parted, and revealed a huge alien creature, like a giant snake slinking across the sky. Instead of a head, it had a suckered, tendrilled hollow stump, yet it seemed to be looking for something, despite no evidence of eyes.

'It is a Lamprey.' The Doctor winced at this thought – the legendary time wraiths were brutal and unflinching in their desire to absorb chronon energy. How had they traced him here?

Chakiss was beside him now. 'Isn't it magnificent?'

'What's that noise?' the Doctor shouted back. It seemed to be a heartbeat, terrifyingly loud.

'A pulsebeat,' Chakiss hissed. 'Look.'

The Lamprey was bearing down, not towards the Doctor as he had expected, but towards Helen, who began screaming. The Doctor wanted to run to her aid, despite the time distillation, but Chakiss held him back.

'No,' he shouted. 'It's come for her. It's her destiny!'

The Doctor pulled free. 'What do you know of this?'

'I brought it here. I was sent to find this woman, then call the Lamprey.'

'Why?'

'None of your business, Doctor.'

And suddenly it was all over. The noise and the accompanying Lamprey were gone, the house was restored and the guests were milling about again, as if nothing had happened.

The Doctor looked around, trying to find Helen, but now the party seemed to be in honour of the old dowager he'd met earlier. Certainly she was the centre of attention.

Chakiss was behind him, hissing over his shoulder.

'She's gone, Time Lord. Everything has re-set itself and you failed in your mission.'

Angrily the Doctor swung around to face him, but instead of Chakiss there was a small furry creature carrying a tray of drinks.

He sought Melanie, who was back with Chakiss's fellows, and again, he pulled her away.

Melanie was indignant, her green cheeks flaring slightly.

'I was doing well, there,' she said grumpily. 'Telling them all about our adventures with the Zarbi and the Proctor of Darruth!'

'No you weren't,' the Doctor said quietly. 'You were just repeating yourself.'

Before she could respond, he starting weaving his way back, away from the dining room and out to the hallway where Chakiss had been.

'Remember where the TARDIS is?'

'By the spaceport,' Melanie responded, sulkily. 'I was having a good time back there.'

'I don't care, Melanie,' he snapped.

She looked shocked, so he took a deep breath. 'I'm sorry. I know you were. Trouble was, it was the second time you'd told them that story in minutes, but you don't remember. For all I know, on a million myriad worlds in a million universes of chances never taken, left turns instead of right turns, a million more Melanies are telling that story, too. All I do know is this: we need to be on Carsus now. I know who Rummas's enemy is, and it's not good.'

Melanie was immediately her normal self again. 'So, we'd better get going then. I can party another time.'

The Doctor put an arm around her shoulder and activated the control that summoned the shuttle that would take them back to the Narrah spaceport. 'I hope,' he said, 'that we can indeed have a better party next time.'

But deep down he wasn't sure if 'next time' might ever exist.

Chapter Eleven
Noise Annoys

The restaurant was the scene of a disaster. Wave after wave of chronon energy was pouring from the two Lampreys as they circled, almost entwined each other, sending shockwaves right, left and centre.

Only the raised table area was safe (although the mirror had been a casualty of the flying bottle of Moët and both were now in hundreds of shards on the floor).

Mel and the Doctor were trying to protect Natjya Tungard, while Pike tried to calm Monica Lamprey down.

'Trouble is,' Mel yelled over the noise the two aliens were making, 'how can he tell which is which?'

'What's going on?' screamed Natjya, pointing at the customers below.

Mel looked down. One minute the patrons and staff were frozen in time, a second later a wave of energy washed over them and they were rotting skeletons. A second later, another angry wave, and they were mewling babies, then back to normal, then just dust and so on.

'There's nothing we can do for them,' shouted the Doctor. 'And we can't move ourselves or we'll get caught up in the same temporal distortion!'

The noise was incredible and Mel wasn't sure if it was a real tsunami of chronon energy or the actual angry cries of the battling Lampreys.

The Doctor yanked Pike away. 'Stay back,' he pleaded. 'In this state, they'll kill you!'

'Monica won't. I have looked after her all these years!'

'Don't be stupid. Any belief you had that she was ever an innocent child you helped place with foster parents is a lie! She's a Lamprey! She can...' they ducked as the table went crashing over their heads, 'she can alter her form at will. She just became a baby because it suited her purpose. Her intelligence has always been the same!'

'Why Joseph?' Natjya said, while Mel tried to keep her wheelchair upright under the onslaught.

'He's a fantastic chemist,' Pike replied. 'He has discovered elements and compounds previously unknown. He'll help mankind move on, recover from the damage the war did to Europe!'

Mel looked at the Doctor. 'Rummas said he achieved nothing!'

The Doctor just shrugged. 'Then either he got it wrong, or Tungard's discoveries remain unknown or... or he lied!'

Joseph Tungard had said nothing all this time. He was sat in a corner, ignoring the violent maelstrom erupting around him. He just stared forward, rocking slightly. Natjya suddenly flopped out of her chair, despite Mel's ministrations, but it was a deliberate move. It brought her face to face with her husband.

'Why?' she asked. 'After all we went through to get here? All we built up? Why *her*?'

Joseph looked into her face, as if seeing her for the first time. 'I'm sorry,' he said, almost too quietly for anyone to hear.

But Mel did, although it was a strain.

Natjya grabbed his hand. 'Is it because of the TB?'

Joseph stared open-mouthed for a moment, then: 'You know?'

'Always. I may be a bitter old cripple, Joseph, but I am not stupid. And I hear everything. Except… except the fact that my husband has been involved with a younger woman.'

'An alien actually,' Mel added, unhelpfully, and then wished she hadn't.

'If I were dead,' Natjya cried, 'would it be easier for you? Would you prefer that? You deserved better than me, I know.'

'No,' yelled Joseph suddenly. 'I love you, I don't love her. It was just… just…'

'Sex?' prompted Mel.

'You're not helping, Mel,' said the Doctor, joining the group.

Pike crawled over to Natjya. 'You should have died months ago, Natjya. It was Monica's temporal energies keeping you alive. She never realised, but I did.'

'So if she leaves Earth,' Mel asked, 'Mrs Tungard dies naturally?'

Pike nodded.

'Then she must stay,' said Joseph.

'No,' Natjya snapped. 'No, I don't want to stay alive like this. You must let me go, Joseph. Move on. Start again with someone new. Just not… not that!'

And the two Lampreys stopped their screeching, their fighting. The noise abated, the winds vanished.

And every human being in the restaurant, bar those near them, was dead. Just dust, aged beyond existence. The interior of the restaurant was a pile of dust. Chairs, tables, everything.

'See what you've done, Sir Bertrand!' the Doctor pointed angrily below them. 'Because you can't keep control!'

The Lamprey that he was addressing surveyed the area, and then in a blur of movement resumed the familiar form of Sir Bertrand.

The other Lamprey reared up, but Sir Bertrand threw his arms up. 'Be gone, Monica Lamprey!' he bellowed and in a flash of light it vanished.

'I've sent her back to the Vortex,' Sir Bertrand said. He took the Doctor's arm. 'I'm out of practice, Doctor. You must track her down, if she communicates with other Lampreys, you may find my Helen. Save her. As the offspring of a Lamprey and a human, she'll be a unique being.'

The Doctor nodded sadly. 'Yes, able to co-exist in both dimensions more easily than pure Lampreys.' He turned to Pike. 'Did Monica disappear periodically?'

Pike shrugged. 'Yes, occasionally, but never for very long.'

Mel helped Natjya Tungard back into her chair. 'It would seem that way to you, wouldn't it? I mean, if she can manipulate time, well, it'd probably seem like just a few seconds to you.'

The Doctor agreed. 'Silly of me, of course. She might have been years in the Vortex, in the Spiral itself, replenishing her energies and then returning to Earth to search for Helen.'

'How did she know of her?' asked Pike.

'She'd sense it from the centre of the Spiral, in the same way a shark can sense blood from miles away. But when she came back here, those senses were confused.'

'She called you a Time Lord, Doctor,' said Sir Bertrand. 'Are you?'

'Yes.'

'Then you have a... what's it called? TARDIS?'

'Yes.'

'Then go. Now, please. Track her down.'

Mel looked at him, taking his hands in hers. 'You must come with us, help us find your daughter.'

But he shook his head. 'I'm tired. It's has been many years since I assumed my true shape, since I suppressed my memories. Tonight has taken all my energy, particularly exiling Monica just now. I... I really do need to rest. Please, you must go.'

The Doctor accepted this, and began to lead Mel away. As they walked through the dust towards the doors, he looked back at Sir Bertrand. 'Remember this. This is what happens if you lose control. Make sure these people haven't died for nothing, Sir Bertrand. Never, ever let yourself do this again.'

Sir Bertrand hung his head ashamed. 'I'm truly sorry, Doctor.'

Joseph Tungard finally scrambled up. 'I must come with you, Doctor. I know how to stop Monica.'

Natjya grabbed his hand. 'No, not yet.'

He bent down to her and kissed her forehead gently. 'If I can't bring her back, you will die. I don't want that, even if *you* do.'

Mel whispered to the Doctor: 'Can't Bertrand's energies keep her alive?'

The Doctor shrugged. 'I presume not, otherwise he'd have said so. It must be something unique to Monica, to the amount of time the two women have spent together.' He then raised his voice. 'Professor Tungard, if you are coming, we should leave. Now.'

Joseph was at their side in a moment.

From the raised dining area, Sir Bertrand watched the three figures ease open the door and leave. Natjya just stared at the closed door, and the Lamprey in human form almost felt sorry for her.

Almost.

Doctor Pike let out a breath. 'We ought to get out of here. If the authorities turn up, we'll have a hell of a job explaining this.'

'Not a problem, Doctor Pike,' said Sir Bertrand, and took the man's hand. 'No problem at all.'

With a gasp and then a scream, Pike saw his hand wither, shrivel and turn to powder. His eyes were gone before he could even take in the fact that his entire body was being eaten away by the ravages of time, and he was dead in less than a second, reduced to no more than a thimbleful of dust.

Sir Bertrand looked at Natjya, helpless in her chair, and laughed.

'You,' snarled Natjya. 'Of course...'

'Me,' replied the Lamprey. 'I can't believe I pulled that one off so easily. Like all Time Lords, the Doctor was so easily fooled.'

And Sir Bertrand shimmered and became who he truly was. Monica.

And Monica lent down, took Natjya's face in her hands. 'You've held him back, all these years, Natjya. But your husband, and more importantly, the knowledge in his head, is going to enable me to seal the Spiral for ever. And all that resultant beautiful, frustrated, angry chaotic energy will be mine to feed on for eternity. Goodbye. Fool.'

Monica placed a kiss on Natjya's lips and reduced her to even less dust than she had Pike.

'Feeding time's over,' she then said straightening up. 'Time to begin the chase anew!' Monica looked up to the ceiling. 'I'm coming for you, Doctor!' And in a flash of light she resumed her Lamprey form and vanished straight into the heart of the Spiral that formed the axis of the space–time vortex.

The final battle was about to begin.

Chapter Twelve
Harmony in My Head

The TARDIS made an uncomfortable landing. After a moment, the Doctor, Melanie Bush and Joseph Tungard emerged, the two humans throwing looks at the Doctor that suggested he might have said, with an alarming gift for understatement, that the trip back to the Carsus Library would be quick, easy and uneventful.

It had been none of those things.

Indeed, it had started when, on entering the TARDIS, Mel had seen, once again, a multitude of identical (and some not so identical) Sixth Doctors milling around, seemingly unaware of each other. Her Doctor had immediately smacked the TARDIS console, as if it were the Ship's fault. When that didn't resolve anything, he glared at Mel and Tungard.

'Well, that's not right. Have you touched anything, Mel?'

'No of course not,' she retorted, with a loud 'what do you mean?' kind of tut.

He glanced up at the scanner, and Mel saw a number of TARDISes, Police Box-shaped TARDISes at that, hovering out there. 'Not right at all.' He turned the scanner off, and as the little screens closed over it he eased himself past an oblivious Doctor (this one in shirt sleeves, reading a book called *The Lost Empires of the Planet Chronos*) and pressed some more switches, but still the multitude of phantom Doctors were there.

Tungard was just staring around him, his mouth hanging open. 'But it was so small...' he said.

Mel was going to respond, but instead Tungard held his hand up. 'My friend Emile was hypothesising about such infinite possibilities,' he said. He looked back at the double doors. 'I mean, if Emile was right, then between those doors and the outer doors is some kind of dimensional gateway that keeps everything together. And this interior is in a wholly different place than the exterior.' He looked almost accusingly at Mel. 'But why's it so small? Surely, this kind of structure would allow for endless internal configurations?'

Mel just pointed silently at the internal door.

'Ah,' said Tungard, comprehending. 'Infinite?'

'Pretty much.'

'And these Doctors crammed in here?'

'Not a regular occurrence,' Mel said, thinking it wise not to point out it had happened once before, on a smaller scale, only a few hours ago.

The Doctor was being distracted by another version of himself, trying to input coordinates at the console, but his ephemeral fingers made no impact. Nevertheless, it was annoying the real Doctor. 'Not again,' he murmured and then, with a shrug, stood exactly where the other stood, creating a kind of bizarre double-exposure look to them both, each one making the same actions, but a few seconds apart.

'Doctor,' Mel finally said. 'This is freaky and a bit alarming.'

The Doctor looked back to her, but didn't stop working. 'I'm not so sure. You see, I've been pondering that Carsus itself is the centre of all the problems. Rummas brought us here to stop them, but I think he might be the actual nexus at the heart of the matter himself.'

'You know, I've no idea what you're talking about,' Mel said.

The Doctor sighed. 'Thank you Mel, you're a great help.'

'It's not my fault if things keep happening and no one tells us what's going on. Poor Joe here is as bemused as I am.'

'No, I'm not actually,' Tungard said quietly. 'I'm guessing that if that Lamprey creature that pretended to be Monica can manipulate multiple timelines, then all these versions of you, Doctor, are just ghosts, afterimages of where you have and haven't been, yes?'

'Well,' the Doctor said. 'That was informative, but not entirely accurate. You did however,' he added with a glare at Mel, 'at least make an effort. So thank you.'

Tungard gasped and Mel noticed that one by one the faux Doctors were disappearing, until only two, totally identical ones were left.

'We took our eye off the ball,' Mel muttered.

One Doctor looked at another. 'One of us ought not to be here,' he said.

'You think?' replied the other.

'Indeed. But which of us is it?'

'Well, we could work it out. I mean, I came aboard the TARDIS with Mel and Joseph Tungard. What about you?'

The other Doctor chewed his lip. 'Oh I see. So after we left Carsus, we went to Earth. We met up at the restaurant and the Lamprey attacked us.'

The other Doctor took up the story. 'When Sir Bertrand exorcised Monica, we all headed here to go back to Rummas at the Library.'

'So did we.'

'Oh yes of course. All of which means that unlike all the others that were here but aren't...'

'...you and I are separated only by the tiniest change in reality.'

'A minute change. We must think on something that has confused us in the recent past.'

'A word or phrase out of place that'll make sense to one of us but not the other.'

Mel and Tungard were getting more alarmed by the second. 'Come on Doctor. Doctors. Two minds are better than one and all that.'

'That's it! The party!'

The other Doctor frowned. 'Which party?'

'Oh come on, we can't be that diverse.'

'No I mean, I've been to so many...'

'Helen Lamprey's sixteenth. Ipswich. Earth. Yes?'

'Yes, been there, done that.'

The Doctors looked at Mel, then one spoke. 'Mel, how's Anabel?'

'Oh, look! Just who on Earth *is* Anabel?' Mel asked.

'Ah ha! I'm the anomaly!' the Doctor who'd asked exclaimed and promptly vanished.

Mel looked at the remaining Doctor. 'I hope to God you're my Doctor.'

'Look at it this way, Mel. I don't know who Anabel is, either.' The Doctor pressed some more switches and declared they could now proceed to the Carsus Library in safety.

At which point the TARDIS lurched from side to side and all three people were thrown to the floor.

'Some days,' Mel muttered staring at the ceiling, 'I wish he'd never open his mouth!'

* * *

So, there they were – the TARDIS having made its uncomfortable landing – stood in the Reading Room with Rummas, and Misters Woltas and Huu. Telling them everything that had happened.

A look passed between the two Custodians and the professor and then Rummas sighed. 'Doctor, I think I need to show you something. Please follow me.'

Mel was going to follow them out when she saw Tungard spot the computer system she'd tried hacking into earlier.

He'd already grasped the basics of it by the time she wandered over. 'Is this the future?' he asked her quietly. 'A future of time machines, displaced temporal monsters and this box of tricks?'

'It's a PC,' Mel said quietly, trying to remember how she'd felt when first confronted with technology way beyond her 1989 experiences. 'A Personal Computer.'

Tungard laughed. 'What is it really?'

Mel just squeezed his shoulder and felt him sag.

'This,' he said after a few moments, 'this is a computer? But... but...'

Mel tried to think what computers meant to someone from 1959, thirty years before it meant ALGOL, IBMs, BBC Micros and LocoScript 1 to her. While travelling with the Doctor, Mel had quickly become acclimatised to developments in technology, but that's because her background was in that field. As a chemist, albeit one who seemed to have harnessed whatever it was Monica Lamprey needed, Joseph's grasp of microcircuitry was going to be limited and the leap of technology she had taken would be more a leap of faith for poor Joe.

'What does this... PC do exactly?' he asked.

Remembering her attempt to cheat the future earlier, Mel

considered lying, but in the end she just hoped he would be stronger than she'd been and accept that the future was best left a closed book.

So she told him.

And before she could breathe, he'd typed his own name in.

Mel, at least, could be reassured that he'd learn nothing other than the fact that his life was destined to be unremarkable.

At least that's what Rummas had said earlier.

The computer screen, however, said something entirely different:

Joseph Piotr Tungard. (B) 1924, Earth Prime. Romanian chemist, fled Soviet persecution to Great Britain in the 1950s where he began teaching at a London college. Whilst there, he discovered three new atomic elements that, when combined, opened the causality loops, enabled unfettered access to the space-time vortex and unleashed the Lampreys previously imprisoned in the Spiral at the apex of the Vortex. As a result of his discoveries, the Lampreys gained unlimited access to all of time and space across the multiverses, reaching back to the creation, or forward to the destruction, of each universe, plus every interstitial point in between, wherein they wreaked havoc and unravelled reality whilst feeding on the chaos energies released as each divergent universe self-destructed. As such, to the few trillion survivors within the eighteen known surviving universes (out of the unrecordable amount that existed previously), he is known as the Architect of Chaos. Many attempts have been made by surviving time-sensitives to go back through time and assassinate Tungard prior to his ascent to maturity but all have failed, his timeline is fiercely guarded by the multitudinous Lampreys.

'That explains a lot,' Joseph Tungard muttered, thinking of the car crash and all that. He sat back in his seat and let out a deep breath. 'I don't think I like this future of yours Miss Bush,' he said after a moment's silence.

'There are times I'm not too keen on it myself.' Then an idea struck her. She asked Joe to move and sat down herself, typing in her own name. She selected Earth Prime under planet but instead of requesting a history, she typed Known Relatives into the search engine. The number started at 131 and started climbing so she pressed the halt button and rephrased it. Known Close Relatives, although this might include the likes of her father's ghastly sister's family, and the lovely Hallams on her mother's side, it'd keep it closer to her own time period.

After a few seconds the computer suggested it had found twelve. Mel considered this before hitting Continue. Her mother and father, various aunts and uncles and cousins. That gave her eleven. So where did the twelfth come from.

She hit Go and watched the expected list take shape.

And stared at the screen. And saw the name she'd heard a couple of times recently, despite it meaning nothing to her. And felt the colour drain from her cheeks.

There was the entry for herself, Melanie Jane born 22/07/64. So who the hell was Anabel Claire, born 04/10/62?

'Oh my god, Professor Tungard,' she breathed aloud. 'I've got a sister I've never met.'

'Of course you have my dear,' said a new, feminine voice behind her.

Mel swung around to find Joseph Tungard held in a neck-pinch, unable to move more than his bulging eyes, staring in fear.

'I do hope his being here means that we've finally got rid of Rummas. Forever?'

'No,' Mel hissed. 'We stopped you.'

Monica Lamprey, in her human form once more, laughed and tossed her hair back over her shoulder. 'Don't be foolish, young lady. You saw what you wanted to see, or rather what I wanted you to see. Now, you two really are a nuisance. Joseph here, I still have a use for. But you, darling Melanie Jane, are a repellent retrograde, a distraction. But you are also the Doctor's companion.'

'He'll do nothing to help you,' Mel shouted.

'Of course he will, you fool,' Monica spat. 'Because if he doesn't, you'll never get back. I see you've discovered the most important thing in your life. The one thing that marks you out as different to the myriad of other Mels that populate the disparate multiverse.'

'I don't get it...'

'They all have a sister called Anabel. But you? That was your trigger moment, the incident that marked you out as special and unique. The path not taken is all because of Anabel. Would you like to know what that is?'

'I...'

'I'll take that as a yes?' smiled Monica and immediately transformed into her Lamprey form. 'Goodbye Melanie Bush of Earth Prime,' she cried. 'I doubt you'll want to come back again!'

And the last thing Mel was aware of was a rushing sound, a tumultuous wind akin to the one she'd heard during the battle in the restaurant.

And then everything stopped.

Forever.

'If I had a map of your pentagramical Library, Professor Rummas,' said the Doctor, 'would I be right in assuming I'm stood at the epicentre, where everything comes together?'

'You would.'

'And would I be right in assuming that what I dismissed as Mel's paranoid ramblings about similar structures on other worlds are, in fact, wholly justified and that the Lampreys can use them to access those planets?'

'You would.'

'And would I be right in assuming that you've known this all along, and could have saved all of us a great deal of stress if you'd told me this before?'

'You would.'

'One last query, old chap. Would I be right in thinking that if I were to abandon my deeply held beliefs about violence and aggression and just let go, that I could probably punch you on the nose before Mr Woltas and Mr Huu could get anywhere near to stopping me?'

There was a brief pause, before a more sheepish 'You would' emerged from Rummas's mouth.

The four of them were stood in a chamber that was as different to the rest of the Carsus Library as could be possible. Brightly lit with fierce halogen bulbs, it had gleaming white walls, bare, although one area contained a small bank of consoles. These had an array of blinking lights and blank computer screens.

It was quite large and at the dead centre – and thus dead centre of the whole library – was an inverted conical aperture leading downwards in the floor, protected by two parallel waist-height rails. The clean surface of the downward cone was the same as the walls of the room, except where it was broken every so often by irregularly placed smoked-glass semi-spheres, roughly the size of ping-pong balls.

The Doctor stared into the depths, trying to see the point at which the bottom converged upon itself, but it was a long, long way down and he couldn't focus upon it. 'If I were someone else, Rummas,' the Doctor said quietly, trying to unclench his teeth, 'I might assume that you were some bumbling fool who had *accidentally* stolen from Gallifrey, during one of your "procurring for the Library" sojourns, one of the most devastating pieces of apparatus in the entire universe – no, sorry, multiverse. However, as one of my oldest friends, I'm placing a guess here that you in fact not only know precisely what this device is, but have used it yourself. And that you, personally, are responsible for everything that has happened here due to your own stupidity, vanity and utter disregard for the laws of time, chaos and any other number of unbreakable tenants of logic and reason instilled in us by the likes of Delox, Borusa and our others tutors at the Academy.' He slowly turned to face the professor, fixing him with a stare that would have had a cobra and a mongoose running for their lives. 'Am I right?'

Rummas couldn't hold the Doctor's gaze for more than a second, and eventually nodded wordlessly.

'Sorry,' the Doctor said. 'I didn't catch that?'

'I... You have to understand Doctor that I –'

'Understand? Understand? UNDERSTAND!' the Doctor exploded. 'You arrogant, ignorant imbecile, Rummas! All I can understand is that when you asked Mel and I for help and we started experiencing multiple time spillage, I honestly assumed that the Lampreys were behind everything. But of course, everything has to have a start point. That beautiful moment when chaos is unleashed upon creation, when something triggers that first incident. The incident that rampages throughout the chronology of existence, unstitching it and then restitching it in an unfamiliar, unique and ultimately catastrophic way. And the person who fired that trigger is you, when you used this bizarre machine.'

The Doctor didn't stop, didn't let Rummas get a word in. 'And you two Custodians, did you know about this? Were you part and parcel of this obscenity, this assault on existence? Or were you just two stupid chumps obeying without question the orders of this utter cretin stood here? Well?'

It was Woltas who answered. 'Yes, Doctor. We knew. By the time the Professor... all of us realised what was happening, it was too late.'

Huu continued. 'Because of our unique position on the cusp of the Vortex, we knew we couldn't do anything to reverse the process.'

'Well of course you couldn't. Once you'd given the Lampreys access to the linear universe, they'd just pop back to the microsecond before you did something and stop you. Every action you three have taken has not only been anticipated by the Lampreys, but actually negated before you've done it.'

'We have done nothing,' Rummas said.

'Well of course you haven't,' the Doctor yelled at him. 'The Lamprey has ensured that. For all you three know, you've tried stopping it a million times but she's stopped you a million and one.'

'That's why I needed you, Doctor,' pleaded Rummas. 'We are part of the process now. But you, you're an outsider, you are an undisciplined, unpredictable element added to the equation. And you've saved the day already.'

This threw the Doctor somewhat. 'Explain.'

'This machine,' Rummas indicated the conical pit and the computer banks nearby, 'is, as you rightly guess, a portal into the Vortex. Or in fact the Spiral at its nexus.'

'Yes, the most powerful, destructive natural force in creation,' the Doctor added, just to make the point. His anger hadn't subsided.

'Yes, yes, yes, all right! But by accessing it, we can control things, set them right. Keep the Lamprey in a prison effectively.'

The Doctor couldn't believe his ears. 'Has aeons of wandering around dark and dusty corridors rotted your brain, Rummas? You can't hold the Lampreys, control them. She/it/they are time, she/it/they are fluid, she/it/they co-exist everywhere. She's/it's/they've been jumping through time forever, living entire lives on a planet then sucking it dry.'

'Not entirely the full story, Doctor,' said Woltas.

The Doctor threw his arms up in a surrender gesture. 'Oh please enlighten me further.'

'We know she's been searching for something. A lodestone to anchor herself, or themselves, at a fixed point so they can access the multiverses simultaneously rather than in the haphazard manner they do now. By having a central base, they don't expend so much energy.'

'And?'

'And,' Woltas continued with a sigh at the interruption, 'and so they've found it. We reckon there's a splinter of the lodestone in one in five universes. So they've been kidnapping four time-sensitives from four universes, and in the fifth they find the lodestone, usually the offspring of someone who has bred with a Lamprey.'

'Helen?'

'Yes,' Rummas took up the story. 'Yes, except there's a Helen Lamprey on all those fifth realities. It's not random, it's deliberate. With one exception. The Helen on Earth Prime...'

'Was Sir Bertrand's, not Monica,' the Doctor reasoned. 'Okay, how does that help us?'

'One of two ways. Sir Bertrand's Helen is either the weak link or she's the ultimate power.'

'No, the ultimate power is Monica. She's the prime Lamprey – possibly every other Lamprey, regardless of its own individuality can be traced back to being an alternate of her in the first place.' The Doctor crossed to the computer bank. 'And so you what? Plan to draw Monica here, by using any number of Helens as bait, then trap her in the Spiral?'

'Exactly,' Mr Huu said. 'The plan was then to seal the Spiral with what you call Monica encased within it. For eternity. And we could guard it here.'

'That's why we... *borrowed* this catchment device.' Rummas was at the Doctor's shoulder now.

'And when,' the Doctor asked, 'does this great fishing trip take place?'

Rummas laughed. 'But that's the joy of it, Doctor. It doesn't have to. We followed your adventures on Earth Prime. The battle in that café...'

'Restaurant,' the Doctor snapped. 'I can't see Mr Bernard Walsh appreciating you calling his establishment a "café ". He's quite particular.'

'Anyway!' Rummas cut in. 'Anyway, we saw what happened and when Sir Bertrand cast Monica into the Vortex after their battle, we were ready.' Rummas punched a switch, and the smoked-glass semi-spheres pulsated and a low humming echoed around the whole chamber. As the Doctor watched, the walls of the inverted cone faded to be replaced by the concentric circles of the Spiral, undulating as they rotated, making him feel almost seasick.

And then tiny beams of light criss-crossed between the semi-spheres, forming the strands of a net. And etched into the net, solidifying as the net increased in density and intensity, was the Lamprey exiled from the London restaurant, lying apparently dead, hanging on the solid light strands. Rummas clapped triumphantly! 'We've won Doctor! You see, we have the lead Lamprey here already! I wanted you to see this before you left us.'

The Doctor took a deep breath and frowned. 'But if you've already caught and killed Monica, why are there still disruptions? All the me's in my TARDIS?'

Mr Huu answered that. 'A stone sinks in a pond Doctor, but the ripples don't stop, until they hit the edge of the banks, rebound and gradually smooth out. Bearing in mind that space–time is almost infinite, those ripples Monica caused will go on for a while. We estimate, in your terms, about another eight years before everything settles down. But it's not a problem – we can shunt you, Miss Bush and your TARDIS eight years into your own future in the wink of an eye and build in a non-return loop, guaranteeing you never visit those eight years again. Easy.'

The Doctor looked at Huu, at Woltas and Rummas, all smiling at their great plan having come to fruition. A multiverse saved, the Lampreys dead.

'Good work gentlemen,' he said. 'Great work even, assuming you've not made one mistake.'

Rummas threw his arm around the Doctor's shoulder and pointed victoriously toward the captured, unmoving Lamprey before them. 'We have made no mistake, Doctor. And really the destruction of the creature is all down to you.'

'Yes,' the Doctor said. 'And that's what worries me. It worried me in the restaurant and it worries me even more now.'

Mr Woltas sighed. 'You are a killjoy at times, Doctor. What mistake?'

The Doctor shrugged off Rummas's arm angrily, crossed to the Spiral and looked down at the Lamprey caught below.

The Doctor shook his head slowly. 'The mistake, gentlemen,

is that you didn't tell me of your plan. Because I was working on one of my own, a way to draw Monica out into the open. My plan worked, yours backfired.'

Rummas stomped towards him. 'Nonsense, Doctor. I'm sorry if we're stealing your thunder, but we won!'

The Doctor held the guardrail tightly, until his knuckles turned white. It took all his strength, all his will not to lash out at these three incompetent, ignorant losers.

Instead he leaned his head forward and whispered to Rummas, trying to keep his voice level and calm. Trying not to let any anger show. 'What if, gentlemen, that Lamprey you've caught, that is lying down there dead as a doornail, is not Monica? What if the Lamprey that was exorcised from Earth was Sir Bertrand, and Monica, being like all Lampreys a temporal metamorph, took on Sir Bertrand's form to fool me, Mel and oh I don't know, any moronic librarians who happened to be watching?'

Rummas would have none of it. 'That is Monica. I know it is!' But his voice quavered, betraying the fact that this was an outcome he'd not foreseen.

'No, Professor Rummas. I'm pretty sure that's Sir Bertrand. Which means Monica is still at large, and very likely back here, bumping off people at various temporal points.'

'Why do you think that, Doctor?' asked Woltas.

'Because if I had Monica's power, guile, cunning and determination to win, that's exactly what I'd have done. And because I do have her cunning, guile and determination to win but, alas, not her power, I'm fairly confident you've just murdered the one Lamprey on our side who could have helped us win.'

* * *

The word home has a few meanings for Melanie Jane Bush.

First and foremost, it's the place her family reside at. Number 36 Downview Crescent, Pease Pottage, Sussex. That's the home that says safety. That's the home that says love.

Then there's the TARDIS. That's the home that says friendship – that exemplifies why she loves being with the Doctor, seeing unique and wonderful things that so few others get the chance to. Oh yes, it's a home that invites danger into her life on a regular basis, but it also invites in satisfaction.

For every Zarbi and Proctor of Darruth escapade, there's a trip to the (literally) singing sands of Cousus VI. For every encounter with the Daleks and their attempts to erase civilisation, there's an encounter with the Pakhars and their attempts to improve civilisation.

Then there's the flat in Goldhawk Road she shared with Leonora, Julia and, in those final few months, Jake. That's where friendships were formed, growing up was achieved and virginities (of just about everyone who ever stayed for more than a week) were lost. The Shag Palace, the other students called it – a name that Mel outwardly objected to because she had her prim and proper appearance to keep up but, deep down, thought was fab. And of course once Jake arrived, well... that was something that was never spoken of back in Downview Crescent.

Then there was the one she lived at during her primary school years, a few miles east of Pease Pottage. Number 14 The Lawns, Ardingly, the big house where old people came at Christmas for carol services, at Easter for more songs and in late June for Harvest Festival, when the house was always left full of tins of sweetcorn, evaporated milk and rhubarb that no one ever truly wanted.

Home, all four of them, was truly where the heart is.

Mel had always been told that she'd been born at The Lawns (well, okay, in Hove Hospital, but that was hair-splitting) – it being the house that Mum and Dad had bought after moving down from the North-east because Dad got that finance job. And she had always believed that, after all, the first photos she had of herself were stood next to the old green Austen parked in the drive, when she was about four.

Four?

Four? How many parents don't have photos of their kids before they were four?

Four?

No, wait, she remembered having her third birthday, playing at the top of the stairs with her Etch-a-Sketch. Of course, along with that Spirograph, Mel could never actually draw anything, but she loved making squiggles and bizarre shapes that, in her mind at least, were dogs and cats. And the joy was that she could pick up the Etch-a-Sketch and shake it. She lost the pictures she drew but was fascinated by the sound it made as the tiny fragments of graphite rattled around inside.

And then there were the Letraset Action Transfers, and Major Matt Mason and… no. No, those were later.

Not when she was three.

So why no photos of that third birthday?

Or the second? Or first? Or pictures of her in baby clothes in the hospital.

Let's face it, unlike most students coming down from university to start life, Alan and Christine Bush were hardly poor. The fact was, they'd both been older than their contemporaries and both had stinking rich parents. Although they made sure they stood on their own two feet, if they'd ever needed it (and Mum was always so proud that they never did), money was available.

So, what, they couldn't afford a camera? Yeah, right...

Mel could still see herself at the top of that staircase, shaking the Etch-a-Sketch and...

Hang on, those aren't the stairs at The Lawns? The Etch-a-Sketch memories go hand in hand with brown carpeted stairs, with gaps between them.

Now she's seeing thinner steps, steeper. Blue, slightly threadbare carpet, solid with a wall on either side and a white bannister up the left side.

And there's a noise associated with these steps, despite the fact that she's never seen them before.

Except she obviously has, because this is a memory. And that's her, sat at the top in a white jumper thing, with no booties on.

But she's not three.

There's no Etch-a-Sketch anywhere in sight.

She's younger and she's staring at the bottom of the stairs, where they curve slightly into the hall. She can see the front door. White wood with red outlines on the panelling. But only on one side for some reason.

Kooky Art Deco? Hardly her memories of her parents' choice of art. No, look closer, that's not actually outlining the panelling, it's just splashed against the corner. And the bottom step's been painted red too. Clashes with the blue carpeting.

Why are mum and dad there suddenly, yelling at each other? And looking up at little Melanie Jane Bush, aged eighteen months (give or take a few weeks).

No, not yelling at each other, yelling at her? Yelling at Mel? Seems unlikely, Mum was one of those weird semi-hippie parents that didn't believe in aggressive parenting. Mel couldn't remember ever having been slapped, smacked or even yelled at. But she was being yelled at now, in a memory she's never had before, at the top of stairs in a house she's never seen till now.

So why does she suddenly know that the address of the house she's in is number 8, Gosling Street, Croxdale?

A house she's never been to in a County Durham town she's never been to.

Dad's with her now, carrying her away from the landing. He's shaking her. No, no he's not, he's just shaking. And Mel's crying because... because Dad's crying? Dads don't cry! Mums cry sometimes but for a dad to cry, something really awful must have happened. But what?

Mel tries to bring it back, someone warm and comforting speaking behind her, moving towards her. The feeling of something touching her little eighteen-month-old left leg. A blur as something goes by her head really fast and yet curiously slow.

A noise like a biscuit breaking.

Quick. Sudden. Then silence, then the screaming starts.

Oh my god.

Anabel.

They say that most babies can't remember much before their second birthdays, often their third.

Unless it's some kind of trauma that's been buried, never referred to again.

Anabel.

Just as the computer in the Reading Room had said. Melanie Jane Bush, born 1964, a sister for eighteen-month-old Anabel Claire Bush. Sister. Eighteen months later, three-year-old Anabel Claire Bush lay broken at the bottom of the stairs of 8 Gosling Street, Croxdale. Broken like a biscuit.

Killed by Melanie Jane Bush.

The same Melanie Jane Bush aged twenty-six(ish) whose

suppressed memories have just come flooding back, alongside a torrent of tears, anger, frustration and shock.

No one had told her.

No one had taken her to the grave (presumably in Durham somewhere).

No one had explained she'd had a sister once, but an accident at the top of some stairs had robbed her of this.

No one had ever said, 'No, you're not an only child, there was another.'

And all Mel wanted to do now was to be at home in Pease Pottage with her parents and ask them 'Why have I been denied this important part of my... our lives? Why?'

And instead, some vicious cow of a trans-temporal alien, hellbent on eating the multiverse, is laughing at Mel's distress, deliberately tormenting her out of sheer sadistic amusement.

So Mel stopped her tears. Mel stopped the heavy, painful breaths that punctuated her sobs. She took a deep breath and thought that if Anabel's death had been erased, compartmentalised, filed away for 26 years, then it could be once again.

And so Mel opened her eyes, letting them dry and focus on the Reading Room as it resolved around her.

She turned to face Monica, who'd now let Joseph Tungard go. He was sat on the floor, holding his neck. Mel just caught in her peripheral vision vast red welts on his skin where Monica had gripped him too tightly.

'So Miss Bush,' sneered Monica, 'how does the truth grab you?'

Mel smiled tightly.

'Screw you. Bitch.'

And she smashed Monica straight in the face with all the power that her pent up anguish, frustration and fury possessed.

Chapter Thirteen
A Different Kind of Tension

How long had they been stuck here? How long had they been drip-feeding their life energies into the unconscious girl suspended in the middle sarcophagus?

'How long?' DiVotow screamed into the blackness.

He was surprised to receive an answer.

'Not much longer,' hissed a voice in his ear. There was no one there, no room for anyone to be in his little prison capsule thing, but the voice was there all the same. 'I promise you freedom soon.' If he took any comfort from that phrase, it was dashed by the mocking laugh that followed.

DiVotow lifted his head and then slammed it back against the rear of his prison as hard as he could. It hurt. So he did it again. And again.

Then he stopped to catch his breath, and looked to his left. He could see Kevin staring back at him, frowning. Then he seemed to wink at DiVotow and started doing the same head banging.

DiVotow started again.

'What are you boys doing?' That was Haema's voice.

'Fighting back,' DiVotow yelled.

* * *

The Reading Room was in tatters, the cyclone that had erupted at the centre of the room was ripping books from shelves, then the shelves from the wall.

The computer was already a million fragments in the wind, and Joseph Tungard had hidden behind a heavy leather armchair that had yet to be scooped up in the maelstrom.

Of poor Miss Bush, he could see nothing. One minute she'd been talking to Monica, then it was as if she'd gone to sleep, but only for a second or two. Then she'd awoken, angry at Monica and so had thumped her.

If she'd been expecting Monica to drop, she was sorely disappointed, and instead, Monica had dropped any pretence at humanity and once again become the screeching creature she'd been back at the restaurant in London.

The restaurant. Natjya. He wanted to be back with his wife.

Damn you, Monica. Damn you for disrupting our lives.

Tungard desperately searched the wreckage for any sign of Miss Bush, but it was as if she'd ceased to exist the moment Monica transformed.

Monica was searching for him, that he knew. He'd spent enough time with her, embracing her, wrapping his body around and into hers that he believed he knew her quite well. Of course, he'd had no idea she was an alien time-destructor, hellbent on universal domination, but apart from that side of her personality, he knew her. He could certainly predict her moods.

The question was, did she still need him? Was he important or did she have the knowledge she wanted from him? Was he to be consigned to hell and damnation like poor Miss Bush? Or was he still useful?

He thought back to those misty, almost dreamlike states where he'd been in this place before. He'd put them down to nightmares, rich English food. But of course they'd not been dreams at all. Oh my God, no they weren't were they? They were real. She'd brought him here to kill a man. A man with many twins, or... of course, he was getting a grasp of what the Doctor had talked about in his wonderful contraption earlier. It was the same man, but in different time zones, different realities. Different decisions.

Did that mean that somewhere, in another reality not on 'Earth Prime' as the computer referred to it, there was a Joseph and Natjya Tungard living happily in London, him with his students, her not sick, not bitter, but doing what she wanted. Or another reality where they never left Romania. Where the communists never came. Where Emile and Hilde Schultz lived in safety with their two beautiful boys who could grow up into a safe, free world?

And Joseph Tungard knew that he would never discover the answer to those questions because he was fated to die here, in this strange room of books and computers and screaming aliens.

Because that was his punishment for aiding the embodiment of the most destructive force ever born.

The armchair in front of him was tossed aside, as if made of paper.

He wasn't even aware of where it ended up, just the gaping maw bearing down on him, eyeless, featureless, with those tendrils throbbing in the wind. But he knew that somehow it was staring at him.

'Hello my love,' said Monica's voice from somewhere deep within. 'Don't worry, I still need you and your fascinating mind.'

And Joseph closed his eyes, not wanting to know what was going to happen next.

What actually happened was that Monica Lamprey, in her

alien form, was interrupted by the opposite door being flung open.

She/it looked up and absorbed the information.

Framed in the doorway, huge multicoloured coat billowing out like a mainsail caught in a tempest, giving him the look of a demented (well, all right, *more* demented) Captain Ahab, was the blasted Doctor. And with him, Rummas and those foppish associates of his.

'Where are my friends?' the Doctor yelled at her.

'Haven't a clue,' Monica lied. 'You want them, Doctor, you find them.'

And Monica vanished into thin air.

Thus a hundred things, some large, some just tattered fragments, dropped to the floor instantly.

After a beat, Joseph crawled out from his corner. 'Doctor?' he tried to shout, but it only came out as a hoarse, terrified whisper. 'Doctor?'

'Tungard?' The Doctor was beside him in an instant. 'We heard the commotion and came back. Where's Mel?'

Tungard shrugged. 'I'm sorry. She gave Monica a great big wallop and then all hell broke loose.'

'Literally,' said the Doctor grimly. 'So, Rummas, I rather think that makes my point. You don't have Monica in your trap, you have the one person sent to keep her in check. Well done, Professor. Is there no end to your talent for getting things wrong?'

Rummas was silent but Tungard noticed he was too ashamed to look at anything. The other two men with Rummas were already stood amid the chaos, sifting through, trying to find books in one piece.

'The greatest library in history,' one said angrily. 'And she destroyed it without hesitation.'

The Doctor was beside him in an instant, angrily smacking to the ground the few books he was carrying. 'You don't get it, do you, Huu? None of you understand it. This library is irrelevant. You, me, every living thing in the cosmos is now irrelevant because you, Professor Rummas, are so vainglorious and self-obsessed that you couldn't see beyond your own reputation. A reputation I might add that's now in as many tatters as this first edition of whatever this is.' He kicked at what seemed to be a hand-written edition of something, pages floating up and then back to the floor. 'Oh such delicious irony,' the Doctor then said, and trod on the book as he stormed out. 'Professor Tungard,' he called. 'If you'd be kind enough to join me?'

And Joseph Tungard scrambled up and headed out after him, stopping only to see that the book the Doctor had referred to was Jane Austen's *Pride and Prejudice*. Hand-written. Worth a small fortune.

Once.

But not now.

Probably not ever again. Because if Monica Lamprey had her way, such things would never exist, or have existed.

Melanie was somewhere else.

She half wondered if she was dead – punching your foe on the nose was never a good idea. A foe that can rewrite history with a thought was pretty much the last person you punched on the nose.

And then something occurred to her. If Monica Lamprey was really that powerful, why did she need Joe Tungard? After all, she could flit back in and out of time, creating duplicates of herself to kidnap Helen Lamprey and no doubt do the same on other planets in other universes, so why did she need to take Joe Tungard to Carsus to stab Rummas with a knitting needle?

She could see that Tungard had something to offer in the chemistry stakes – some new elements that gave her access to something or other (she wasn't sure if the Doctor had explained that properly but as her eidetic memory wasn't bringing anything up, she guessed not). So why was he committing the murders? Why was Monica scared to get her own hands dirty?

'Because,' she said out loud suddenly, 'anything she does herself becomes part and parcel of time and whilst she can rewrite everyone else's timelines, rewriting her own could result in destroying herself!'

'That's a possibility,' said the Doctor. 'Wonder why I didn't think of that.'

'Yeah, before we hiked halfway around the planet Janus 8,' said another familiar voice. 'And who are you?'

Mel stared at herself. Or something that she knew was her, yet was clearly different. And the Doctor – it was the scarred one she'd seen in the TARDIS.

'My name is Mel. Melanie Bush. Hi.'

'Hello Melanie Bush,' said the Doctor, smiling, his one eye twinkling. 'I like the name Mel. I wonder which Earth you're from?'

Mel was going to say 'Earth Prime' but somehow that sounded like bragging. After all, wouldn't everyone assume theirs was the 'prime' Earth anyway?

'Oh, quite a nice one,' was the best she could come up with.

'Mine stinks,' said her duplicate, scratching her closely cropped scalp. 'I'm Melina. Or Technician 38.'

'I prefer Melina,' said the Doctor. 'Come on, the TARDIS is this way.'

'Where are we?' Mel asked, looking around, trying to get some bearings.

'Janus 8,' said Melina grumpily as if that answered everything. When it clearly didn't, she added: 'Some bumwipe of a planet out of the Empire's reach, thank Jupiter.'

The Doctor sighed. 'I've told you Melina, we may not even be in your universe, so it's no wonder the Empire isn't here. Besides, it'll be a long time before one of your Caesars gets you past the barrier of intergalactic travel. Too consumed...'

'... with dominating everyone on Earth. Yeah, yeah,' Melina said, then whispered to Mel. 'Heard it all before. Only met him a few days back and he's bored the life out of me. Still, if it gets me credits back home with the Praetor, it'll be worth it.'

'I selected you for this mission, dear girl, because I knew, somehow – or though for the life of me I've yet to see any evidence to support this – that you were... destined not to stay on Earth.' The Doctor pointed at Mel. 'And the presence here of your duplicate rather confirms that.' He smiled at Mel, which reassured her that despite his facial blemishes, this was still the Doctor, albeit one with better fashion sense. 'I assume you travel with some temporal alternative version of yours truly?'

Mel said she did.

'And is he as sophisticated, elegant and remarkable as I?'

'Or is he just as big a blowfish, with an over-inflated sense of self-importance, forever going on about how being a Time Lord is the coolest thing ever?' Melina asked, rather unkindly. Mel sensed that there was little warmth between these two, despite the Doctor's attempts.

It made her feel homesick for her own Doctor.

'Ignore her, sweet Mel,' the Doctor said. 'I freed her from bondage but alas she has no frame of reference by which she may judge her new-found freedom. By eliminating drudgery and poverty from her life, I've taken her from all that is familiar and safe, no matter how desperate. She's yet to acclimatise.'

Melina shrugged. 'Too right, Doc.'

Mel decided she liked this Doctor but wasn't keen on Melina. There by the grace of God go I, she told herself.

'So Melanie Bush,' the Doctor smiled at her. 'How did you end up here. With us? Did Rummas send you to check up on us?'

'No. Not at all. We were on Carsus, we'd trapped Monica, or so we thought. Turned out she'd tricked us and I, um, well, I hit her.'

'Hit her?' laughed Melina. 'I'm beginning to like you, girlie.'

'I'm not proud of it actually,' Mel said.

'Indeed,' agreed the Doctor, 'violence is never the answer.'

'Anyway, I think she zapped me here in anger. And you two?'

Melina laughed. 'Oh, Rummas gave us a task, asked us to find a party girl called Helen. We failed. Couldn't find her at all. Then something happened to the sky, as if something was up there...'

'Trying to break through but couldn't. No idea what, so we decided to go back to Carsus,' the Doctor completed.

'The Lamprey,' Mel said. 'That's the creature this Monica I hit became. I think. It's very complicated.'

The Doctor said he knew how she felt but once they were back in the Library, everything would be made clearer by Rummas.

'I wouldn't guarantee that,' Mel said.

'By Jupiter, we agree on something at last,' Melina said. 'See, Doc, told you he was a couple of sesterces short of a denarius.'

The Doctor was unlocking the TARDIS door, and then cursed. 'It's always getting stuck,' he said and slammed his shoulder against the door, so it finally opened. Taking some deep breaths after the exertion, he motioned for them to go in.

Mel found herself in a bizarre variation of her more familiar TARDIS, this one all wooden and stained glass, with parquet flooring and sculptures and artworks littering the walls. 'This is beautiful, Doctor,' she said. 'Our TARDIS is nothing like this.'

'Ah yes, of course,' the Doctor nodded. 'That would make sense. Especially if the Roman Empire didn't have a grip on your version of Earth, but does your Doctor share my penchant for all things Earthly?'

'I'm sure he does,' Mel agreed. 'But this is fantastic. Though I don't understand how the Roman Empire never fell?'

'Lucky you,' said Melina. 'Some of us will have to get used to it. Again.'

The Doctor closed the doors and looked at both versions of the same girl. 'Infinite combinations, infinite alternatives,' he said quietly.

He pressed some switches on his wooden version of the TARDIS console and they dematerialised.

'Where now, Doc?' asked Melina.

'Back to Carsus?' asked Mel.

The Doctor held up a hand to quieten them both. 'Listen, carefully, this is very important. You need to know this.' That last bit seemed to be directed at Melina rather than both of them.

'I can see where this is going,' Melina sighed. 'A lecture and no doubt it's all to do with your "friend" the Lamprey. Thanks for nothing.' She smiled at the Doctor. 'Hey Doc, couldn't you just take me home again?'

Mel had had enough. 'Look, why are you so pissy all the time, Melina?'

'You what?'

'Well, I mean the Doctor has rescued you from being a slave as far as I can see. Why so keen to go back, and why are you always so grouchy?'

Melina pulled Mel to one side, so as to stop the Doctor overhearing their conversation. 'Listen, I don't know what life was like for you on your world, but on mine, I take orders. I don't ask questions, I don't think for myself, not because I can't, but because I mustn't.' She sighed. 'The Empire is all-knowing, all-seeing. My parents, my sister, we are a family unit. If one drops for any reason, the others suffer. There's no replacement for the lost earnings, no state supplement like there is for the Praetorian Guard or the Senators. So while you might think it's great that your Doctor took you away from whatever drudgery you endured, by whisking me away, he's potentially crippling my family.'

Mel stared at Melina, and then, for reasons she couldn't explain to herself, gave her sidestepped duplicate a huge sisterly hug.

'You have a sister?' she said. 'Anabel?'

'Yes. Don't you?'

'No. No, not any more.' She leaned back, to look Melina straight in the face. 'So there's always a pay-off somewhere.'

After a few more seconds, Melina disentangled herself and walked out of the control room.

Mel felt a hand on her shoulder. It was the Doctor. She looked straight into his damaged face and realised she could see beyond that. To the inner beauty behind it. This, too, was a different Doctor. Calmer, gentler, less explosive and... emotional than hers. Much as she loved the Doctor to death, this version suggested a slightly less acerbic and confrontational man.

How long before that got boring, she thought. I'm better off with mine.

She touched his face. 'May I ask?'

He smiled, and it reached his single blue eye that gazed at her. 'I had a friend, a warrior queen from the New World. A part of Earth that...'

'America we call it,' Mel said.

He nodded. 'Of course. She was Brown Perpugilliam. Peri. She was strong, forthright and brave. She... she died despite my attempts to save her from a barbarian king, Yikkar, who decided she was his property.' He sighed and went silent, then looked at the ceiling, refusing to catch Mel's eye. 'I told lies about her afterwards, you see. Gave a more heroic account of the battle, made my injuries seem more like a war wound gained battling an old enemy. But the truth is Yikkar tortured me with a red hot sword before letting me go. I could have regenerated, but that would have been...'

'Vanity?'

He nodded. 'And Peri deserved better than me changing myself just to forget her.' He then stared towards the door through which Melina had disappeared. 'I think I made the wrong choice there. She resents me, all this. But somehow, I was drawn to her...'

'It's fate, I guess,' Mel said. 'Every Doctor has to have a Mel.' She took his hand. 'Mine had a Peri from America, too. I'm not sure what happened to her, I'm not sure he is either. It strikes me that no matter what universe we're from, some things take the same path, it's just the scenery that differs.'

He laughed. 'I couldn't have put it better myself. He's lucky, your Doctor. To have you.'

* * *

Joseph Tungard decided that if he ever got home, he would let himself go mad. After all, it had to be a better option than all this. It was bad enough he was on an alien world (and how easily he accepted that absurdity), a world that was the inter-section for a million, million (and maybe another million) different versions of the same universe. But right now, he was seeing something even he hadn't contemplated before.

Two identical Doctors.

Both in that ridiculous multicoloured coat, both trying to speak louder and more angrily than each other. Both standing near their police box flying machines.

And the new one who had been waiting for them in something the Doctor he knew had referred to as the Spiral Chamber.

Once they'd both yelled about how dangerous Professor Rummas was, and how stupid, daft, ridiculous, untrustworthy and irresponsible (the only thing they'd agreed on so far was their new-found dislike of Rummas), they moved out of the big bright room and back into a corridor where the police boxes were 'parked'.

This new Doctor had two companions, a tiny girl of about four, and a girl who was a similar height to Miss Bush, but of reptilian descent.

Reptilian descent! Add that to parallel worlds, time ships and Lampreys.

The green girl was carrying the tiny, more human-looking one, who was sleeping. 'You any good with children?' she asked him in perfect English.

So perfect it reminded him of –

'Mel, isn't it?' he said, taking a gamble.

'Yes,' she smiled broadly. 'Have we met?'

'No, I know another Miss Melanie Bush.'

'Oh,' said the green Melanie. 'I'm not Miss Bush. I'm Miss Baal.'

'Hello, I'm Joseph Tungard. All this is my fault. I think.'

'It most certainly isn't,' snapped the Doctor (but Joseph had no idea which one). 'You are an unwitting pawn, Professor Tungard. Don't, for even a split second, believe this is in any way your fault.'

'But I worked with Monica. I dreamed about... well, killing Professor Rummas. At least, I thought they were dreams.'

'About that,' said the other Doctor. 'Why? I mean, he's an idiot, but he's our idiot.' There was a beat. 'He is a Time Lord in your universe, yes?'

'Oh yes,' said the Doctor who had assured Tungard of his non-complicity. Tungard realised that was 'his' Doctor then.

Suddenly there was the most godawful racket and another police box popped into existence beside the other two.

So that was what it looked like when the TARDIS he'd come in had materialised. Interesting.

The door opened and Miss Bush appeared.

'Doctor?'

'Mel? My Mel?'

'I think so.'

The Doctor hugged her. 'I hope so. I'd hate to end up with the wrong one. I rather like mine.' He winked at Melanie Baal. 'No disrespect.'

She shrugged, and shifted the weight as she moved the girl in her arms. Tungard realised he'd never answered her question and offered to take the child from her.

From behind Mel, another Doctor wandered out of the police box. This one was very different. Dark clothes, a scar on his face. And a new Mel, Tungard was sure of that. He could see the pattern forming now.

A door opened onto the corridor and Professor Rummas emerged. 'I've left the Custodians trying to clear up the mess Monica Lamprey made and I –' He stopped as he took in three Doctors, three Mels, and Tungard holding the child.

The Doctor, the real Doctor, poked Rummas in the chest. 'Well, now you've three of us here. How many more should we expect?'

'I don't know what you –'

The scarred one joined in. 'What my counterpart means, Professor, is how many other Doctors and Mels have you sent to save a Helen?'

Rummas sighed. 'Three hundred and eighteen, so far. That I know of. Of course my own personal future is closed to me, so I can't –'

'That's it!' a Doctor exclaimed, but Tungard didn't note which one.

'What is?' said the miserable-looking Mel with little hair.

'Of course!' That was the real Doctor. 'He's a Time Lord, bursting with chronon energy.'

'Yes I can see that,' said the identical one, 'but what does that mean?'

'Don't you see?' asked scarred-face. 'That's what Monica Lamprey fears.'

'Yes,' said Mel Bush. 'She does. Before she sent me off to Janus 8, she said she hoped that the professor was finally dead.'

'Janus 8? What were you doing there?' asked Melanie Baal.

'Long story. Actually, no it's not,' Mel Bush corrected herself. 'I actually don't know.'

One of the Doctors (oh this was getting complicated now) said he did. 'By shunting you into a universe not your own, she created a hole into it.'

'But why?' That was the cropped one.

'Because Melina,' said scarred-face, 'she expected to find a Helen on Janus 8, but there wasn't one.'

'So she had no access.'

'So she used Mel to create an access port.'

'But it was irrelevant. Presumably she'd wormed back through time, found no trace of a Helen and given up.'

'Information exchange?'

'Oh yes, right away.'

All three versions of the Doctor touched their foreheads, repeated the word 'contact' and, after a few seconds, relaxed.

'All up to speed?'

'Very much so.'

'Indeed.'

Rummas clapped his hands then. 'Enough Doctor. Doctors. Mels.' Tungard watched the professor carefully as he looked first at the scar-faced Doctor and, what was her name? Melina? 'There ought to have been a Helen on Janus 8,' he was saying. 'That's why I sent you there.'

The real Doctor nodded. 'But there wasn't. Her scheme is, one hopes, weakened by this.'

'By one girl?' asked Melina.

'One's enough,' said the other Doctor. 'Somewhere she has a... a place. A subspace area inaccessible via normal time. There she must be using the powers inherent in this in-bred Helen girl to draw the multiverse in, destroy each universe and feed off the resultant chaos energy.'

Melanie Baal shrugged. 'One question, why?'

'Greed, Mel,' said her Doctor. 'Pure and simple.'

'And why, if she's after Helens, did she want a Kina?' Melanie Baal pointed at the girl Tungard was rocking back and forth.

'Helen's the centre-point, through which she'll run the energy. But to actually create access portals to drain energy, she'd need normal time-sensitives.'

'Like Kina? Ah.'

'Ah indeed. Somewhere in this subspace chamber, as the other me just called it, there may be tens, dozens, even hundreds of innocents. Time-sensitives forced to drain their own life energies into Helen, to create the portals.'

'That's evil,' Tungard said.

'And you helped her,' said Melina. 'Apparently.'

'Be nice, Melina,' said scarred-face. 'Professor Tungard's role was far more important than we realised.'

'My chemicals you mean?'

The real Doctor nodded. 'To some extent, yes. But she was... um, involved with you, yes?'

'You mean, they were having an affair?' asked Melanie Baal.

Tungard found himself nodding. 'I was completely in love. I was a... a fool.'

The Doctor wandered over to him and put a hand on each shoulder. 'Not a fool, Joseph. Love is a wonderful, exhilarating emotion and although it can often make us do foolish things, one should never feel foolish for having those feelings.'

Mel Bush joined her Doctor. 'Okay, but why did Monica do it? Use him I mean?'

The Doctor looked at his fellow selves. 'Agreed?'

They nodded.

'Professor Rummas is a Time Lord, like me. Us. He exists on Carsus and as a result can coexist in multiple timelines in the same place. By going through and systematically killing his different selves, the amount of chronon energy present in the Library drops. When it reaches a certain point, it's safe for the

Lamprey to actually exist here, and unchallenged – which with no Rummas and no chronon energies, unchallenged it would be – it can use this place, having used Helen to rip open the time portals, to drain the universe into the one place capable of storing all that chaos energy. Providing a storehouse that she can feast on for ever. And when stocks dip, she nips back in time somewhere, changes a few things and thus creates another ten dozen divergent timelines, then rips them open and eats the energies from them.'

Rummas spoke suddenly. 'No, you've got it wrong Doctor. I can stop it with the Spiral Chamber! You saw what it did to the other one, your Bertrand Lamprey. It died. Monica can be killed the same way.'

The Doctor was clearly aghast at what he saw as Rummas's, well, stupidity, but for the life of him, Tungard could only agree with his fellow scientist. If Sir Bertrand Lamprey was dead in whatever this 'Spiral Chamber' was, then surely Monica could be treated the same way.

The Doctor spoke very slowly. Clearly. As if dealing with a very stupid child. 'You stole the Chamber because Monica wanted you to. She's been playing you since Day One. You think you've tricked her but she's outside linear time and no matter how much you can observe outside normal time, you, personally cannot really see outside your own time. It's the powers of the Carsus Library that enabled you to see those ghost images of your murdered other selves, but you couldn't interact with them could you?'

'Well, no...'

'You couldn't divine the exact death dates because you are still living your life. She saw you build it and, in all likelihood, has found ways to influence its construction. That's why Sir Bertrand ended up there, she sent him into it. Knowing it will kill the one Lamprey not spawned by her. The last survivor of the original race that wasn't a temporal image of herself! You've not set a trap, you've been trapped, and by giving Monica access to the Spiral, here, on Carsus, you've multiplied her power by, oh, an infinitesimal and exponential rate. Well done, Rummas. You've given her the universe and she's made sure the *only* thing that could stop her, your accumulated other selves' chronon energy, can't stop her.'

The scarred Doctor walked up behind the first. 'You've handed her creation on a plate and there's nothing anyone can do to stop it.'

The real Doctor took a deep breath and turned away from Rummas to face his other selves. 'Oh yes there is. Chronon energy, remember. Overfeed her and she'll cease to exist forever. We just need to give her some.'

After a second, they both nodded. 'We'd need help.'

'Well,' said the real Doctor. 'We're at the centre of temporal reality here. It's not going to be difficult to get it, is it?'

What happened next was a bewildering blur as far as Mel was concerned. Right now, the Doctors and Rummas huddled all huggermugger, shouting, whispering, scheming and arguing again. Rummas seemed to be the butt of many snide comments but Mel couldn't feel too sorry for him.

Besides she and her new friends had been given a new task. Rescue Helen and the time-sensitives. The Doctors had explained that the chemicals Professor Tungard had discovered were what enabled Monica to create her little pocket reality outside of normal time. The combination of those new elements created a breach in normal space, apparently.

As they would, Mel joked, but the Doctor hadn't laughed. 'Just accept this Mel,' he'd said dangerously. 'Tungard has found a new method of exploring subspace, hundreds of years before anyone should. That's what Monica has exploited. That's why she kept him alive and why we need him.'

'So if she can access all of time and space, why can't she see what's going on here. Right now, I mean? And stop it.'

The Doctor was grim. 'Well, for a start, the sheer amount of temporal energies flitting around Carsus effectively blindsides her. Like looking for a particular snowflake on a field covered in snow. So, she can get the general area, but specifics become less... discernible.' He beamed, and Mel felt relieved. Until he added: 'At least, I hope that's the case, because if she can spot individual snowflakes, we are in something of a pretty pickle.'

And so the plan, it turned out, was that Woltas would show them to a science area of the Library, and Joe would be able to mix his concoction again, open the gateway to subspace, and a Doctor or two would nip in and rescue as many people as possible.

'"As many..." What does that mean?' Mel's reptilian duplicate had asked, aghast. 'Surely we get everyone out.'

It had been her Doctor who answered that. 'It may not be possible. We have to weaken Monica and whilst it'd be nice to save everyone, there may be millions. Which wouldn't be possible in the time we've got.'

'I thought that time wasn't a problem on Carsus?' Melina had snapped.

'Subspace isn't Carsus,' her Doctor said. 'Time moves there in a linear fashion, as it does for us, so every second counts.'

Mel's Doctor had assured her they'd make every effort.

It was the scarred one who was asked to stay behind with Tungard to operate the chemical gateway.

'Sounds like magic to me,' Mel said.

'Exactly what chemistry is,' said Melanie Baal's Doctor. 'Add chemical one to chemical two and it changes state. Professor Tungard has found a way to alter different states in different ways, that's all.'

The Doctor told Tungard to call them when he was ready and wandered back to the Spiral Chamber.

Some hours had passed now and Tungard finally said he was ready.

Mel looked at her two new friends. Well, associates. 'Are we all thinking the same thing?'

'Yup,' said Melanie Baal.

Melina shook her head. 'Oh I'm thinking it, but it's madness.'

Mel took her arm gently. 'Melina, they need every minute here.'

Melina grimaced. 'Go on, before I change my mind.'

Tungard finally twigged what they were talking about. He turned to little Kina. 'Kina, can you find the Doctors please? Now!'

The little girl nodded and scampered out of the room.

'I won't help you,' he said.

Mel shrugged. 'Seems to me that if I pour this, onto this and then...'

'No! No, Mel, don't!'

'...add a bit of this...'

There was a flash and as the smoke cleared, it formed a smoky arch.

And beyond the arch was a dark somewhere.

'Cool,' said Melina.

Tungard was distraught. 'I won't let you go through.'

'Just keep it open for us, Prof,' said Melanie Baal and walked through. Melina followed.

Mel watched them go then turned back to Tungard. 'We all

have to do our bit. You've done yours.' She pointed to the smoke archway. 'Just keep the reaction going for us.'

For a moment Tungard locked eyes with her, and she kept his gaze, daring him to back down.

Much as she liked him, she knew ultimately he was weak, especially where women were concerned.

She was right. His eyes dropped. 'Go on. And good luck. I'll be here for you.'

And with a silently mouthed 'thank you, Joe', Mel followed her duplicates.

With a sigh, Joseph Tungard watched them go through. Just as he had so many times when Monica had done this in his dreams... no, not dreams. He knew that now. She'd manipulated him. Coerced him. And he'd been weak and let her.

But never again.

'You're so right my love,' said Monica, suddenly beside him. 'Never again.'

And Joseph realised she was kissing him.

He tried to pull away, to call out, but she held him tight in an embrace, his lips pressed against hers.

And he felt his legs go, started to slip downwards.

What was happening to him?

Suddenly he was free of Monica. Free of her and floating backwards.

'Darling?'

He turned to see Natjya. Natjya dressed in her wedding dress, young, beautiful. Walking.

'Natjya, you look... beautiful...'

Natjya and Joseph Tungard on their wedding day.

'I love you.'

The happiest day of his life.
'I love you too.'
Happy...

Chapter Fourteen
Thunder of Hearts

How long had they been walking?

'Well, this is fun,' said Melina, lying.

Melanie Baal shrugged. 'Who cares. We've a job to do. So long as Tungard doesn't let us down, we'll be fine.'

'Yeah, and my whole life has probably been waiting for this moment.. To walk though an impossibility into an absurdity.' Melina stopped and looked around. 'And to top it all, we're lost.'

'How can we be lost?' asked Mel. 'We don't know where we're supposed to be.'

'Oh great,' said Melanie. 'This was your idea.'

'I thought it was yours, greenie,' said Melina.

'That's enough,' Mel shouted. 'Bickering won't get us anywhere.'

There was silence as they stared at each other. After a few moments, Melina laughed. 'You know, I reckon we all thought the same thing then. I mean, how couldn't we?'

'I doubt it,' Melanie said.

But Mel nodded. 'Melina's probably right. Oh we thought it in different ways, depending on the way we've grown up, but at heart, we're the same person, coming to the same conclusions but by different routes.'

'I'm not that pompous,' Melanie said.

'I'm not that gobby,' Melina added.

Mel laughed. 'We're all the same.'

'Yeah, 'cept our backgrounds are different.' Melina snorted. 'I mean, my family are slaves, her family are... scaly and your family are poseurs.'

'You're all charm,' Mel sniped.

'Wonder where I get that from,' Melina responded, and it took Melanie Baal to stop them going further.

'Enough,' she shouted. 'If we can't play nice, let's not play at all. Let's turn around, go back to Carsus and let our Doctors do this.'

'No!' the other two said in unison, then laughed.

'Accord at last!'

Mel waited a beat as Melina stomped ahead, then tapped Melanie on the shoulder. 'Good move.'

'It's just my cold-blooded nature,' she said, but without any hint of humour.

'Was it difficult?'

'What, being a pick-n-mix baby? Yeah, school wasn't a picnic, and uni was worse, but Mum and Dad were good and ensured I was okay. And it's not like I was the only one.' They began walking after Melina.

'Your sister?'

'Nah, Annie's pure. Mum married Baal after her first husband died.'

Mel stopped cold. That hadn't occurred to her. 'Al... Alan Bush died?'

Melanie nodded. 'An accident at home, I think. Mum doesn't talk about it much and Annie doesn't remember him at all. So my dad's her dad really.'

'Annie. Short for Anabel, yes?'

'Yeah. Got a photo of her in the TARDIS. Reminds me of home. Called Anabel in your reality?'

'Was. I never knew her. Died in an accident at... at home.'

'Freaky. Annie always reckons the reason it's never talked about is because she was involved in some way. Poor kid, I'm always saying that even if that was so, Mum doesn't seem to hold it against her.'

Mel smiled sadly. 'I can imagine how she feels though.'

'Can you?'

'Yeah. A little. Come on, let's catch up with –'

Mel was stopped by a cry from ahead. It was Melina.

The two girls ran at full pelt in the direction Melina had taken, but obviously got separated because both found themselves entering a circular chamber through opposite entrances.

'Freaky,' said all three Melanies together.

Above them were four sarcophagus-shaped constructs, floating in mid-air, connected to a central star-shaped fifth, via transparent tubing.

All five were rotating in unison, however, and so every so often but always simultaneously Mel could see the occupants.

One, smaller than the others, seemed empty; one contained a teenaged boy; another an older man and the third, a girl. The star-shaped one held a recognisable figure.

'Helen Lamprey,' said Mel and Melanie together.

'So that's her,' Melina responded. 'All this, just for her?'

Melanie pointed to the empty one, small enough for a child, perhaps? 'Kina?'

Mel nodded. 'Can we get to them?'

'Shoulders?' Melanie and Melina said together, then Melina added, 'We have so got to stop doing that!'

Melanie climbed onto Melina's shoulders, and Mel began scaling both of them, amidst 'ouches' and 'hey, where's that foot going?' but it was pointless. Even at full stretch, Mel was still a good arm's reach too low.

Meanwhile the constructs kept rotating.

'By Jupiter!' Melina suddenly squealed. 'Hold tight, girls!'

Instinctively, the other two Melanies did as bidden. Mel looked down and saw that Melina was being lifted onto someone else's shoulders. A boy.

'Hi,' he said quietly. 'I'm Marlern Jarl. Hopefully you can get Haema down, yeah?'

Mel shrugged. 'Maybe now.'

She reached up to the nearest sarcophagus and her fingers found no way to access the interior. 'I doubt someone as powerful as this Lamprey uses a key,' Melina said sullenly. 'Try the tubes.'

'I was going to do that,' Mel snapped back. 'Give me a chance.'

With Marlern's help, they eased slightly to the left and Mel was able to grab the tube running from the girl's sarcophagus, but although it moved slightly, it didn't give way.

'I've an idea,' Mel shouted.

'Yeah but it's risky,' Melanie said back.

'Gotta be done, though.' That was Melina. 'Hey, boy, step back.'

Marlern, probably already confused by the strange communication going on around him, did as asked, and Melina jumped from his shoulders, bringing Melanie down too.

But Mel hung onto the tubing, now a good twenty feet above their heads.

'Yeah, we'll catch you,' Melina said in response to an unspoken question.

Mel didn't exactly have faith in that thought, but still started swinging back and forth on the tubing.

What happened next was loud and painful, but the bottom line was that Mel found herself lying in Melina's arms, caught with expert timing and not a little bit of unexpected strength ('Hey, we Roman slaves work out a bit,' said a voice in her head).

On the ground beside them were five shattered sarcophaguses, including the star-shaped one, and a load of tubes flapped about above their heads, momentarily sparking.

Each occupant staggered out, unhurt but shaken.

'Who are you?' asked the younger boy, as Haema and Marlern embraced. 'I thought the creature had killed you,' she said.

'She ignored me,' Marlern said.

'You're not a time-sensitive,' Melina guessed. 'Irrelevant to her. Essential to us. First mistake our Monica's made.'

The older guy was trying to revive the girl in the star-shaped device, but nothing doing.

Instead they watched as she thrashed from side to side. Mel watched as, with every slight movement, an afterimage remained so that it looked like there were loads of her, each one moving a split second after the other.

'Helen Lamprey,' she breathed, then dropped beside her. 'Helen. Be calm. Please.'

As if reacting to her voice, Helen indeed stopped and it took nearly a minute before all the ghostly afterimages caught up and settled into just the one body.

'My god,' said Melanie. 'How many Helens from how many realities are contained in that body?'

'You what?' said the guy who'd crouched beside her.

'Complicated,' Melanie said.

'I'm Mel,' Mel offered her hand.

'Kevin,' he replied. 'That's DiVotow and Haema.'

'Thanks for getting us free,' said DiVotow. 'I'm not sure how much more I could have taken.'

Melina crossed over to them. 'You're not free yet. We need to get out of here before Monica comes looking for us.'

'Bit late for that, kiddies,' snarled a new voice behind them all.

Mel sighed. 'Spoke too soon, Melina. That's Monica.'

'Who's she?' asked Kevin.

And Monica transformed into her full Lamprey.

'Oh,' Kevin continued. 'Right – *her!* Right. Run!'

And he scooped the unconscious Helen into his arms and they began to run to an opposite exit, where Melina had come in, but suddenly a duplicate Lamprey was stood blocking it.

'My domain, my world. My creation. I go where I please.'

'Like... hell...' said a new voice, and Mel looked down to see Helen stirring. Helen raised a hand and a blast of energy smashed the Lamprey out of existence. 'Hi Great Auntie Mummy Granny Monica, I'm Helen. And that was pure chronon energy. Enjoyed it?'

Helen then stood up, easing Kevin back. 'Oh and I'm a Lamprey, remember.' And she transformed into a smaller version of Monica's alien form. 'That exit,' she yelled, chucking another ball of chronon energy and dissipating another Monica.

The assembled gang needed no second warning and led by DiVotow and Melina, they ran.

Mel paused to see what Helen was doing and watched aghast as she transformed into human Helen again and dashed after them.

Monica wasn't far behind, gliding through the darkness, screeching in fury.

Marlern called back to Mel. 'She's used the others because they're time-sensitives, right? Whatever that means?'

'It means they're important to her plans, yeah,' Mel replied, breathlessly.

She wasn't as fit as she thought.

Then she realised Marlern had stopped running. 'Keep going,' he shouted.

'Marlern, no!' That was Haema.

Mel tried to grab her, but Haema ran back the other way towards Marlern.

'We'll give you what time we can!' Marlern shouted and vanished in a cloud of dust particles as the Monica/Lamprey swept straight into him.

Haema didn't say a word, she just died as quickly as the Monica/Lamprey brushed past her.

'Mel! Come on,' screamed Melina from the front. 'I can see the way we came in!'

A new voice bellowed out encouragement.

'Come on Mel! Mels!'

It was the Doctor's voice. One of them at least.

Mel could see her two counterparts escape to safety, leaving the two guys and her.

DiVotow was out, then Kevin, but could she make it before the Monica/Lamprey caught up with her?

And how were they going to stop her getting out anyway?

Or had Tungard come up with a solution?

Mel saw the bright light of the lab as she ran towards the smoky arch.

She saw Melanie turn to Melina. 'Kick over the experiment!' she screamed. 'Disturb the elements!'

Melina was indecisive. 'It'll hurt,' she said, no doubt already feeling the considerable warmth as she reached out.

'That's not the answer,' cried the Doctor as Mel bundled straight into him.

'I'm out,' she gasped.

And seeing that Melina had failed, Melanie Baal threw herself at Tungard's experiment and vanished in a sudden bright flash.

The smoky arch was gone, trapping the Monica/Lamprey inside.

But so was Melanie Baal and Mel could see by the Doctor's reaction this wasn't her Doctor, but Melanie's.

Melina just stood there, staring at where Melanie had been. 'I... I...'

Mel threw her a vicious look. 'You're all talk,' she said bitterly and walked out of the room.

The Doctor, her Doctor, found Mel sat in the wrecked Reading Room a few moments later.

'It wasn't Melina's fault,' he said gently.

'No, I know,' Mel said. 'It was mine. I led them in there.'

The Doctor let out a quiet laugh. 'Three headstrong Mels? I think you lead yourselves. Poor Kina was quite worried.'

'Where is she?'

'Safe. With DiVotow and Kevin, being looked after by Misters Woltas and Huu. Somehow, they'll get them home when this is all over.'

'All over?' Mel threw her arms around, gesticulating to the destroyed room. 'How is this ever going to be all over? Joe Tungard's gone, apparently. So's Melanie Baal and those two kids I barely knew. But have we stopped Monica?'

The Doctor sighed. 'No. No, we haven't.'

'I know. It was a rhetorical question, Doctor. How long do you think she'll be trapped inside Joe's subspace thing?'

'Honestly?'

'Honestly, please.'

The Doctor smiled grimly. 'I doubt she's there now. She'll be coming here soon, that's why we locked the youngsters up.'

'And Helen?'

'Helen's... helping us.'

'She's bait you mean. Using her chronon energies, that's what you meant earlier wasn't it. The collected selves of Rummas are too weak, so you need someone else with thousands of displaced temporal energies within her. I think that's really selfish of you.'

'Well...'

'Worse than that, it's despicable, Doctor.' Mel stood up. 'I want to go back to the TARDIS, now please. I don't want to watch you sacrifice her.'

The Doctor walked to the doorway. 'The TARDIS is that way Mel. You've got a key.'

And Mel started walking as indicated. 'See you later, Doctor.'

'Goodbye, Mel,' he replied, softly and closed the door behind him.

Mel took a deep breath, placed her hand on the handle and –

There had been something in his voice. Something in the way he spoke. Something as he said. 'Goodbye, Mel'...

'Doctor!'

She suddenly realised how wrong she'd been.

Helen wasn't the bait.

Helen wasn't a Time Lord with multiple selves scattered across all of time and space, across countless universes.

Helen was a key, she could open the aperture.

The only person with the necessary chronon energy was...

'Doctor!' she screamed, rushing back across the room and through the door he'd left by.

Which of course took her somewhere else entirely.

She raced down a corridor.

Seven minutes. All these buildings were the same and through the centre of each, Helen would draw... would draw dozens, perhaps hundreds of Doctors.

Just like her Doctor, ready and able to sacrifice themselves, their special Time Lord life energies, to stop the Monica/Lamprey.

Mel turned a corridor and ran straight into Mr Woltas.

'The Spiral Chamber,' she snapped. 'Where?'

'Well, I –'

'Damn you, Woltas,' Mel finally snapped. 'Just tell me!'

Chapter Fifteen
Time's Up

Thirty minutes later, she and her Doctor stood together in the Spiral Chamber. Mel realised she was holding the Doctor's hand tightly. Almost too tightly. She didn't understand what was going on, but she felt a... not exactly a thrill but a sense of excitement she could almost taste. That sense you get in anticipation of something that might be good, but could go bad. That moment before you enter through a door into the first day of a new job. The feeling as you sit in a car ready for your first driving lesson. The awful, gut-wrenching but delightful sense of excitement and dread as you kiss someone special for the first time, not knowing if it's what either of you really want but knowing it's the only way to find out. That moment she could remember first spending the night, asleep with Jake, curling up behind him in bed and easing her arm around him, gently stroking his chest, loving it but aware that in a second he could move her arm away and thus tell her exactly where their relationship was.

Or wasn't.

As a child she was told to call it 'butterflies in your tummy'.

As an adult, she was taught that it was a mix of adrenalin and endorphins released into your system.

Being an adult takes all the fun out of life, it seemed.

Right now, all those feelings were raging through Mel and she hoped that, like the arm-around-Jake's-chest analogy, it would be all right in the end.

But the look in the Doctor's eyes told her it might not be.

Not this time.

Oh God...

Beside him were the other two versions of him she'd come to know. The scarred one in the cloak and the friendly one whose version of Melanie had gone.

How sad the surviving Doctors looked.

She stared at her Doctor. Funny how she thought of him like that – these were all her Doctor really, who was to say which was the right one. Well, obviously it was hers.

Her mind briefly thought about the sacrifices that had been made to get them here. Apart from the reptilian version of herself, there had been Haema and Marlern, together till the end. Joe Tungard, so appalled by what he'd learned about becoming the Architect of Chaos on the Reading Room PC. Sir Bertrand Lamprey, grieved for by Helen, who had learned now the truth, and the final fate of her beloved father.

And that's what the Doctor had become to Mel. A father figure. She could see that now. Especially during those moments where she longed for home, for her parents – and although that sadness would never go away, in so many ways the Doctor had supplanted them.

It was a mutual need – Alan and Christine Bush had one another, but the Doctor had no one. And nor really did Mel.

Except each other, caring and looking out for one another, with that confidence and mutual honesty, that familiarity that allowed them to finish one another's sentences. Thoughts, even.

Once she feared it might be love. Now she knew it was solid friendship, paternal and good.

And for the first time in their (oh how many months was it now?) travels, Mel wondered if this might be it.

The strain the Doctor was already facing, even with a couple of time-lost duplicates, was phenomenal and demanded more than he could reasonably be expected to give, surely.

Professor Rummas was watching from the left side of the crucible, ready to open the Spiral and reveal the Lamprey. Or Lampreys.

No one could be sure whether there was one still alive or sixty million, dragged in from alternative existences.

Helen was stood directly on the edge of the inverted Spiral cone itself, gripping the handrail tightly. She said nothing to anyone, she knew what was expected of her. To be the bait, to open the Spiral one last time and draw the Monica/Lamprey in, and any temporal versions of her out there. All of them, like moths to the flame.

Of course, the Monica/Lamprey creature wasn't that stupid but it would come nevertheless. It still needed Helen, and would easily destroy anyone who got in her/their/its way.

At least, that was the supposition. It was a dangerous guessing game – the future, the present and the past of literally countless realities hung on what Helen, and then the three Doctors, would do next.

And the multitude of others that could be drawn here once Helen opened the way.

Mel was going to speak some words of encouragement to the Doctor. Doctors. But Rummas caught her eye and jerked his head across the chamber, trying to get her to see something.

And Mel gasped as she saw what had caught his attention.

Helen was writhing violently now, the Spiral's concentric

circles were rotating. It had started, and just as before, the delayed afterimages of Helen's every move were showing.

But that meant help was on its way.

Mel just hoped the help arrived before the reason it was needed.

And there they were. Stood opposite, grouped around the far side of the Spiral Chamber's inverted cone were more identical Doctors. A majority had similar clothes as her one, but there were a few variants. And not everyone was accompanied by a Mel, although many were.

One Doctor, hands behind his back as he gazed at the crucible in wonderment, was stood with a pretty young brunette in a bright pink tee, and clashing blue shorts.

Nearby, a Doctor in a coat made up entirely of differing shades of blue was with a woman in her fifties. Mel's attention was then drawn to an identical hued Doctor further back with the same woman, although this one had metallic implants down the left side of her head, arm and chest, like some kind of cyborg. Another Doctor was talking to – Mel couldn't quite believe this – what appeared to be a penguin.

There were perhaps twenty, no wait, surely thirty Doctors in total. No, every time Mel thought she'd counted, another Doctor and companion would be there. How long before there were hundreds? Of course, that might, this one time, be advantageous...

After a moment, her Doctor looked up and across the giant covered dish and took in the spectacle opposite. The other two Doctors followed suit.

'As I said. Infinite combinations of infinite diversions,' the scarred one murmured. 'Fascinating.'

The Doctor, Mel's Doctor, reached down to the crucible's control panel and said, simply, 'It's time.'

'Are you sure about this, Doctor?' Mel asked, knowing the answer but still praying he'd suddenly think up another way.

However he just nodded. 'I made a mistake, Mel. I trusted Rummas and the others knew what they were doing.' He smiled weakly. 'When I think of all the friends I've had over the years, I thought of myself as a really rather splendid judge of character. And yet, when it mattered most, when I thought the fate of the entire history, present and future of everything was being overseen by sensible people, I got it wrong. As a result, I... we... have to bear the consequences because we're the only people here with the power to have a hope of defeating Monica.'

Mel knew he was saying it just loud enough for Rummas to hear, but didn't want to catch Rummas's eye. She might go further than the Doctor, any of these Doctors, had gone and actually wallop him.

Just as she had Monica. And look where *that* had got her.

'What's going to happen?' Mel heard herself ask. 'Why are they all here?'

Rummas had crossed the room to join her. 'It's a sacrifice, across time and space. Across universes and multiverses. Across dimensions and –'

'Oh do belt up,' snapped a voice Mel recognised behind her.

It was Melina, leaning against the doorway, her eyes red where she'd been crying.

Mel was going to be waspish, to say something along the lines of 'Oh, finally decided to join us?' but couldn't. Didn't want to.

What was the point – Melina was feeling wretched enough. Mel knew that as well as she knew... well, herself really.

Instead she held out a hand, and felt Melina's slip into it. An odd feeling, holding your own doppelgänger's hand.

She squeezed it reassuringly and heard a whispered 'thank you' from Melina.

There really was a first time for everything.

'Ready?' asked the Doctor.

'Ready,' boomed back a chorus of about thirty Doctors, making it very loud.

Rummas actually seemed to jump with surprise. He then looked back at Mel. 'This may not work, you know,' he said.

'Cheery git aren't you,' Melina responded.

'If he... they fail?' Mel asked.

Rummas shrugged sadly. 'He's giving up his chronon energy, it'll draw it out of all of them. The hope is that it'll overfeed and burst before too many Doctors die.'

Melina squeezed Mel's hand tighter but didn't let go. She still needed that reassurance. But her tone of voice belied that. 'What do you mean, die?'

Rummas swung around on her angrily. 'What the hell do you think is going on here, girl? You think I want to see this? A Time Lord sacrificing not just this life but possibly all his future ones, maybe his past ones, everything he's got, just to save a universe that really doesn't deserve saving.' Rummas was actually crying. 'He's my friend, too!'

Mel felt the butterflies throw themselves around the pit of her stomach that little bit harder and faster. But before she could speak, the crucible cover slid back, revealing a kaleidoscopic vortex and slowly spinning spirals.

A slight column of air shot upwards, blowing Helen's multiple images haywire.

It had started.

Helen was trying to hold tight, but it was no good.

'Let go, Helen,' Rummas screamed. 'Get back here, you've done your bit!'

But Helen didn't move. 'Maybe I can do more,' she hissed, each word a tortured breath. 'Maybe...'

And Rummas was behind her, pulling her away. 'Let him... them do their job!'

As Helen fell back to safety, the three Doctors stepped forward, a movement echoed by the nearest Doctors opposite. The harsh wind blew now into the Doctors' faces, while the vortex below illuminated them with an intense halogen light.

'Look,' said an alternate Mel opposite, and sure enough, one of the spirals fractured and split as a Lamprey oozed out. Within a few seconds, another five or six had done likewise.

Then another blast of light and air, and hovering above the crucible, twisting in a column of bright light was what Mel knew was the main Lamprey, the big one, the progenitor of the remaining Lampreys. The one which all the others were just shades of. Echoes.

'Monica,' she said quietly.

'So Doctor, we meet once again,' it spat, 'and you've brought me some presents.' But all the Doctors intently ignored it, staring down at its smaller duplicates still within the Spiral. 'That was a joke,' it said. 'Presents as in past, present, future. Lots of versions of your present self and – oh never mind, maybe one of your past incarnations understands humour,' it snarled.

Meanwhile a crackle of blue light etched from a Lamprey below, back against the rim of the inverted cone, like slow forked lightning, but no one moved.

'Professor Rummas,' the Monica/Lamprey addressed the elderly librarian. 'No lives to offer up like this Doctor friend of yours? You may have no future regenerations, but a few past ones might make for a good appetiser. Yes?'

'You are an abomination,' he yelled. 'The antithesis of everything that's good across the omniverse!'

'Why, thank you, Professor,' the Monica/Lamprey giggled. 'You say the sweetest things.'

And a blue fragment of electricity shot from its body and hit Rummas squarely in the chest.

He staggered back, which clearly surprised the Monica/Lamprey creature. 'Wow, you are tasty old man,' it said. 'I'll have more of that, please.'

Mel considered running forward, blocking the path of the lightning, knowing that a second blast would most likely destroy Rummas forever.

But someone else was their first. She felt Melina slip out of her grip a split second before she would have released her hand anyway.

Melina stood defiantly in front of Rummas and Mel felt a pang of pride.

Deep down, they were the same person after all.

'Why don't you sod right off back to where you came from,' Melina bellowed furiously.

On the other hand, Mel decided, that wasn't her kind of approach, but it was pretty heartfelt and echoed her own sentiments.

And Melina was gone, utterly destroyed by a snaking tendril of blue light from the Monica/Lamprey.

Mel, Helen and Rummas stared at the spot where she had stood in shock.

And the Monica/Lamprey laughed. 'A crumb, a morsel. Barely worth eating,' it laughed. 'But it shut her up at least.'

Mel was going to say something but Rummas weakly tugged her trouser leg, looking beyond her.

Mel looked back towards the cone area in shock.

'Contact,' said the Doctor, her Doctor.

And the others, possible dozens, maybe hundreds of them, all replied, holding their right hands up, palm to the front, and closed their eyes.

'He needed the time,' Rummas said quietly. 'Poor Melina. That was my role.'

'Self-sacrifice as a distraction?' asked Mel. 'Seems a bit extreme to me.'

'You don't get it,' snapped Rummas. 'This isn't some non-sensical danger like the Daleks or the Cybermen. This creature, this filth is going to destroy everything, past, present and future, just to feed its bloated existence. The Doctor is going to sacrifice himself to stop it. My life, yours, Melina's. Worth nothing in comparison to buying time for the Doctor.'

The Monica/Lamprey was squirming around in its column of light.

'What are you doing?' it screamed. 'What's going on?'

'Can I help them?' Helen asked, but Rummas shook his head.

Connecting the palms of all the Doctors was a beam of light, criss-crossing in all directions, creating a network of power and energy, although each Doctor was notably weaker by its doing so.

'Chronon energy,' Rummas mumbled. 'Without it, a Time Lord will age and die. It keeps him together as he crosses the timelines.' He looked at Mel. 'It infects those that travel with him, too, keeping you young, stopping your personal chronological energy from going haywire.'

'And it's the only thing that can stop the Lamprey?'

Rummas nodded. 'It will absorb so much, too much hopefully.'

'But the Doctors? Won't they die?'

'Each and every one of them,' he said slowly. 'Each and every one sacrificing himself so that his own personal universe can live on.'

Mel saw the blue-coated Doctor and his cyborg companion suddenly stagger back and vanish.

And Mel knew that their universe was safe, no longer another victim of the Lamprey. But minus its champions. Sacrificing themselves so that others could live.

Only the Doctor would do this. Doctors.

In unison the Doctors lifted their palms slightly, their faces grimacing with the strain, various respective friends and companions looking on with as much fear on their faces as Mel guessed was on hers.

Another Doctor blinked out of existence, and Mel noticed that another materialised to replace him. But as a couple more faded away, she noticed fewer and fewer replacements were arriving. This was a losing battle, and there was nothing she could do to help. How useless she felt right now.

The remaining Doctors gritted their teeth harder, bringing the latticework of energy upwards, drawing the smaller Lampreys below towards it. They were spitting out blue lightning but to little effect. A couple more Doctors expired, but now none replaced them, so the others took the strain that bit more to compensate.

The scarred Doctor, unaware that his version of Mel was gone, lifted his head and stared at the Monica/Lamprey, which was thrashing about angrily above their heads, spitting blue fire, which everyone bravely ignored. 'Had enough yet?'

'You are pathetic, Time Lords,' it yelled. 'You think this can stop me? You are just feeding me, giving me the power I need!'

One by one, the smaller Lampreys flew upwards and into the lattice of energy, and were vaporised as they hit it, but the Monica/Lamprey didn't care, shouting: 'All the more for me!'

Mel could see there were no more Lampreys below, and the Monica/Lamprey was notably larger now, swelling up as the chronon energy the Time Lords were disseminating was being drawn into it.

Their palms were much higher now, and there were probably only about six Doctors left.

The nice one to her Doctor's left, whose Mel had been part reptile, fell back with a gasp as blue lightning hit him and he too vanished.

Rummas sighed. 'It's not working,' he said quietly. 'The Lamprey can cope!'

As if in response, the various Doctors stopped emitting their energy beams, gasping for breath as they did so.

Above them, still framed in the column of halogen light beaming up from the centre of the Spiral, the Monica/Lamprey gloated.

'I've beaten you. The omniverse is my restaurant. Time is my menu!'

'To coin a phrase,' gasped the scarred Doctor, '"Belt up"!'

And he, like so many before, disappeared in a blue flash, and Mel felt a pang of sadness.

But her Doctor was still there, stood alone on one side of the crucible, staring at his equally intent duplicates gathered on the other side. In some ghastly tableau, like puppets, they nodded, three times, but as one. No fluctuation, no missed beat.

Then before Mel could stop him, her Doctor climbed on to the side of the crucible and reached into the light, and grabbed the Lamprey.

It screeched and squirmed in his grip.

'How! How can you touch me! I'm intangible. I am across all time and space. I am everywhere at once.'

'No,' the Doctor said, pained, exhausted and just a little

angrily. 'You are trapped here. By me. One solitary individual against your omnipotence. And I will beat you.'

'How?'

'Because I am... the... Doctor!'

And he threw himself into the spiralled crucible, dropping downwards into the dimensionally transcendental abyss, accompanied by the screeching Monica/Lamprey, sending shards of blue light around them as they fell.

One more Doctor, hit squarely in the chest by some blue light disappeared forever, but the others ignored this.

'Doctor... no...' whispered Rummas. 'Oh no...'

Mel didn't understand what was going on.

She wasn't helped when the remaining alternative Doctors pointed their palms into the crucible and let rip. Every ounce of chronon energy they'd previously shared poured into the apex of the Spiral, shattering the sides, gouging away the spirals, and hitting both the Doctor – her Doctor – and the screeching Monica/Lamprey, feeding them both so much energy.

'Nothing can take that much energy.' Rummas hauled himself up off the floor, joining Mel staring over the edge of the cone into the destruction below.

The spiral vortex was rent, torn open in multiple places, the energy from the assembled Doctors battering the two figures, distorting them along every dimensional plane, stretching, flattening, plumping, bloating, twisting and twirling them in so many directions.

It was like a nightmarish hall of mirrors, Mel unable to tell where the Doctor began or ended, trying to ignore the shriek of primal agony that emerged from the crucible.

And then with one final column of bright, almost burning, light that spat upwards it was finished.

The last Mel and Rummas saw of the Monica/Lamprey was a flattened, two-dimensional image, twisting in pain at the heart of the column of light that slowly but surely split apart, atom by atom it seemed, silently evaporating as it hit the edges of the chronon energy beam until nothing was left.

The Spiral Chamber was now silent and still. No spirals, no vortex, just a straightforward twenty-something-foot-deep cone, with an inverted apex.

And huddled, fetal, at the bottom, was the Doctor. Battered, bloody and unmoving.

Out of the corner of her eye, Mel saw the surviving alternative Doctors, companions, even the penguin stop still, then bleed away as one TARDIS, always a blue police box she noted, seemed to envelop each duo and then disappeared, leaving the room empty bar herself, Rummas and the Doctor.

She threw a look at Rummas. 'Where's Helen?'

But she knew the answer. Helen was still a Lamprey. Had been a Lamprey.

'Not just bait,' Mel spat, 'but a sacrifice as well.' Then Mel was clambering over the handrail and jumping down into the blackened, Spiral-less cone before Rummas could stop her, sliding down to the Doctor's huddled form.

'Doctor?'

His eyes flicked open. 'Did we win?'

'All of you. They've all gone now, off in their TARDISes.'

'And the Monica/Lamprey?'

'Dead. Destroyed in the Spiral, obliterated by it completely.'

'Poor Helen,' he breathed. 'I'm sorry.' He coughed. 'Rummas?' he shouted hoarsely.

'He's fine,' assured Mel, but then realised it wasn't a question addressed to her.

'Yes?' came Rummas's response.

'Check the timelines and all the universes. Get Mr Woltas and Mr Huu to double-check everything. There should be no trace of the Lampreys anywhere. Otherwise, we've failed.'

Rummas hobbled away, to do just that, and Mel helped the Doctor to his feet.

She was sure he was different, certainly less heavy. Indeed, he seemed small in stature, his hair was lank, and his pallor greying.

'You look like death,' she said helpfully.

'Thank you for those kind words of encouragement. I've just stopped the end of creation, and all you can do is tell me I don't look so good.'

Mel laughed and they slowly, very slowly in fact, bearing in mind how tired and drawn the Doctor was, crawled out of the destroyed inverted cone, out of the chamber itself and into the Library.

'Where now?' Mel asked once they were in the corridor.

'I need a bit of a sleep. Let's get to the TARDIS and away from here.'

'But Rummas?'

'Can look after things here. The Lamprey is gone. I can feel it in my bones.' He squeezed his arm and winced. 'Painfully so, in fact.'

Mel looked around, then closed her eyes, trying to bring up in her mind a plan of the Library. Then she smiled, opened her eyes and pointed towards a corridor to the left.

'TARDIS. Seven minutes that way.'

The Doctor let Mel take his weight. 'Seven minutes, eh? What would I do without you?'

'What would the universe do without you?' she countered.

'Let's hope... let's hope we don't find out...'

Chapter Sixteen
Everybody's Happy Nowadays

The TARDIS control room had never seemed so bright, so warm. So inviting.

Mel was all but dragging the Doctor inside as she looked around her. As if by magic, part of the far wall opened up and a long bed emerged – perhaps the TARDIS could tell its pilot was desperately ill, Mel decided.

The Doctor waved a hand almost irritably towards the bed and it was absorbed by the wall once again. 'I'm fine, Mel.' He glanced up to the ceiling as Mel closed the doors behind them. 'No, really, I am.' He then smiled at Mel. 'We didn't do too badly, did we?'

'We?' laughed Mel. '"We" did nothing. You, on the other hand, just saved the multiverse. Literally for once.'

'For once? Mel, we save the multiverse once a week! Don't we?'

'Not usually, no. You're usually satisfied with a race, or a planet. A galaxy at the most.' She could tell he was masking his pain behind his bonhomie, of course. 'But seriously, Doctor, I think you need to rest. The Lamprey really took it out of you. Again, literally!'

The Doctor took a deep breath and stood proudly by his precious TARDIS console. 'Nonsense, Mel, what harm could possibly befall one such as I?'

At which point he began coughing and spluttering. Mel ran to his side instantly, trying to pat him on the back. Being considerably shorter than he, this merely resulted in a few ineffectual thumps to a couple of middle vertebrae. He gently eased her hand back. 'You know, I think some rest might be in order after all.'

'Doctor's orders?' suggested Mel cheekily.

He nodded and smiled back at her.

And Mel's heart went cold.

She'd been travelling with him long enough to be able to read the Doctor well by now. This avuncular man who she trusted with her life. A man whose moods and quirks she could pretty much predict these days. A Time Lord – so much power contained in such a frail body, despite its appearance of... well, pretty solidness anyway.

But who really knew what made Time Lords tick? Even these days, Mel was aware that she couldn't entirely be sure of how well the Doctor might be.

Having witnessed that final struggle as the Lamprey was extinguished, she was forced to question whether the Doctor should have accepted that constant absorption of energy and light. Could his form really have just taken that punishment and then shrugged it off as easily as he made out?

'Doctor, listen to me. Rummas warned you what it might take to stop it.'

The Doctor was leaning on the TARDIS console, gripping it tightly enough that his knuckles were white with the strain.

'So what? Okay, I might not be able to regenerate twelve times. Eleven, ten maybe. Who cares?'

'You should.'

'Why? Look at the scanner Mel, look at that. All those stars and worlds and races and civilisations. They could all have gone the way of poor Professor Tungard if I'd not stopped it. As sacrifices go, I could afford it and I truly believe it was worth it.'

Mel was at his side. She placed a hand on his and drew it away quickly.

'Doctor, you're ice cold. I mean, absolutely frozen.'

'Really? Can't feel it myself.' His gaze was still on the scanner. 'Mel, can you press that blue switch please.'

'Why?'

'Because I asked nicely?'

Mel did as she was told and instantly the TARDIS roared into life, the central column rising and falling as they left Carsus for what she hoped would be the last time.

A few seconds later, it stopped and the scanner just showed space again. Mel frowned but the Doctor smiled, albeit weakly.

'Hover mode. I just want to look one last time at the local cosmos.'

'One... last... what d'you mean, *one last time*?'

The Doctor finally pried his hands away from the console, trying to work the fingers but to no avail. He stared straight at Mel and she suddenly realised she was facing not a man in his mid-forties as he normally appeared, but a tired, drained man, who just this once she could believe was 900-plus years. His blue eyes were grey, the crow's feet more pronounced and his hair had a few grey roots and curls, especially at the temples.

'We did good, Mel. I'm honoured to have had you at my side one last time.'

And he fell to the floor with a loud crump.

Mel was at his side in a second, resting his head on her lap, massaging his temples. 'C'mon Doctor, no time to be sleeping.' She looked up at the scanner.

All those stars, still twinkling.

All the planets still revolving.

All the life that owed its continued existence to a man, a wonderful, brave man it had never known.

Might never know.

She realised she was crying and a tear dropped onto the Doctor's face. His skin was very grey now. His eyes flickered open and he smiled tightly.

'Don't cry Mel. It was my time. Well, maybe not, but it was my time to give. To donate. I've had a good innings you know, seen and done a lot. Can't complain this time. Don't feel cheated.'

Mel couldn't understand what he was saying. He couldn't be... couldn't be dying.

Had letting his chronon energy be absorbed to that degree really destroyed him. Finally?

'No...' she whispered. 'It's not fair!'

'Yes. Yes it is...' she heard him say, but the words seemed to be in her head rather than coming from his closed mouth.

She suddenly found herself remembering their initial meeting in Brighton. An initial enmity that had given way to respect, admiration and finally a great enough affection that she had given it all up to join him aboard the TARDIS. To travel the universe.

The TARDIS lights seemed to have dimmed a fraction, as if it... as if she knew. Understood.

Mel wished she did.

Then the TARDIS lurched violently, once, twice, three times. The Doctor was rocked out of her hands and he curled up, facing the bottom of the console.

'Local... tractor beam...' he said aloud this time, trying to raise his hand. Trying to reach up, grab the console and haul himself upright.

Mel watched for a second, convinced that he'd succeed. Of course he would, if they were under some sort of attack, the Doctor would leap into action and save the day again.

He had to.

'Doctor!' she whispered as, instead, his arm drooped and he was still once more.

His skin was the colour of granite now and Mel was sure it was blurring slightly.

Had to be her own tears, distorting her vision.

The force of the tractor beams – another one rocked the TARDIS again – had sent her a couple of feet away from the Doctor and the floor seemed to be at a severe angle.

She tried to crawl towards him, but another blow, then another and Mel suddenly wondered if this was what it felt like to be a deep-sea diver, going down too rapidly. Getting the bends. She felt, somehow, that the TARDIS was indeed going down, being dragged through space, like a rollercoaster car in freefall.

And then it was all over. The TARDIS landed with an enormous juddering thump, but in her ears, in her mind, it seemed as if the noise was still going on and she knew then, that she had failed the Doctor.

He was dying in front of her eyes and her own brain was closing down, trying to block off the effects of the crash-landing, or whatever it was, by making her sleep.

She would fight unconsciousness. She'd been knocked out before, she knew that she could catch it, stop it...

She knew she could...

She knew...

No... no it wasn't fair...

Wait!

The TARDIS door was opening. How? No one had operated the door controls. They must have been forced.

Mel could barely keep her eyes open, the darkness that wanted to consume her was winning, and she was losing the battle.

Let it go, she heard her inner voice say. Sleep.

With a final effort, Mel rolled onto her back, facing the doorway.

As unconsciousness took a hold, she was sure there were people there.

They moved towards her and as she finally succumbed to complete sensory deprivation, she heard a strident female voice barking out an order.

'Leave the girl. It's the man I want.'

Acknowledgements

Spiral Scratch couldn't have come about without the help of the following, mostly unwilling, participants. If you enjoyed this book, the credit's all mine. If you didn't, blame the following:

John Binns, for being part of my life. It was *always* fun. Thanks, from me and Hugh Manatee.

Justin Richards, Sarah Emsley and Vicki Vrint, for being patient. For redefining the word 'patience' in fact.

Jason Haigh-Ellery, for his understanding, which is always appreciated, if rarely acknowledged by me.

Colin Baker and Bonnie Langford, for the inspiration.

Richard Atkinson, for being in the spare room.

Richard Beeby, for the downloads, Ipswich and crooked curtains.

David Brawn, for letting me plagiarise myself.

Barnaby Edwards, for being arty.

Jacqueline Farrow, for being a Cat Among the Pigeons.

Scott Handcock, for some classic suggestions.

John McLaughlin, for being as fab as always.

Paul Magrs, for words of encouragement. All eight of them can be found in this book. Including 'lobster'.

David Southwell and Sean Twist, for much inspiration.

Tom Spilsbury, for telling me the sun ain't gonna shine any more.

About the Author

Gary Russell lives in south-east London but dreams of escaping to the smog-less countryside. This is why he enjoys watching those daytime TV programmes where people move from cities to idyllic country cottages with three acres of land and the nearest neighbours ten minutes away. Were he to live in such a place, he'd probably write even more *Doctor Who* books to alleviate the loneliness, so count yourself lucky that he's stuck in London! Amongst his written works are a handful of *Doctor Who* novels, a book about the making of the 1996 *Doctor Who* TV Movie starring Paul McGann, programme guides to shows such as *The Simpsons* and *Frasier* and a best-selling series of books about the *Lord of the Rings* movie trilogy. He's currently working on a volume about the 2006 *Lord of the Rings* stage extravaganza, plus a couple of *Space 1999* novels.

Apart from all this writing stuff, Gary produces the *Doctor Who* and *Bernice Summerfield* audio ranges for Big Finish Productions, which takes up 99 per cent of his time, the remaining 1 per cent is dedicated to collecting Action Figures, buying too many CDs and watching *Neighbours*. And at school, they always said he had such potential...

Coming soon from
BBC Doctor Who books:

Fear Itself

by Nick Wallace
Published 8 September 2005
ISBN 0 563 48634 1

A new adventure featuring the Eighth Doctor

The 22nd century, and a few short years of interstellar contact have taught Man a hard lesson: there are forces abroad that are nightmare manifest. Powerful, unstoppable, alien forces. It's a realisation that deals a body blow to Man's belief in his own superiority, and leaves him with the only option he has ever had – to fight.

When the Doctor and his friends are caught in the crossfire, they find suspicion and paranoia running rampant, with enemies to be seen in every shadow.

The fight against alien forces is no job for an amateur, and for a Doctor only just finding his way in the universe again, one misstep could be fatal.

New series adventures
coming soon from BBC Books

DOCTOR·WHO

The Deviant Strain

By Justin Richards
ISBN 0 563 48637 6
UK £6.99 US $11.99/$14.99 CDN

The Novrosk Peninsula: the Soviet naval base has been
abandoned, the nuclear submarines are rusting and rotting.
Cold, isolated, forgotten.

Until the Russian Special Forces arrive – and discover that
the Doctor and his companions are here too. But there is
something else in Novrosk. Something that predates even the
stone circle on the cliff top. Something that is at last waking,
hunting, killing...

Can the Doctor and his friends stay alive long enough to learn
the truth? With time running out, they must discover who is
really responsible for the Deviant Strain...

Featuring the Doctor as played by Christopher Eccleston,
together with Rose and Captain Jack as played by Billie Piper
and John Barrowman in the hit series from BBC Television.

DOCTOR·WHO

Only Human
By Gareth Roberts
ISBN 0 563 48639 2
UK £6.99 US $11.99/$14.99 CDN

Somebody's interfering with time. The Doctor, Rose and
Captain Jack arrive on modern-day Earth to find the culprit –
and discover a Neanderthal Man, twenty-eight thousand years
after his race became extinct. Only a trip back to the primeval
dawn of humanity can solve the mystery.

Who are the mysterious humans from the distant future now
living in that distant past? What hideous monsters are trying to
escape from behind the Grey Door? Is Rose going to end up
married to a caveman?

Caught between three very different types of human being –
past, present and future – the Doctor, Rose and Captain Jack
must learn the truth behind the Osterberg experiment before
the monstrous Hy-Bractors escape to change humanity's history
forever...

*Featuring the Doctor, Rose and Captain Jack as played by
Christopher Eccleston, Billie Piper and John Barrowman in
the hit series from BBC Television.*

DOCTOR·WHO

The Stealers of Dreams
By Steve Lyons
ISBN 0 563 48638 4
UK £6.99 US $11.99/$14.99 CDN

In the far future, the Doctor, Rose and Captain Jack find a
world on which fiction has been outlawed. A world where it's
a crime to tell stories, a crime to lie, a crime to hope, and a
crime to dream.

But now somebody is challenging the status quo. A pirate TV
station urges people to fight back. And the Doctor wants to help
– until he sees how easily dreams can turn into nightmares.

With one of his companions stalked by shadows and the other
committed to an asylum, the Doctor is forced to admit that
fiction can be dangerous after all. Though perhaps it is not as
deadly as the truth...

*Featuring the Doctor as played by Christopher Eccleston,
together with Rose and Captain Jack as played by Billie Piper
and John Barrowman in the hit series from BBC Television.*

New series adventures
also available from BBC Books

*Featuring the Doctor and Rose as played
by Christopher Eccleston and Billie Piper
in the hit series from BBC Television.*

The Clockwise Man
By Justin Richards
ISBN 0 563 48628 7
UK £6.99 US $11.99/$14.99 CDN

In 1920s London the Doctor and Rose find themselves
caught up in the hunt for a mysterious murderer.
But not everything is what it seems.

The Monsters Inside
By Stephen Cole
ISBN 0 563 48629 5
UK £6.99 US $11.99/$14.99 CDN

The TARDIS takes the Doctor and Rose to a destination
in deep space – Justicia, a prison camp stretched over seven
planets, where Earth colonies deal with their criminals.

Winner Takes All
By Jacqueline Rayner
ISBN 0 563 48627 9
UK £6.99 US $11.99/$14.99 CDN

Rose and the Doctor return to present-day Earth, and
become intrigued by the latest craze – the video game
Death to Mantodeans. Is it as harmless as it seems?
And why are so many local people going on holiday
and never returning?

Recently published
by BBC books:

Monsters and Villains

By Justin Richards
ISBN 0 563 48632 5
UK £7.99 US $12.99/$15.99 CDN

For over forty years, the Doctor has battled against the monsters
and villains of the universe. This book brings together the best –
or rather the worst – of his enemies.

Discover why the Daleks are so deadly; how the Yeti invade
London; the secret of the Loch Ness Monster; and how the
Cybermen have survived. Learn who the Master is, and – above
all – how the Doctor defeats them all.

Whether you read it on or behind the sofa, this book provides a
wealth of information about the monsters and villains that have
made *Doctor Who* the tremendous success it has been over the
years, and the galactic phenomenon that it is today.